Ever since Ryan Sutcliffe was a child, he has been obsessed with storytelling and fascinated with achieving the first dream he ever had, to be an author. From a young age, he showcased his writing and storytelling passion by writing comics for his beloved Nan to read and as he's grown older, that passion and desire to become an author has never faded. All he has ever wanted to do since he was a young boy was to create stories for people to enjoy and lose themselves in.

Find more updates about Ryan's works on his Instagram @ryan_sutcliffe_books

Ruth Kelly
'Goodnight and God bless'

Barry Sutcliffe
Jack Pickles

For my mum ,dad, brother,and Syd. Thank you for all your love and support over the years.
For my loving friends, I thank every one of you for your support.

For Heather Hudson. Thank you for developing my passion and love for writing.

.

Ryan Sutcliffe

THREE GRIFTERS

AUSTIN MACAULEY PUBLISHERS®

LONDON * CAMBRIDGE * NEW YORK * SHARJAH

A CIP catalogue record for this title is available from the British Library.

ISBN 9781035861415 (Paperback)
ISBN 9781035861422 (ePub e-book)

www.austinmacauley.com

First Published 2024
Austin Macauley Publishers Ltd®
1 Canada Square
Canary Wharf
London
E14 5AA

I would like to thank Josh Sutcliffe, James Barker, and Roberts Zarins for posing as the book's cover art.

I would like to thank Mark Sutcliffe for reading through my first draft.

I would also like to send a special thanks to my family and friends. I don't know where I'd be in this crazy world without you all. I'm lucky to have every one of you, and forever grateful. Your support and belief in me means the world.

I would finally like to thank Austin Macauley Publishers for taking a chance on a kid with a dream.

Table of Contents

Part I: 'The Rise'   **11**

   I: 'The Balance'   15

   II:'The Murderous Affair'   30

   III: 'Icarus'   44

   IV: 'The Spark'   51

   V: 'The First Meeting'   61

   VI: 'The Proving Moment'   71

   VII: 'To Silence the Silencer'   77

   VIII: 'Two Hearts as One'   87

   IX: 'A Dark Night'   92

Part II: 'The Moonie Effect'   **95**

   X: 'Enter Paul Moonie'   97

   XI: 'A Step Too Far'   107

   XII: 'The Truce'   111

   XIII: 'Two Pints and an Orange Juice'   115

   XIV: 'Dog Food'   125

   XV: 'A Brothers Reunion'   130

   XVI: 'The First Dance'   141

   XVII: 'The Light Diffused'   154

   XVIII: 'An Ego's End'   159

Part III: 'The Fall'   **167**

    XIX: 'Facing the Truth'   *169*

    XX: 'To Kill a Rat'   *178*

    XXI: 'Dissension'   *187*

    XXII: 'McHay's Escape'   *196*

    XXIII: 'Stepping Out of the Shadows'   *198*

    XXIV: 'Keys to the Empire'   *202*

    XXV 'To Restart a War?'   *205*

    XXVI 'The Crumbling of an Empire'   *209*

    XXVII: 'End of the Road'   *217*

    XXVIII: 'A Ghost in the Shadows'   *226*

    XXIX: 'The Parting of Ways'   *231*

    XXX: 'What Comes Now?'   *236*

Part I
'The Rise'

Trust can be a dangerous game. It is the most destructive tool for anyone to use. It deceives itself in the name of loyalty. Forget what you see in films; not one gangster has loyalty. It's only the ones smart enough to survive this life that do. Things weren't always this bad. The path you choose in life really does matter. Ever heard of the saying, 'How the mighty fall'? Well, here's how. This is the story of the infamous Three Grifters...

Before we board this train of guns, love and deceit, indulging ourselves in the bleak, worn-out world that was England in the late 1980s is pivotal.

The grey skies hung high above the broken, worn-out and ever-ageing cities as the intense industrial age slowly began to become a distant memory. Every city during this time in England was trying desperately to find a role in this post-industrial world of change. There was a change brewing and Manchester was no different.

However, our story's roots don't begin in Manchester in the 80s. They begin in a city 44.6 miles from Manchester, in the city of Leeds. A moment that will start it all...

Leeds, 1972

A young, skinny, shaven, and inexperienced Vincent McHay stands across from the home of his boss's most detested adversary. Shaking and constantly watching over his shoulder, McHay watches on as the house gets overtaken by a forceful blaze. All at the doing of his actions.

"Have you rung the fire brigade?" A nearby neighbour calls over to McHay. McHay is too transfixed in his work to answer. Guilt is slowly beginning to seep into him.

"Hey, pal, I'm talking to you," the neighbour says. Growing frustrated with McHay's ignorance, the neighbour approaches him and lightly shakes his shoulders. This breaks McHay from his momentary trance.

"Have you rung the fire brigade?" He asks again.

McHay hangs his head low and walks away without saying a single word. His work here is done.

I

'The Balance'

Manchester, 1986

"Do you know why I drink shandy, Acey?" The chubby, always well-dressed, well-trimmed, hair slickened, and expensive watch-wearing Hunter Smith asks his protégé, Tony 'Ace' Johnson, who is dressed in his usual attire of a black leather jacket with a black shirt and a black fedora. They both sit waiting in the lobby of the luxurious 'High Horse' hotel.

"Why's that, Hunter?" The black-haired and green-eyed 'Ace' asks.

"Because it has a perfect balance. The lager represents the dark, the lemonade is the light. Half is the Devil, half is God. You and I are shandies, we always have that balance. But sometimes all it takes is a little too much darkness and we lose sight of the light," Hunter educates 'Ace' as he sips more of his shandy down his fat neck. Hunter always talks like he is a prophet. Ace puts it down to his oversized ego. Ace has always been of the belief that the minute you start acting like a prophet is the minute that your fate is sealed to be forever doomed.

"I'll drink to that." Ace cheers his pint of lager, hoping it will stop Hunter from lecturing on more.

Tony 'Ace' Johnson has been under the mentorship of Hunter for years now. Hunter has known Ace since he was a little child, having been best friends with Ace's father from childhood. When Ace's parents were killed in a car accident, when Ace was twenty-two, Hunter took Ace in and raised him under his wing supplying him with a roof over his head and food on his plate. When Ace was ready, Hunter then supplied him with work, starting him off with simple chores like driving around Hunter's associates, shopping for supplies and picking up items for him.

Then, five years ago, Hunter decided to get Ace more involved in his business. Hunter gifted him the nickname of 'Ace' as he is Hunter's secret weapon, always getting the job done and never failing him.

Hunter runs a small group of debt collectors in Manchester. The group are locally referred to as 'Hunter's Merry Men' and they include the right-hand man, Ace. Then under Ace is the experienced, suit-wearing, and witty Vince McHay. McHay models his appearance after Hunter with a similar well-trimmed beard and chubby physique. As well as Ace and McHay, there's Jasper Jace Reeves, also known as 'JJ'. JJ and Ace always wear leather jackets, and both gained the nickname 'leather lovers' from Hunter like they are some sort of 80s wrestling tag team.

JJ is Ace's best friend having both grown up together during their school years. The blonde and humorous JJ always enjoys having a laugh and often uses his comedic side on jobs; however, when pushed too far, he can get aggressive fast and many times Ace has had to pull JJ off a client and calm him down. There is no balance with JJ; he's either the funniest man in the room or the angriest. And he can switch it up without a second's notice. Lastly, and very least, there's Flacco. The Italian-born Flacco is useless and clumsy. He has scruffy uncombed and lengthy brown hair and always smells of sweat.

Flacco, and his English-born mother, Dorothy, came to Manchester four years ago after Flacco's father, Alessandro, was murdered by the Italian mafia. Ace has little trust in Flacco, it's rare that he ever completes a job he is sent on and then lies to the group about the littlest of things. For example, he once told JJ that his first job was as a train conductor. A statement that was later made redundant by Dorothy. To this day, JJ doesn't understand why Flacco lied about something as little as that. It's just who he is.

Hunter and Ace are at the hotel awaiting the arrival of a 'Mr Alonso'. Mr Alonso owns a restaurant nearby under the name 'Big Al's', and to keep his restaurant running after a small fire last year, he borrowed an excessive amount of money from the leader of one of the many drug gangs in Manchester, 'The Cheetas'. The leader of 'The Cheetas', Bradly Owens, came to Hunter and requested his services. Hunter's organisation has a very small but well-respected presence in the city.

"He's taking his sweet ass time, 'H'," an irritated Ace exclaims as he checks his £1500 watch that Hunter gifted him four years ago for his thirtieth birthday.

"Good things come to those who wait, Acey. And even better things come to those who wait with a pint in their hand," Hunter says as he attempts to ease Ace's rising tension with a little humour.

"What if he knows we are coming? Maybe he got tipped off," an anxious Ace follows up.

"You think too much, Ace. You can't afford to think too much in our game, it will never end well. The only people who know we are here today are us two and Owens. Relax," Hunter replies to his paranoid understudy.

Ace rises to his feet and begins to pace around in the lobby.

"Ace, will you just sit down and relax?" Hunter is growing more annoyed now as he doesn't want Ace's persecution complex to bring them any unnecessary attention and thus destroy their plan.

Ace begins to survey the room with his shark-like eyes. In the corner sits an elderly man wearing a flap cap and reading a local newspaper with a headline that reads: 'Moonie's New Club Continues Construction After Workers' Strike'. A few steps west from the elderly man is a hotel worker approaching the reception handing the blonde receptionist some paperwork.

Hunter looks over his shoulder at the stressed Ace. "Ace, I swear you will be the death of me one day! Take a seat, you are making me bloody nervous," Hunter tries one last time to get Ace to return to his seat but Ace ignores him. Hunter storms up out of his seat and gets up close to Ace, talking ever so silently so the receptionist is unable to hear them. "Acey, sit back down! We can't have this job compromised. We have a big payday riding on this one. It is a simple job. Don't make it more than it needs to be."

Hunter's words hit Ace and he realises how over the top he is being. Ace has always been an anxious individual. Even from a small age, he often found his overthinking and paranoia taking control over him. Many people put it down to him losing his parents at a young age, others just think that he thinks too deeply.

"Everything okay, gentlemen?" The tall, curvy, blue-eyed receptionist asks.

"Everything is great, thank you, darling," Hunter replies smiling at her.

"Sorry, H, I just get stressed. I hate waiting," Ace replies sitting back down.

"No, you think too much. Live a little," Hunter says as he continues to sip his shandy.

Ten minutes later, in stumbles a completely intoxicated, balding, middle-aged Italian man. Hunter nods over to Ace to get his attention on the drunken fool.

"That him?" Ace asks.

"That's our guy," Hunter says as he places down his shandy and stands up. Ace does the same.

The drunken Mr Alonso stumbles into a nearby table knocking off an expensive lamp that shatters onto the ground. The receptionist ascends from her chair to clear the mess but Hunter waves her off.

"Don't worry about that, sweetheart, we will sort it. Does this man have a room here?" Hunter, acting like he has no idea who Mr Alonso is, enquires.

"Yes. That's Mr Alonso, room…room 132," she replies as she checks her check-in documents.

"Okay, me and my friend here will take him up. What floor would that be on?" Hunter asks as Ace looks on impressed with how Hunter is handling the situation. He's using his charm to get the associate into his room where they will be alone to finish their job. They've barely had to put any effort into this one.

"That would be floor five," the receptionist replies.

"Perfect. Acey, get on the other side of him." Hunter and Ace carry the inebriated Mr Alonso into the elevator.

As the elevator ascends the ten-floored hotel, Mr Alonso stands in between both Hunter and Ace. He lightly sways side to side in the middle of them.

"Thank you, boys, I'm a little drunk," Alonso thanks the men for escorting him to his room.

"That's okay, pal, because in the morning you are not going to remember this next part," Ace replies.

"Next part?" Alonso questions.

Ace pulls out his knuckle dusters from the inside pocket of his leather jacket. He tightens his fist and repeatedly punches Mr Alonso in his genitals. Alonso falls to the floor of the elevator crying in antagonising agony.

"I love it when you do that," Hunter laughs.

"My best move. It works every time." Ace smiles as he kicks the already grounded Mr Alonso in his stomach.

"Ey, you don't kick a man when he's down, Ace. You've already done your job getting him down there." Hunter scrapes Mr Alonso off the floor as the elevator reaches the fifth floor. The two of them then continue to carry Alonso to his room.

"What was all that about?" Alonso spits out a small patch of blood as he speaks.

"You'll find out soon enough. Now shut your mouth!" Ace sharply responds.

"Charming," Alonso says.

"Give me your key," Hunter orders Alonso as they reach the door to room 132. Alonso roots into his blazer pocket and pulls out his room key only for Hunter to snatch it off him and open the door. Ace kicks Alonso into the room where he faceplants the floor.

As he steps inside, Ace picks up a bright yellow Kalanchoe which is planted on the oak drawers to the left of him as he enters. The room is kept well and tidy with the bed neatly made and the carpet well-treated.

SMASH! Ace relocates the Kalanchoe over Alonso's balding head. The pot shatters and cuts the drunken fool.

"Always hated yellow," Ace remarks referring to the colour of the plant. Hunter switches on the 'Sharp 13' television and slightly increases the volume to dilute the upcoming and anticipated screams of agony from Alonso.

"Here, tie him to that chair." Hunter delves into his blazer pocket and pulls out a small bundle of string. He throws the string to Ace who ties Alonso tightly to a red chair sitting in the corner of the room.

Sweat begins to dribble down Alonso's bleeding forehead as he comes to the realisation that he is in immediate danger. He suspects that Hunter and Ace are here to collect the money he owes Owens. His rear end clenches tightly in fear as Hunter and Ace dominantly stand in front of him.

"Any beers in this place?" Ace asks.

"Some in that first drawer," Alonso directs Ace over to the drawers where Ace retrieves a bottle of red wine.

"Wine? Really?" Ace mocks Alonso.

"It came with the room," Alonso replies.

"I don't care." Ace violently smashes the wine bottle against the wall, damaging the vibrant wallpaper. He then handles what is left of the daggered wine glass and holds it under Alonso's sweat-glistened neck.

"Now, Mr Alonso, please do not lie to us. Do you know why we are here?" Hunter calmly asks the nervous and fearful Alonso who is now shaking slightly.

Alonso scans Hunter's and Ace's faces before looking down at the shattered wine bottle which haunts the bottom of his neck like a shark swimming on the seabed stalking its prey above.

What do I tell them? Will they kill me? I'm dead. How do I get out of this? These thoughts race through Alonso's mind as he desperately attempts to grasp a way out of his current situation. Then suddenly he loses his breath and his sweat rapidly escalates.

"He's freaking out. What's happening?" A confused Ace looks on not knowing if Alonso is having a heart attack or not.

"He's in a state of panic. He's having a panic attack. The wine glass is too much, Ace, I've told you about your approach to these jobs. It's far too much!" Hunter takes the shattered wine glass from Ace's hand and throws it on the floor before holding Alonso, who is now shaking more furiously, by the shoulders.

"Alonso, Alonso, you are going to be fine. Snap out of it," Hunter says before attempting to slap some sense into him.

"It's not working," Hunter claims.

Ace quickly enters the bathroom and empties a toothbrush holder before pouring ice-cold water into it. He then returns to the sight of Hunter shaking Alonso back and forth. "Stand back, H." Ace launches the water on Alonso's bloody and worrying face. Miraculously, this manages to slow down Alonso's attack and after a few minutes, he slowly comes back to his senses.

"Alonso, just communicate with us and everything will be okay. We will only harm you if you make us," Hunter says as he wipes Alonso's face with a towel that Ace hands him from the bathroom.

"Now, Mr Alonso, do you know why we are visiting you today?" Hunter softly asks.

Alonso looks up and realises that the shattered wine glass is now on the floor.

"I…I think so, yes," he reluctantly replies.

"Good. Now we are getting somewhere. Mr Alonso, we are here on behalf of one Bradly Owens. Mr Owens has been very patient with your situation. He's already extended your debt three times. But now, he has had enough. Me and my associate over here have come to collect what you owe him," Hunter addresses the reasoning for their aggressive visit.

"Please don't hurt me. I have told Mr Owens that I need more time. My business needs time to get back on its feet again. Rome wasn't built in a day," Alonso responds not knowing how Hunter and Ace will react.

"Rome wasn't built in a day. That's funny. You're from Rome, aren't you, Mr Alonso?" Ace asks. Alonso nods. "You have been back there recently to visit your family?" Ace follows up. Alonso shakes his head. "Well, if we don't get what we came for, you will be going back there in a body bag. You understand?" Ace threatens Alonso's life even though he has yet to make his first kill, unlike

Hunter who has two kills to his name. Although he has threatened this, Ace has no intention of killing Mr Alonso. In fact, the very idea of killing anyone makes Ace feel uneasy and sick.

"I understand but I DO NOT HAVE THE MONEY," Alonso stresses.

"We know you don't have the money, Alonso. We are not here for the money, we are here for that." Hunter points at a golden necklace Alonso is wearing. The necklace is a gold figure of the Italian goddess of the Moon, Jana. Jana has two faces; one faces the past and the other faces the future.

Alonso looks down and holds his necklace tightly.

"That covers what you owe. Mr Owens says if you hand that over, then your debt is cleared." Hunter can detect Alonso's reluctance to comply. "You don't really have a choice, Mr Alonso. It's the necklace or the body bag. Your call," Hunter continues.

Alonso thinks deeply for a few moments. The necklace means a lot to him as it was passed down to him through five generations of his family. Handing it over would bring him great shame to his family. On the other hand, he wishes to see his family again and not put them through the grief of losing him. Ultimately, he chooses his life. He slowly removes the necklace and hands it over to a smiling Hunter.

"Pleasure doing business, Mr Alonso. Now go take a bath, you stink." Hunter pats Alonso on his shoulder as Ace unties him from the chair.

The minute Hunter and Ace step outside the room onto the hotel corridor, Hunter slams Ace up against the wall and grips him by the collar.

"I have told you time after time about your approach. It's too aggressive, you need to be calm. We don't want messy, we want results and we only get results when you listen to me. Know your place. I brought you into this world and I can just as easily take you out of it. That's not something I want to do so don't make me," Hunter rages.

"Are you threatening me?"

A furious Hunter rams his fists into Ace's throat. "What was that?"

Ace is struggling to breathe. "Nothing."

"If I want to threaten you, I will." Hunter releases Ace and walks off. Ace stares at the back of Hunter with a slight and ever-growing resentment before following him out of the hotel.

Across the cloudy city of Manchester, the slickened blonde-haired, black sunglasses-wearing JJ Reeves sits in a dimly lit booth in a small, unloved pub known as 'The Blue Moon'.

The pub has been an ornament in the city since the First World War, and when the Nazis dropped bombs in the area during the Second World War, it was the only building left standing in the area.

The current landlady, the fair-haired, caring and loving, Eden Simson, always reserves a specific booth for Hunter and his gang. The pub is deserted today with only a couple of the locals in.

Vince McHay soon joins JJ in the booth, having just ordered two pints of lager from the bar. He slides a pint across to JJ.

"Do you have to wear them inside?" McHay asks pointing to JJ's sunglasses.

"Yes, I do, big un. We can't have people seeing my two black eyes. It shows weakness and we are not men of weakness," JJ sharply replies. JJ is using the glasses to shield the two black eyes that were gifted to him by a butch seven-foot security guard from a job he and Ace were on a few weeks ago.

"I wish I'd have seen that Goliath lamp you." McHay laughs as he sips some of his freshly poured lager.

"You've got foam on your beard, you tart," JJ mocks as McHay wipes his beard clean.

"At least I can grow hair unlike you, you pubescent prick," McHay laughs back.

JJ and Vince are awaiting Hunter and Ace's arrival at the pub. They were told it was important and that they had to attend but they don't know why.

"What do you reckon all this is about anyway?" JJ asks as lager travels down his throat.

"Whatever it is, it can't be good. H sounded out of breath on the phone. My best guess is that something has happened, and we've got to do a hit," McHay responds. Since he is the most experienced member of Hunter's gang, bar from Hunter himself, McHay has a body count of one kill under his belt. McHay was Hunter's first man recruited to the gang many years ago when Hunter operated in Leeds. JJ is the newest member of the gang and like Ace, he has yet to kill a man for Hunter. Unlike Ace, JJ revels in the idea of taking another man's life. He sees it as his initiation into gang life. He views it as him stepping up and climbing the ranks in Hunter's small organisation.

"A hit? Oh, how I've been waiting for this," a slightly eager and excited JJ responds.

"Well, don't. It's nothing like you expect, trust me," McHay coldly debunks JJ's longing hopes. JJ looks up and sees the seriousness deep within Vince's green eyes.

"What was it like? Your first kill," JJ quietly asks.

"At the moment, you feel nothing but pure rage and adrenaline. It's what comes after that gets you and knocks you sick. The two days after the kill are always the most crucial. It is like all the bad feelings and thoughts you have ever experienced in your life all come together and hit you like a freight train. The guilt for the family who is now left with no answers, the paranoia, and the doubt as to whether you covered it up well enough. If you are not careful, it can cripple you. It's not a good feeling trust me, but all you must keep telling yourself is that it's for the greater good. You must keep reminding yourself that the man you've just executed deserves it and the world is a better place with them gone, even if you don't really believe it." Vince's words almost trap him in a reflective trance as he stares down with feelings of immense guilt and regret.

JJ takes a large gulp of lager having taken all that in, then blurts out, "Understood."

The heavy oak doors of 'The Blue Moon' swing wide open and the silhouette of Hunter and Ace stand omnipotently at the entrance. Ace is protectively holding a mysterious black briefcase in his left hand.

"They're here," McHay points out to JJ. Hunter and Ace approach the booth and take a seat.

Hunter has a mile-long smile across his face. "Gentlemen, our rise has begun," he greets them as Ace slams the briefcase down on the table.

"Open it up, McHay," Hunter orders. Vince McHay slowly and curiously pings open the briefcase. It flings open. Inside sits a stupendous amount of stacks of fifty-pound notes.

"Holy shit," McHay says with greedy glee in his eyes.

"7500 English pounds," a proud Hunter announces.

"Shit a brick!" JJ is stunned and spins the briefcase his way so he can admire the fortune. He's never seen so much money.

"You see, JJ, those two black eyes were worth it in the end," Ace laughs. £2500 of that £7500 comes from the job that Ace and JJ got sent on which was to drug and transport a news reporter to a local nightclub owner. The reporter had been destroying the club's reputation in the paper and causing the club to lose punters. It was on this job that JJ received his two black eyes from the reporter's seven-foot security guard. The remaining £5000 comes courtesy of Bradly Owens for the collection of Mr Alonso's necklace.

"Along with this money, Mr Owens is putting the word out that we are trustworthy and reliable muscle. We will soon be big-time, boys." Hunter smiles again with a great sense of excitement for the future of his gang.

"Brilliant. I must say though, H, you sounded panicked on the phone," McHay says.

"That is because, McHay, I have some more news." Hunter stands up before he continues. "Lizzy is pregnant. I am going to be a father," Hunter announces. The boys cheer and congratulate their leader.

"A bloody hit? What a load of crap! You're off your rocker, Vino," JJ mocks McHay for speculating that Hunter's news was about doing a killing.

Hunter pats Ace's shoulder and declares, "Acey, get the drinks in. Tonight, we celebrate."

The celebrations last a solid and definitely not sober twelve hours. During the night, Hunter took Ace over to one side and asked him to be the godfather to his child. Without a second of hesitation, Ace said yes.

A couple of days later

Hunter has sent Ace and JJ on a job collecting debt from a small-time drug dealer who lives in a flat on the outskirts of the city.

Ace parks his grey Pontiac Fiero, which passengers JJ, up in front of a small shabby and ragged block of flats. A block that once upon a time saw love and care that now sees abandonment and decay.

Ace looks over to his left. "Here we are, 'double J', Manchester's finest."

JJ laughs as he pulls out a pack of chewing gum from his jacket pocket. He offers a piece to Ace, who rejects it. JJ then goes into his other pocket and pulls out his signature shades. Ace smiles and then shakes his head as they begin to make their way into the block of flats.

"This place stinks. My shits smell better than this and that's after I've had a curry," JJ proclaims as they ascend the stairs which will lead them to their target's floor.

"You have such a poetic voice, JJ. What did you expect?" Ace replies. The two reach the middle floor and search for the number 20.

Just from standing in front of number 20's door, the two can smell a powerful and overwhelming scent of weed. BAM. BAM. Ace pounds the door as JJ cracks his neck in anticipation.

"Room service, motherfucker," JJ shouts.

The door opens but not all the way as the inside chain lock is applied. A young-looking man greets the two with only half of his face visible as he furtively looks out. The man looks to have long black hair and his build is scrawny.

"Evening, baby cakes," Ace greets him as JJ stands smiling behind. "Know who we are?"

"No, I think you have the wrong flat." The man goes to shut the door, but Ace kicks the door back open as JJ pulls out his knife and points it at the man.

"Now, kid, unlock the chain and let us in. Don't make us do something we don't wish to do," Ace calmly orders the man who is now sweating in panic.

"Okay. Sorry. One moment." The man closes the door and unlocks the chain before welcoming Ace and JJ into his drug-infested home.

The interior of the flat is everything that Ace imagined it would be: dark with the curtains drawn, furniture stained, crumbs indented into what was once a white carpet, and bongs laid out on the stained coffee table.

"My, my, what a place you have here, kid," JJ sarcastically says before he pushes the man harshly down on the nearby couch. "Now sit down, son."

"Listen up, fuck face, do you know why we are here?" Ace questions as he removes his black fedora and slaps it down on the man's head. The man sits in silence. "I don't like to ask twice, do I, JJ?"

JJ slightly pulls his shades down and kneels looking the man in his eyes. "No, you do not, Acey."

"Therefore, I think it's in your best interest to answer my question." Ace grips the man's shirt.

"I think so, yes," the man nervously spits out.

"Ah, he's not so much an oblivious arse stain as we thought," JJ cheers.

"Double J, run him the story just in case the weed has gone straight to his thick head, and he's got a bit foggy on the details. Why are we here?" Ace says.

JJ smacks his hand hard on the man's shoulder before explaining why they have paid their visit today. "Well, what a story it is. Once upon a fucking time you, you rat bastard, borrowed money from my lovely boss, Hunter, in order to cover rent for this palace of shithousery. The debt was due two months ago but because our boss is such a sweetheart, a handsome one at that too, and goes way back with you as you helped him once on a job, he extended your deadline. A deadline which was due yesterday and you failed to comply with it. So now he's sent his two best heavies to deal with your dumb ass. What a story. I'm thinking of selling the rights to Hollywood," JJ explains.

"You should. Although it's not set to have a happy ending," Ace responds.

The man takes a humongous gulp before responding. "Listen, I have the money, I do. I just forgot the date yesterday that's all."

JJ obnoxiously laughs in the man's face.

"What, do you think we are stupid now?" Ace slaps the man across his face before continuing. "We won't be leaving this building until we have that money in our hands, no matter how many of your bones we have to break."

"I have the money I swear. I slept in yesterday that's all," the man pleads.

"You didn't sleep in. I tell you what you did, you got on that white shit and that bong and got wasted. Because all you are is a pathetic joke, everyone knows it that's why no one buys any of your drugs. No one trusts you. Why H hasn't put you in the ground yet is beyond me. JJ, raid this dump and get our money."

JJ begins to raid the man's flat, trashing the place even more than it already is and collecting money and other goods along the way.

"Why are you taking my things? It's just the money. It's all under my bed."

Ace slowly walks over to the man and takes back his fedora. "We will take what we want, it's compensation." Ace begins to beat the man in his chair so hard that he falls out of it and crashes to the floor.

JJ runs over to kick him but Ace intervenes.

"You don't kick someone when they're down. He gets the message. You go get the money."

JJ heads into the bedroom to collect the money from under the bed.

Twenty minutes of beating the man senseless later, Ace and JJ head back to the car.

"Good job in there, JJ." Ace pats his best friend on the back.

"We make a great team, Acey, always have since we were kids." They get into the car.

"There's no one I would rather have by my side, JJ, you are a brother to me," Ace tells JJ, who smiles after hearing that.

"Dam straight, brother."

"We will be running this gang in no time," Ace says.

"No, no. I'd much rather be the right-hand man than the leader. Heavy hangs that head."

"Speak for yourself," Ace laughs.

About two hours west of where Ace and JJ are conducting their business, McHay has been sent down to 'Big Stu's Gym' on a job for Hunter. Last week, Hunter had been given word that an old client of his, and a regular of the gym, Ben Riven, had been bad-mouthing him around the area and thus attempting to diminish his reputation.

'Big Stu's Gym' is well-admired and has gained many members since its inception in 1969. It is usually a busy place, especially this time of the day. McHay would much rather handle the business in a private place like Riven's home but Hunter wants to make a statement and he wants it to be seen. In his mind, such a disrespectful act as bad-mouthing him deserves the most public humiliation to return the favour.

McHay doesn't want to let Hunter down and he wants this done quickly. In and out. Before entering the gym, he closes his eyes and takes in a deep breath before counting down from three and then exhaling. He grabs the handle and opens the door.

The gym is rammed at this time, and every machine in immediate sight is in use. McHay has been shown a photograph from Hunter prior to his visit so he can easily identify Ben's 5ft 11" pale white build.

Like looking for a needle in a bloody haystack, McHay thinks to himself.

"Can I help you, Sir?" A butch male worker standing behind the welcome desk asks.

McHay doesn't answer. He continues scanning the main room.

"Sir? Can I help you?" The worker asks again.

This irritates McHay as it breaks his intense surveillance of the room. "What do you want?"

"I'm just wondering if there is anything I can help you with, Sir. It's not often people come here in suits," the worker responds.

"Mind your own business. What I'm here for doesn't concern you."

"It does, it's my gym."

McHay's attention is soon diverted by a male voice yelling out, "I said I don't need a spotter, so do me a favour and PISS OFF!"

McHay looks over in the direction of the shouting; it's his man. Ben Riven. "I've found what I'm looking for," McHay says as he heads in the direction of Ben Riven who is currently lying on a bench doing some bench presses.

"Ben Riven," McHay calls over as he reaches him in mid-bench press as he is about to raise the bar from his chest level for another rep.

"Piss off, I'm busy."

"Not anymore," McHay says as he grabs the bar and applies all his pressure on it forcing it down. Ben continues to try and raise it but McHay's strength outweighs Ben's tiredness and pains. McHay crushes the bar down onto Ben's chest and continues to apply his pressure.

"Dude, who the hell are you? What do you want?" Ben struggles to get his words out of his mouth as his chest is slowly crunching under the weight.

"If I get word that you bad mouth Hunter again, I will be back and I will be less forgiving." McHay eases up and lets go of the bar.

"I'm sorry," Ben replies.

But before McHay can respond to Ben's apology, the worker from the desk comes up behind McHay and gets him in a headlock. "You, my friend, have got yourself banned from here," the worker tells McHay as he begins to head for the door with McHay still in his grip.

The grip is so tight that McHay is steadily closing his eyes ready to pass out.

"Hey!" A voice calls out. McHay can barely hear it as he is about to embrace unconsciousness. SMACK! The grip on McHay is suddenly loosened and he falls to the floor. He hears the worker come crashing down behind him.

"Come on, pal. We need to go," says a brown-haired, muscular man who stands over McHay offering out his hand to help him up. The man has a long nasty scar running down his nose that looks like it's been there for quite some time.

A confused McHay looks up and sees blood on the man's knuckles. He takes the stranger's hand. The two, in fast fashion, flee the gym and head out to McHay's car.

"Thank you for that," McHay says.

"Don't worry about it, Ben is a prick. He deserved what you did to him. Everyone in that gym hates him, he's too arrogant," the stranger replies.

"You risked your neck for me, I won't forget that. What's your name?"

"Darren. Darren Swade."

"What's with the scar Swade?"

Darren smiles and replies, "Everyone has a story."

"That we do. Well, I hope we meet again someday, Darren Swade," McHay states as he shakes Darren's hand.

II

'The Murderous Affair'

January 23rd

Vince McHay pulls up his light grey Buick Roadmaster outside of house number 14 on Ramsden Avenue. This is Hunter and his fiancé, Lizzy's, house. He checks his hair in his rear-view mirror and quickly licks his right index finger before scanning it through the front of his hair. He neatens up his tie and then exits his vehicle to approach the house.

As he makes his way to the front door, he notices how well-kept the flowers which sit under the window are. Before he can knock, the door swings rapidly open. Stood in front of him is Lizzy who is showing a curly, blonde and big-breasted lady out of the house. This is Lizzy's sister, Amanda. Amanda catches McHay's eyes staring at her.

"Oops, sorry." Amanda looks up at McHay and apologises for getting in his way. McHay gracefully moves out of the way to let Amanda pass. "I'll see you next week, Liz," Amanda says as she begins to make her way to her car.

"See you, Amanda, take care," the brunette and well-toned Lizzy replies. "Hey, Vince." Lizzy hugs Vince as he enters the house.

"Hi, Liz. Congratulations by the way. You guys will make great parents," McHay congratulates her.

"Thank you, Vince. He's in the basement," Liz directs McHay to the basement where Hunter waits for a meeting. Every meeting the gang holds takes place in Hunter's basement. Vince begins to make his way towards the basement but then stops himself and turns back to Lizzy.

"Erm, Liz, who was that woman by the way?" A curious yet slightly love-struck McHay questions.

"Amanda? That's my sister. Yes, she's single." Lizzy smiles.

"What? No, no, I was just wondering that's all." McHay nervously laughs.

"McHay, I saw the way you looked at her. I'll write her number down for you," Lizzy excitedly says as she rushes to get a pen. "Take it easy on her though. She's had a rough time recently." She writes Amanda's number on a notepad before tearing off the page and handing it over to McHay.

McHay descends the steps that lead into the basement. The basement has substantial space. It consists of a pool table, a dusty old dart board, and a television. The true heart of it though is the bar which is based in the corner. In the middle of the room sits a table with five chairs, this is where the business gets done.

Hunter and Ace, who arrived ten minutes before McHay, are sitting at the table waiting patiently for the rest to arrive. Ace is fiddling with a pack of cards, randomly shuffling them for no apparent reason other than easing his boredom.

"Ah, Vince, come take a seat," Hunter notices Vince has just entered the room.

"Gentlemen," McHay nods at them both.

"What took you so long?" Ace asks.

"He's always late, it's his thing," Hunter defends McHay.

"Well, as we know, boys, the party doesn't start until I arrive," McHay cracks a joke.

Suddenly, the three men hear the sound of a toilet flushing followed up by the sound of feet jogging down the basement stairs.

"I must know where you get that toilet paper from. It smells so divine," comically says JJ.

"What would you rate that one, JJ?" Ace asks.

"I'd have to say, the shape was a miserable three but the smell, well the smell was an astronomical ten," JJ replies which prompts Ace to laugh.

"Lovely," McHay remarks. JJ passes McHay and pats him on his back.

"I didn't wash my hands either, McHay." JJ sarcastically blows McHay a kiss as he takes his seat.

"Well, what are we waiting for?" McHay asks.

"Somewhere to be, big un?" JJ questions.

"Yeah, a date with your gal. I'm going to blow her back out," McHay quickly fires the banter back.

"Ah, Gab left me, man," JJ hangs his head low.

"Shit sorry, man," McHay tries to heal the wound that he just exposed.

"We are waiting for Flacco," Hunter pipes in redirecting the conversation.

"Frigging Flacco!" McHay shows disdain towards Flacco. Ace smiles and sips his bottle of beer, remaining neutral.

"Why the frig have you asked that silly bastard to come here?" JJ also disapproves. "He's a waste of time."

"It's about time we brought him along. He needs to take that next step now and become more involved. Now we are getting bigger, we need more hands," Hunter explains his reasoning.

"H, that's all well and good if Flacco wasn't such a useless dildo," JJ defends his position of disapproval.

"For the first time in history, I agree with JJ on this one, H. The kid is an idiot. I mean come on, Acey, what do you think?" McHay notices that Ace is silent on the matter, so he tries to get him involved.

Ace puts down his bottle of beer. "Listen, we all have to start someday." Deep down Ace agrees with McHay and JJ but doesn't want to oppose Hunter as he knows that Hunter is excessively stubborn and won't change his mind. Arguing would just be a waste of time.

"Boys, just trust me on this one, okay? I'm not going to throw him straight in on the big stuff. I'm just going to slowly phase him into our operations more that's all," Hunter lectures.

The gang's hatred for Flacco is immensely justified. Flacco is a college dropout twenty-one-year-old pain in the ass. Hunter took Flacco on a year ago as the gang's driver and errand boy. But the gang soon came to the realisation that Flacco is just a liability, always showing up late with some gibberish story as to why he's late. As well as this Flacco is also known to run and leave his fellow men behind when things get too heated.

For example, six months ago, Flacco was the getaway driver for Ace and JJ who had been sent to collect some debt from a rival of Hunter's, Eric Jones. The job got intensely heated when Jones pulled a gun out on Ace and JJ. Sat in the car with the engine running, Flacco saw this all unfold through the window of the house. He rapidly drove off thinking the worst, leaving Ace and JJ to find their own way back to Hunter after they wrestled Jones down and knocked him out. Since that day, Ace, JJ and McHay have refused to trust or even work with Flacco again. Trust is everything.

Hunter, however, believes that there's still potential in the young Flacco and puts his running away antics down to his inexperienced youth.

Five minutes pass before Flacco enters the basement in a smart and newly bought black leather jacket with his black hair gelled up so much that it appears shiny.

"Arrival of the prick," JJ remarks.

"What happened this time? Wrestling more bears?" McHay mocks Flacco's late appearance.

"Or flirting with Nuns?" JJ adds whilst laughing at his own joke.

"Nah, I was balls deep in mummy McHay," the cocky Flacco fires back as he joins the gang at the table. He spins his chair around backwards and sits on it that way rather than the normal way to sit on a chair.

"Simmer down, children. H, why are we here then?" Ace redirects the purpose of the meeting and wants to get to business.

"Well, gentlemen, now that we are all here, I have an important job to discuss with you all. A job which is out of our usual debt-collecting realm. Now, last month Lizzy's best friend, Eva, had a drunken one-night stand with a Latvian man who goes by the name Adrians Andris. Eva is a married woman with three children and the one-night stand was just that, a drunken mistake after a long day. She very much loves her family. Adrians is now blackmailing Eva into paying him monthly instalments of £500 in return for his silence," Hunter explains. "If Eva fails to make a payment, then he has threatened to tell Eva's husband about the one-night stand. This will tear her family apart. This guy is a real piece of crap."

"And where do we factor into all of this?" A curious Ace asks.

"Well, Acey, we are going to pay Adrians a visit and get him to leave Eva and her family alone," Hunter replies.

"Wait. Did you say his name is Adrians Andris?" A slightly concerned JJ checks.

"Yes. Adrians Andris," Hunter, looking slightly confused at JJ's response answers.

"This is bad, H, we shouldn't get involved," a fearful JJ warns his boss.

"You all smell that? I think JJ has just shit his pants." McHay laughs.

JJ doesn't respond to McHay's words, he just looks sternly at Hunter. "He is a very dangerous man, H. He is Paul Moonie's head of security. You don't mess with any man who is associated with Paul Moonie. As far as this city is concerned, Paul Moonie is Jupiter."

"Jupiter?" Ace wonders aloud.

"The King of all other Gods," JJ follows up.

"Paul Moonie? I have heard many stories about that man," Flacco echoes JJ's concerns.

"Yeah? Every story you've heard is true," JJ warns.

"I can handle Paul Moonie. Our job is simple, we pay Adrians a visit. We bruise him up a bit and threaten him. You can even wear masks to hide your faces if you are too scared," Hunter firmly states, it's his way or the highway.

"H, you don't realise, Paul Moonie runs Manchester. This is his city. He's the most feared name in Manchester since Margret Thatcher. He is ruthless," JJ stresses the importance of his warning.

"Listen, JJ, if Hunter says he can handle Moonie, he can handle Moonie. Wipe your ass and get to work," McHay defends Hunter, as usual.

Ace watches the room refusing to give his input. He too has also heard many stories of Paul Moonie including one where Moonie once took an iron to a man's face because he parked in front of Moonie's house. Moonie dragged the man into his home and put his head on an ironing board before burning the man with the iron. All over a parking space. The burnt man was a local news reporter but due to Moonie's reputation and connections, the man was fired from the news company and would later leave Manchester.

Ace believes this may end deplorably for the gang but he also knows that Hunter isn't going to listen or change his mind. He's too set in his ways. "When do we make our move?" Ace asks even though he believes that nothing good will come from this.

"Tomorrow. I want this done clean, gentlemen. Do what you must do but don't kill him, and don't make it messy. Flacco, I want you with Ace and JJ on this one," Hunter orders. Hunter will not be taking part in the job, it's rare that he does these days. His excuse is, 'The prime minister doesn't get on the battlefield'. Maybe the country would be a better place if they did though.

"What will I be doing in this dance, boss?" McHay, who always refers to jobs as 'dances', questions noticing that Hunter didn't mention his name with Ace and JJ's.

"You, McHay, are going to be with me. We have been invited to Bradly Owens' birthday drinks at his penthouse," Hunter replies.

How lovely, frick and frack get to party whilst we do all the heavy lifting, an exasperate Ace thinks to himself.

Instead of heading back home, Ace and JJ decide to go for a pint in the city after the meeting commences. They head to a bar named 'The White Lightning' based in the city centre.

As the moon slowly lingers, traffic in the city lowers as more people head out for a night on the booze. After all, it is a Friday night. Manchester has gained a rough reputation over the years with stabbings, riots, and a rise in crime. Most of which occur due to these boozy nights.

As Ace and JJ see 'The White Lightning' in the distance, a drunken man stumbles and falls in front of the two. Neither of them helps the drunken imbecile up and they just walk around his limp body. This is a normal sight for Manchester.

"This Goddam city, what would we do without it?" Ace remarks.

"We would be a lot more sober and probably live a lot longer," JJ laughs.

The bar is busy, full of couples, singletons, and freshly turned legal drinkers. People from all backgrounds are drinking the night away here. The jukebox is flowing, the fruit machine is in high demand, and cocktails are being shaken.

"You see, city bars are so much better than town bars," Ace shares his opinion with JJ as they sit at a table near the bar.

"Why is that, Acey?" JJ wonders.

"Well, look around you, JJ, who do you know in here? No one. In a town bar, you walk in, and I guarantee you get recognised by at least five people who know all about your business. They even know when and where you last took a crap. But in a city bar, well in a city bar, you can be whomever you want to be because no one knows you," Ace voices.

"My God, Acey, you really are a paranoid soul, aren't you?" JJ chuckles. "Anyway, come on, you know I'm right about the whole Andris and Moonie situation, don't you?" JJ wants to know Ace's real stance on the subject.

Ace puts down his bottle of beer. "Listen, all I am going to say is that we have a job to do. I don't get caught up in the politics. What Hunter says is what goes. You know him as well as I know him, he will never change his mind once it's decided," Ace responds.

"But this is Paul Moonie. I know we're getting steam and are on the rise now, but we are not big enough to cross that line. We will never be big enough to cross that line," JJ states.

"I've heard all the stories and I've read all the papers too. But Hunter's orders are final and we must respect that and do our job. We aren't big enough to oppose Hunter. Not yet," Ace voices as he sips more of his beer.

"Excuse me, fellas, got any sniff?" A scruffy-looking nineteen-year-old approaches them.

"Sorry, child, do I look like I carry coke?" JJ snaps at the young man.

"Well, yeah," the teen rudely replies. JJ slams down on the table.

Ace can see JJ's anger growing deeper in his eyes, so he puts his hand on JJ's shoulder and chimes in; "Listen, kid, we don't have any sniff so kindly do one."

"Hey, dude, I was only asking. Don't tell me to do one. Who the hell are you? You look like a shitty virgin version of the Terminator," the teen rages back. JJ turns his head and gives Ace a confused look.

"It's the leather jacket," Ace explains. "This guy thinks he's a comedian," Ace says before he starts to stand up.

"Why are you getting up?" The teen curiously asks fearing that he's about to become involved in a physical interaction.

"Because, kid, we are about to get thrown out of here," Ace softly says as JJ swiftly headbutts the teen before bashing his head several times harshly off the sharp edge of the table.

Ace and JJ are thrown out of the bar to the kerb shortly after.

Ace picks JJ up and they both laugh before continuing up the city to find another bar.

"Well, I've been called many things, JJ, but never once a virgin Terminator," Ace laughs more.

"Arnie ain't got shit on you, my man."

In the distance, they see a large group of people standing outside of a bar that looks full called, 'The Phoenix'.

"Looks like there's a few heads in there. Are we having it, Acey?" JJ asks.

"You are too intelligent to be asking stupid questions, JJ." The two head towards the heavily occupied bar.

Music blasting, people laughing, and bartenders being overworked. This bar is packed. The interior is spacious and lit with blue neon lights. This bar is well known across Manchester for having a 'futuristic look' and is also known to be the place where celebrities stop by for a drink when they are in the city.

"I am not queuing in that," JJ points out to the heavy traffic at the bar. People all crammed and desperate to be served, all looking like zombies scrambling desperately for brains.

"There's a bar upstairs, come on." The two head upstairs to the second floor which is set out very similar to the main floor with the only difference being a stage positioned at the end of the room where a karaoke machine lingers waiting to be chosen by that one intoxicated punter who believes they are half-good at singing. This room is less populated, and everyone seems to know each other in here.

"Erm, Acey, we've walked into a private party," JJ realises this having seen a banner hung saying, 'Happy Birthday Nancy'.

"Then let's party." They head to the bar.

"Two lagers please," Ace orders to the slim male bartender behind the bar.

"Lagers? That's boring," a female voice pipes up from the side of Ace. Ace looks to his right revealing a brunette goddess wearing a dark purple dress. Her sparkling blue eyes look up at him. She's like no one he's ever seen before, yet her presence feels welcoming and familiar. A feeling that he wants to keep and cherish.

"Boring? I assure you, darling, nothing about me is boring," Ace smoothly replies.

"So how do you know, Nancy?" She asks him in order to form a conversation.

"Nancy? Ah, I went to school with her. Yeah, we go way back me and her. What about you?" He lies.

"Ah, I used to work with her. I literally know no one here, they are all relatives I think," she laughs.

"Same!" Ace replies.

The woman moves closer to Ace. "Well, it's a good job we have each other then." She looks into his eyes as she sips her cocktail through her straw. The bartender brings Ace his lagers. JJ sees Ace talking with the woman, so he pays for the pints.

"I'm just going to the toilet. Am I okay to join you guys after, since we both know no one here?" The woman politely asks.

"Of course. We will be sat near the stage." Ace and JJ head for a table positioned near the stage.

"You seem in there, Acey," JJ encourages.

"What? I don't know, mate. It might not be a good idea," Ace responds.

JJ puts his pint down. "Are you crazy? A woman like that is a once-in-a-lifetime woman. She seems into you. You would be crazy to not pursue her!" JJ tries to talk some sense into Ace.

"JJ, a woman like her doesn't belong to a man like me. In a life like we lead. How many people in our game find someone? It's a lot to ask," Ace shows doubts.

"H did. Listen, pal, I'm telling you she's into you. And a woman like that is worth it all. So, get a grip and get to know her." JJ picks up his pint and leaves the table as the woman returns and sits down with Ace.

"I hope I didn't scare your friend off," she says.

Ace smiles. "No, no, JJ is scared of all women not just you. It's nothing personal." They both laugh.

"You haven't asked me yet," she bluntly states.

"Asked you for what?"

"My name."

Ace smiles. "Okay. What's your name?"

"Birtha," she laughs. Her laugh illuminates a feeling of great warmth within Ace. "Ava, my name is Ava Sutton."

"That's definitely better than Birtha. Well, Ava, it's good to meet you, I'm Tony Johnson but everyone knows me as 'Ace'."

Out of nowhere, a drunken relative of Nancy jumps on stage and starts to sing karaoke. The song she sings is slow and people begin to dance with their partners.

"Tell me, Ace, do you dance?" Ava asks.

"No, no, I'm no dancer."

"Oh, I think you are." Ava rises and forces Ace up. They embark on a slow dance.

For the first time in a long time, Ace is lost in the beauty of a woman. His heart is glowing, and he feels an excited anxiety flow through him. As the song ends, he leans in and the two kiss.

As the night draws to a close, Ace walks Ava home safely. They reach her house near Deansgate station.

"Well, this is me," Ava says as they stand outside of her house.

"This is you. Can I see you again?" Ace asks as Ava smiles at him.

"You better. Check your pocket," Ava kisses Ace then runs into her house like a giddy child. Ace goes into his jacket pocket and pulls out a note that has Ava's number written on it. He smiles.

January 24th

The morning sun breaks through giving light to the waking city. Ace's alarm beams off rudely waking him from an erotic dream he's just had about Ava. He wipes his eyes and downs a glass of milk before having a morning urination to clear the lagers he sipped last night from his system. Today is the day he, JJ, and Flacco will pay a visit to Adrians Andris.

After guzzling down his morning coffee, Ace jumps into his Pontiac Fiero and heads to pick JJ and Flacco up.

Ace pulls up to a park that's ten minutes from his apartment. This is where he has arranged to pick JJ and Flacco up. Only JJ is here.

"Where is he?" An annoyed Ace asks.

"God knows. The guy is a liability we know this." JJ gets into the car.

"He has five minutes, or we are going without him," Ace announces.

"So how did it go last night?"

"It went well yeah. Where is this prick?"

"You seeing her again?" JJ has a childlike glee over his face.

"I will be. If you don't mind, I'd like to focus on this job." Ace doesn't like to go into details about girls, he's not outwardly in touch with his emotions. JJ looks at him and smiles. He is delighted that his friend may have found someone.

"There he is." Ace sees Flacco walking towards the car from a distance. Flacco seems in no rush and is holding a white carrier bag in his hand.

"Is that a frigging takeaway wrapper in his hand?" JJ notices Flacco carrying the bag.

"Morning, fellas," Flacco greets the two as he gets into the back of the car.

"Where have you been?" Ace firmly asks.

"I had to get breakfast," Flacco replies as he pulls out a cheeseburger from the bag. JJ turns around and looks at him in disgust.

"Breakfast? You have got to be shitting me. We're working with a Goddam child." Ace isn't impressed. JJ shakes his head and watches as Flacco bites into the burger.

"I can't eat when you watch me like that," Flacco says. JJ just continues to watch him eat.

A thirty-minute drive later, Ace parks up on St John Street.

"Which house is Eva's?" JJ asks.

"That one," Ace points to the right of him.

"So, what's the plan, boys?" The irritating voice of Flacco wonders.

"We wait for him to come to collect Eva's money and then we pounce. Beat him till he bruises, nothing more," Ace orders.

JJ turns to face Flacco again. "Don't run this time," he says. Flacco puts his head down. He's ashamed that he has got this reputation.

"Right, let's go."

Eva greets the men and offers to cook them some food as they wait in the kitchen. Ace and JJ kindly reject the offer but Flacco requests a bowl of cereal.

"You've already eaten, you greedy git," JJ says as Flacco tucks into his cereal.

"I'm a growing man, JJ. A growing man."

"You are a boy," Ace adds his opinion.

"Are you sure I can't get you anything, Ace?" Eva asks.

"I'm all right, thanks, Eva. Listen, it might be in your best interest if you leave until we are finished. Maybe head out to the shops or something. This could get ugly quick," Ace recommends.

"Yeah. Okay, I'll head down to the supermarket and come back in like twenty minutes?"

"Make it an hour to be safe, love," Ace advises. Eva goes to put her jacket on and leaves the house.

"I'll make sure to wash up my bowl, Eva!" Flacco calls out as Eva leaves.

JJ slaps Flacco across the back of his head. "I'll make sure to wash up my bowl, Eva," JJ repeats Flacco's words in a high-pitched voice. "What did we do to Hunter to be working with this baboon?"

JJ then begins looking around the kitchen and he sees a photo of Eva with her husband and kids playing on a beach. He goes over and examines it. "They seem happy," he states.

"Is that photo before or after she got dicked down by this prick? I mean I can't blame him, I'd rail her. She is unbelievable," Flacco claims. JJ puts the photo down and walks over to the sitting Flacco. JJ takes the cereal bowl and pours the milk over Flacco's pants. "You dickhead! Why would you do that?" Flacco complains.

At 10.30 am, Ace hears a van pulling up directly outside of the house. "It's him. Be ready," he says having checked out of the window.

The bald and well-built 6ft 5" Adrians Andris enters the house without knocking. "Payment is due, bitch."

"I don't think so, baldy," JJ says as he sits on a chair a few feet from the door.

Adrians stands confused at this sight. "Who are you?"

"Your worst nightmare," JJ says as Ace comes from behind the door armed with a cricket bat owned by one of Eva's children. He strikes Adrians in the back of his knees which grounds him. JJ then stands and hits Adrians in the face with the wooden chair he's just been sitting on.

"Now, you big slab of meat, you are going to leave Eva and her family alone. You will receive no more payments and keep well away, or these beatings will continue." Ace kneels down to Adrians' face.

"I'm not going anywhere." Adrians spits up at Ace who rises to his feet.

"Flacco, you want to show your worth? Have at him," Ace orders.

Flacco approaches the floored Adrians and hits him several times over in his face. He then pulls his fist back after a few hits and shakes his hand. He's never hit anyone before, the pain is unfamiliar to him. JJ storms over and takes the cricket bat off Ace and strikes Adrians again with it.

"Now, as I said before, you will pay no more visits to Eva or her family. If you do, then we will ruin you," Ace spits back at him.

Adrians, who is now full of rage, suddenly forces himself up and launches JJ into the wall. He then takes out a small black knife and swings for Ace. It's fight or flight time.

Flacco stands there almost frozen. He wants to run but he also wants rid of his running reputation. In a short moment of adrenaline-induced energy, he flings forward and tackles Adrians down as he's swinging for Ace with his knife.

Adrians tumbles to the floor dropping his knife near Flacco.

"Well in, Flac," Ace cheers. Flacco isn't done though. He's high on adrenaline. Fuelled with rage and desperate for approval, Flacco picks up Adrian's knife.

"Flac, calm it." A slight rush of panic hits Ace as he sees that Flacco has clearly lost control of his sanity. This has always been a fear of Ace's. He fears that when someone loses control and order then dangerous and damaging things happen as they know no limitations.

Adrians looks up laughing at Flacco. "You don't have the balls," he says, which riles Flacco up further. He sees an opportunity. An opportunity to show Ace and JJ that he isn't a joke. He sees a chance to show them that he is a man to be taken just as seriously as them. He looks down at Adrians in an exasperated rage. He lunges and continuously stabs Adrians over and over. Ace and JJ are in shock. They rush over and pull Flacco off Adrians, forcing him to stop his relentless stabbing attack.

JJ pins Flacco up against the wall as Ace heads over to the extremely bloodied Adrians. "You've killed him."

"Oh, you idiot!" JJ lets go of Flacco who drops his knife onto the floor. Flacco's eyes are glued onto the deceased body. He is contemplating what he has just done. The room is hit with pure silence for a few minutes as they all stare at the body.

Ace and JJ are stunned. They can't believe what has just transpired right in front of their eyes. Ace knows he must put his shock to one side though and think fast on his feet.

"JJ, get me some bin bags," Ace orders as he gets a meat cleaver out of the kitchen drawers.

"What's our move?" JJ asks.

"I'm going to cut him into parts then put them in the bags. Flacco, head up to the bathroom and get a sponge. You are cleaning this mess."

Flacco says nothing, he just looks at Adrians' lifeless body.

"Flacco!" JJ shouts which breaks him out of his guilty trance.

Thirty minutes later, Ace and JJ have put the bin bags containing Adrians' body parts into the boot of Ace's car. Flacco soon joins them outside having just finished cleaning away all of the blood.

"What have you done with the sponge?" JJ questions.

"Threw it in the bin."

"The bin inside the kitchen? How are you so stupid?" JJ outrages as he storms back inside and removes the blood-stained sponge from the kitchen bin before heading back to the car boot and putting it inside one of the bin bags.

"What do we tell Hunter?" Flacco asks, fearing what the repercussions of his violent actions will be.

"We tell him that we were right and that he shouldn't trust you," JJ snaps back.

"Do we have to tell him about this?" Flacco looks to Ace.

"I don't know. Just let me think."

"Acey, are you crazy? We need to tell H. Adrians is one of Paul fucking Moonie's men!"

"JJ, just let me think. Get in the car, come on, let's go."

"I will not be killed for the actions of this delinquent." JJ opens the car door and is about to get in.

"Shut your dam mouth, JJ! I stepped up in there and saved your ass," Flacco fires back.

"That's it!" JJ slams the car door shut and clenches his fists. "I'm going to kill him, Acey."

"Come on then." Flacco spits onto the floor.

"Enough. Both of you!" Ace shouts as he steps in between them both and diffuses the situation.

Ace knows that telling Hunter would make things increasingly worse, but he also knows that Hunter needs to know something as important as this as the repercussions could be monumental. By telling Hunter, it will also show him that Flacco isn't ready to be as involved with the gang. What should he do?

"We have to tell H," Ace declares after thinking it over in silence as he drives.

"Thank god, he has sense!" JJ approves.

"That's it for me then, isn't it? What will he do to me?" A petrified Flacco responds.

"Whatever he wants to because you, my stupid as shit friend, have just compromised us all. What were you thinking?" JJ sharply asks.

"I wasn't thinking, I just saw red."

"Obviously, you weren't thinking! You absolute dick. You've put us all at risk here."

"I'm sorry okay. I made a bad call."

"That's the understatement of the century."

"I'm sorry."

"Hunter's orders were to beat and not kill. NOT KILL. God help you when we tell him."

III

'Icarus'

Across Manchester in the centre of the city, Hunter and Vince have just arrived at Bradley Owens' birthday party in one of his three penthouses in the North of England.

The penthouse is enormous and is the definition of wealth. Shiny white couches are positioned neatly across the gleaming floor, two polished oak wine cabinets on either side of the door, rare houseplants scattered around, and expensive paintings hang on the walls. One of which catches Hunter's attention, 'San Giorgio Maggiore at Dusk' by Claude Monte. Its beauty mesmerises Hunter who has always had a fondness for paintings.

"Isn't she beautiful, McHay?" Hunter taps Vince on his shoulder to turn and admire the painting with him.

"That it is, H. Magnificent." McHay doesn't share Hunter's passion for paintings he just agrees to please his boss.

"Tell me, McHay, what do you see in this painting?"

McHay looks at the painting intently. "I see the island of San Giorgio Maggiore. It's remarkable."

"Look at the light. It captures the beauty of the light at sunset. The beauty of light in the darkness. In life, you must find that light in the darkness."

McHay looks up at his boss. "Don't get all romantic on me now, H."

"You have Amanda's number. Call her."

McHay nearly chokes on the white wine that was handed to him on his way into the penthouse.

"Lizzy told you about Amanda?"

"She did."

"I am going to call her, I just need to find the right time," McHay defends himself as he slightly blushes.

"Don't wait too long, McHay, there will always be someone better."

Before McHay has the chance to respond, a voice from behind them calls out. They turn around and are greeted by Bradley Owens.

Bradley Owens is a brown-haired and well-built bodybuilder who is the embodiment of masculinity and steroids. As well as owning several garages in Manchester, he also runs his own protein company selling shakes and protein bars all across the United Kingdom. However, all that isn't enough for Owens, he also deals narcotics across Cheetham and other areas of Manchester. He is one of the most well-known and respected drug dealers in the area. Owens always wears a white tank top wherever he goes for any occasion. He likes to remind people of his size to strike intimidation in the hearts of anyone who dares to confront him. He likes people to know that he could beat them. Well, more realistically, he wants people to think that he could beat them.

Although he has built himself a solidified empire within the North of England, most people share the opinion that he is a hubristic man who has fallen lucky.

"Gentlemen, so glad you have made it. You like the place?" Owens grabs another glass of white wine from one of his waiters who is doing laps of the floor offering free wine to everyone.

"It's sublime, Bradley, it truly is. We are grateful for the invitation," Hunter replies.

"You know you fellas are welcome in any one of my homes any time. Did you check out my balcony? It has a great view." Owens points to his right highlighting his outdoor balcony that overlooks the city.

"It looks great, Bradley," McHay complements.

"It's also peaceful. The type of space where nobody would interrupt us talking business," he replies.

"You invited us here to talk shop?" Hunter wonders.

Owens smiles. "You are a man of great intelligence, Hunter, just like me. Shall we?"

Hunter and McHay finish their glasses of wine before following Owens out onto his balcony.

Owens' balcony oversees a breathtaking view of the city. All the busy city life, all of the rising skyscrapers, all of the aging factories, and all of the commuting hustle and bustle in one big view.

"As you know, gentlemen, there is a growing tension between us here in Cheetham and Moss Side," Owens states.

"There's always been a tension," Hunter remarks.

"Well, yes, but now things are far worse. We are sitting on a ticking time bomb before an all-out war breaks out. So, you can understand why a prominent Cheetham representative like myself can't be seen stirring the pot with Moss Side. We don't want a war."

"Where are you going with this, Owens?" A curious McHay wants Owens to get to the point.

"Last week, a Moss Side gang under the name 'Red Syndicate' burnt down my kid brother's off-track betting shop after they had heard he had been bad-mouthing their betting shop for essentially being a front for their money. He was trying to steal their customers by telling them the truth. Anyway, I need you and your gang to burn their shop down in return for what they did. I myself cannot get involved, a war with Moss Side is not good for business. My poor brother isn't Cheetham or Moss Side, he's just a good guy trying to make a simple living."

Hunter scratches his neck, a usual trait of his when he's stressed. "Look, Brad, we are debt collectors. We don't get involved in this sort of stuff."

Bradley pats Hunter on his shoulder. "I got you out of that shadow, Hunter. Because of my connections, people in this city now hold a stronger reputation for you after you did that job for me. Because of me, the 'fugly five' are now the 'famous five'. Do this job as a thank you to me."

"How dare you…" Hunter holds his hand out and stops McHay from finishing his rant. Hunter understands that Owens' words do hold some truth. Hunter's gang is now viewed highly within the city thanks to the word of mouth spread by Owens after Hunter and Ace carried out that job on Mr Alonso. They are now slowly becoming more than debt collectors.

"Double the payment of the last job and you have a deal." Hunter looks Owens straight in his bright brown eyes.

"Money is no object to me, my friend. Looks like we have a deal." Owens offers out his hand which Hunter shakes.

"Whereabouts in Moss Side is the shop?"

"Head back inside and mingle for a bit and I'll bring you all the details in a document I have. It's always a pleasure doing business with Hunter and his merry men." Owens sarcastically pats McHay on his back as he re-enters the party.

"Arsehole," McHay mutters.

Hunter and McHay stay on the balcony taking in the astonishing view.

"What are you doing, H? We shouldn't be getting involved in the heat between Cheetham and Moss Side," McHay, for one of the few rare times, shows opposition to Hunter.

"McHay, times are changing. The 90s are coming and to keep on top, we have to adapt and solidify these connections we have. Look at us, we are on the rise. We are the biggest we have ever been so why stop here when we can go bigger."

Since the early 80s, Cheetham and Moss Side have been bitter and violent rivals. Their attacks on each other had become infamous in the city, nowhere was safe from pubs to cinemas, to even car parks. All of which witnessed a bloodbath between the two sides at some point.

One of the most famous stories of these attacks was in 1983. The host of the attack was a small pub called 'The Soldier's Arms'. It was 2 pm and the pub was packed as Manchester United played West Ham United. Here, a Moss Side gang entered the pub armed with machine guns and opened fire on the brother of a Cheetham gang leader, killing eight innocents in the process.

The wars between the two sides are the most morbid drug wars in the history of the United Kingdom. They had such an astronomical impact on the city that Manchester gained the nicknames, 'Gunchester' and 'Madchester'.

However, from late 1984 onwards, both sides gradually eased tensions. Although, there is still a fragile animosity between the two. All it would take is a little spark to trigger the full-blown breakout of war once more.

"I'm sorry to question you, H, I'm just concerned. If a war is brewing between Cheetham and Moss Side, I think we should just be careful that's all."

"McHay, everything will be fine. I know what I'm doing. We head to Moss Side, start a fire in that place, and head back home. In and out and no one will ever know it's us or Owens behind it. We will make it look like an inside job. And for that easy bit of work, we get a fat pay cheque and a boost in our reputation. All without even breaking a sweat."

McHay feels a little more open to the idea now that he sees Hunter's glowing confidence about the job.

"Now, come on, there's a party to drink at."

As Hunter and McHay rub shoulders with Cheetham's elite, Ace, JJ, and Flacco park up opposite a construction site. The site is in construction to be yet another pub in the city and is based around ten miles from Eva's house.

"We wait here till the sun sets. Then we bury the bags under the floor," Ace lays out his plan.

"Okay, but we aren't taking Flacco with us," JJ responds.

Flacco is annoyed by this. "And why not?" He asks.

JJ quickly turns around and looks at him. "Are you serious? Do not push my temper because I will seriously rip your arsehole out and shove it down your throat!" JJ's words cause Ace to let slip a little chuckle.

"Flacco, you stay here and stay silent. You have caused enough hassle for one day," Ace recommends.

"Yeah, and prepare yourself for the ultimate lashing that H is going to give you, rightfully."

Flacco looks down in shame and worry.

As the sun lowers into a temporary retirement and the night crawls in, Ace and JJ take the bin bags containing segments of Adrians Andris and enter the construction site.

Cement mixers and tools populate the soon-to-be bar room. Walls in mid-construction loom high and the floor is only half laid. *This should be easy*, thinks Ace.

"Here we go." Ace places the bags down and heads over to the recently laid wooden floor. He and JJ meticulously lift four wooden planks which reveal a twelve-foot drop underneath. They drag the bags over and hurdle them down into the hole before re-covering the wooden planks.

"What do you think H will do to Flacco?" JJ wonders.

"H will do whatever he pleases, there will be no stopping him. Whatever he decides, it surely can't be good for Flacco. Hunter doesn't handle being disobeyed well. I should know."

The two head back to the car and embark on the journey to Hunter's house.

At 9.45 pm, Ace, JJ, and the scared-stiff Flacco enter Hunter's basement to break the news to him. The three men take their seats at the table which already homes Hunter and McHay.

"Gentlemen, I hope you have come to tell me that you have dealt with our Andris situation."

Flacco has his head looking down at the ground. With his heart racing, sweat is beginning to break free on the top of his forehead.

"Flacco killed him, H. He lost his head in there and he stabbed him to death," JJ bluntly breaks the news. Hunter spits out his drink in shock. McHay is also stunned by the revelation. Hunter doesn't verbally respond. He remains silent for the time being, letting the information register.

"Flacco killed him? You have got to be kidding us, right? Flacco?" McHay wants to believe that they are wise-cracking them. McHay looks up at Ace for answers.

"It's true," Ace simply says. Hunter stands to his feet and slowly approaches the sitting Flacco, who still has his head held down.

"When I briefed you, I specifically said for this job to be dealt with cleanly. I asked, no, I fucking ordered you not to kill. Beat and intimidate but NOT kill," Hunter begins to remove his belt. Ace, JJ, and McHay feel slightly uncomfortable as they know what comes next won't be for the faint of heart.

"H, I am so sorry. I just got too caught up in the moment."

"Do not H me, child! I took a chance on you when these men doubted me. You have made me look like a fool. You are an ungrateful little insignificant prick!" Hunter violently whips Flacco across the face with his belt several times over which draws blood across Flacco's frail face. "Do you know just what kind of shit you have landed us in?" Hunter strikes again before throwing Flacco back first off the chair, crashing hard on the cold concrete floor.

"H, please, I am sorry. I will make it up to you!" Flacco cries.

"Crying? How pathetic." Hunter lashes him again across his face. "Get a Goddam grip!" Hunter strikes with his belt more.

Flacco lies in a small pool of blood that drips down from his face. After hitting him a few more times, Hunter puts his belt back on and returns to sitting at the table having recomposed himself.

"What did you do with the body?"

"We disposed it under the floor of a construction site," Ace informs.

"Good. Could it in any way be traced back to us if the body is found?"

"We did a pretty good job of cleaning it up, H. We wiped everything and no one saw us," JJ chimes in.

Hunter releases a slight sigh of relief after running his hands through his short hair.

"I need a drink." Hunter stands and heads upstairs towards his fridge where he pulls out a can of beer. He also grabs a towel from the side and throws it down to Flacco when he returns to the basement.

"I don't want any blood on my floor." Hunter sits back down at the table. "We have more business to discuss. We have another job to carry out for Bradley Owens. This one is much different to anything we have done before." Hunter explains in detail to his men the job they are undertaking for Owens.

The reaction is polarising. JJ shares the same doubts that McHay had at first about the job.

"H, if this job goes wrong then we find ourselves tied up in a drug war. A war that we should stay well clear of," JJ proclaims.

"Like I said, JJ, the job is simple, and it won't go wrong. Red Syndicate will not even know we or Owens are behind the fire. It will look like an inside job. Thus, there will be no need for a war to break out," Hunter attempts to sway JJ's thinking.

"Listen, you are the boss, H, and if you want this then we will do it. I'm just not sure if it is a good idea," JJ follows up.

"JJ, we are not exclusive to debt-collecting any more. We are gangsters. This is our rise. The fear of the fall is what stops the rise. We need to not fear the fall, that's how we rise to the top."

Ace doesn't share his doubts with the group even though he also has doubts about the job and doesn't feel it is in the gang's best interest to get involved in a potential drug war. He mentally compares Hunter to Icarus flying too close to the sun.

"Acey, you seem quiet. Do you have any concerns?" Hunter looks over to his understudy.

"It all sounds fine with me, H." Ace sees no point in opposing Hunter as his stubborn set ways means he won't change his mind even if the whole room disagrees with him. It would just be a waste of breath and time to show opposition.

"Good. In two days we make our move."

"I'm also fine with it, boss," Flacco's feeble voice vocalises.

"Fuck off, Flacco."

IV
'The Spark'

One day later, Ace sits in a newly opened, lavish Chinese restaurant with the lovely Ava on their first date. Ava is dressed in a tight pink dress with her hair neatly combed and her lips coated in a delicious red. Ace has decided to wear a black silk shirt for the occasion with his hair slightly gelled up.

The two have just ordered their main meals. Ace has gone for the duck in plum sauce, and Ava has gone for sweet and sour chicken with egg-fried rice.

"So then, Ace, tell me what you do for a living."

"For a living? Well, that is one good question. I'm somewhat of a debt collector."

"A debt collector? That's definitely different," she laughs.

"Well, I figured it's best to be honest with you. After my parents died, a good friend of theirs took me in and raised me. Ever since I have been working for him, collecting debts and running errands for him. I feel like I owe him because if he didn't take me in, I have no idea where I would be." Ace feels that being honest and open with Ava will impress her as it shows trust and that he feels comfortable around her.

"I'm so sorry about your parents. How did they go if you don't mind me asking?"

"It was a car accident. But yeah, I was in a very dark place until Hunter came along. He saved me in many ways."

"Well, I know I don't know you that well just yet, but I'm sure your parents would be proud of you. You seem like a good man."

Ace smiles. "Enough about me, tell me about yourself. What do you do for a living?"

"I'm a wrestler. Former women's heavyweight champion."

"Wrestler? That's also definitely different."

"It's also a lie. You are so gullible." Ava laughs as Ace realises it was a joke and laughs too.

"I'm actually an actress."

"Wow, that's amazing!"

"No, that's a lie." She laughs even harder this time having got Ace again. "For real though, I am a comic illustrator."

"Nice. You worked on anything I might know?"

"Erm, ever heard of 'The Mighty Ten'?"

'The Mighty Ten' is a famous comic book series that has run across the UK since its formation in 1950. 'The Mighty Ten' is a superhero group of ten of the greatest heroes mustered from all over the globe to come together and fight earth-threatening villains.

Each hero in the ten is named according to the number they were recruited with 'One' being the leader. Each hero also has their own speciality power. 'One' has super strength; 'Two' has super speed; 'Three' has laser eyes; 'Four' has invisibility; 'Five' has flight through her angel wings; 'Six' has the ability to turn into liquid; 'Seven' can speak to the dead; 'Eight' has four legs; 'Nine' is the most intelligent man in the world, and 'Ten' is an alien who can teleport.

"Heard of 'The Mighty Ten'? I used to love those books! Nine was always my favourite. It was a great move to change his gender to female." Ace is delighted, and Ava can see this. She looks at him and smiles. She is fond of his unforgotten passion. "How long have you been working on them?"

"About five years now, I love it. Ever since I was a little girl, I have been fascinated with writing and drawing my own comics. My family never had much so growing up, we were always short on money and whatever we got, we had to work so hard for. I remember it was my Nan who bought me my first ever notepad and set of crayons when I was ten. Ever since that day, I fell in love and now it's my job." Ava is extremely content with her life at the minute.

"I'm certain that your Nan is very proud of you." The main meals arrive and they tuck in.

Ace is diving into the duck when Ava asks, "What was your first impression of me when you saw me at that party?"

"I thought who is that girl at this party that I have literally no right being at and didn't get an invite to."

"Wait, you didn't?" Ava laughs.

"Nope, that was a complete and utter gate crash." The two laugh. "Your turn. What was your first impression of me?"

"I thought, woah that leather jacket looks tacky but I can tell those eyes carry some stories."

"I assure you, they do."

"I can't wait to find out about them."

After the meal, Ace walks Ava home again, taking the long route back so that they can see more of the city at night.

The two reach the front of her house. "Well, this is me again." Ava looks up to Ace.

"This is you." Ace holds Ava by the waist and goes in for a long kiss. Ava's lips taste what Ace imagines the kiss of a goddess to taste. It's so good, it should be forbidden.

"I don't usually do this but I feel like we have made a solid connection tonight. So would you like to maybe come in?" She asks smiling.

"Yes. Yes, I think I would." Ace swipes Ava off her feet and carries her into her house where they embrace in a heated half hour of intercourse.

As the sun rises over the vast city of Manchester, Ace wakes up next to the beautiful Ava. He rolls over and kisses her forehead before exiting the bed and going downstairs to make her a cup of coffee and a slice of toast.

He is spreading strawberry jam onto the toast when he hears footsteps coming down from upstairs.

"Morning, you," Ace speaks to who he thinks is Ava.

"Morning, sweetheart," laughs the voice of Ava's housemate, Judy.

"Ah, you must be Judy, right?"

"Indeed, I am. I take it you two had a good night?"

"That we did. Your housemate is incredible." Ace picks up the plate of toast and the mug of coffee and heads towards the stairs.

"Take care of her, she's one of the good ones."

"Don't I know it."

Ace can't remember the last time he has been so infatuated with a girl. The closest he can relate to this feeling is when he was back in school, and he had a crush on a blonde girl called Monica. Monica would go on to break Ace's heart though as she chose his classmate, Eric, over him. But he expects that his feelings for Ava will massively outgrow any that came before her, and he hopes it won't end as painfully as his crush for Monica did.

Five miles south of Ace making Ava breakfast, JJ exits his council estate house and is greeted by Vince McHay standing in front of JJ's parked grey van.

"Morning, treacle tits. It's good to see you out in the open and out of H's ass for once," JJ comically addresses McHay.

"You're hilarious, JJ. I hope you've had a full breakfast. Today is a big day."

"Every day is a big day for a superstar like me, McHay, I have to carry all of your arses."

"Only in your bloody dreams you do."

"So, how do you like the whip?" JJ refers to his newly purchased van that McHay stands before.

"I'm sure it's quite the attraction for the ladies."

"I'll have you know that Patricia here is a modern-day marvel with the ladies."

McHay shakes his head in disapproval.

"You're a pig, JJ." The two get into the van.

JJ turns left at the end of the estate and the two join the main road.

"So how far is this place we are going?" McHay asks.

"It's a warehouse on New Union Street. The guy there is an old friend of mine." JJ and McHay are travelling down to the warehouse to meet a man by the name of Brian Bernard. Bernard is supplying them with six containers of petrol. These containers will be used to burn down the betting shop that is owned by 'Red Syndicate'.

"Tell me, Vino, in all honesty, do you really think that this job is a good idea?"

"I have faith in H and his decisions. He's got us this far, hasn't he? Our names are starting to mean something."

"Jesus Christ, McHay, crawl out of his backside for one minute. He was wrong about Flacco and if it weren't for me and Ace, that incident could have bitten us badly. It still could if the Moonie boys ever go sniffing around it. H is over his head these days. You know it and I know it."

"Look, JJ, what happened with Flacco was just an unfortunate accident that won't be repeated. This dance is simple, and we will never be outed as the ones responsible and in return, our reputation and trust amongst this city will grow even more."

"That's if it goes to 'H's almighty plan'. What if this goes wrong, McHay? We are meddling in a situation that may bring about an all-out war between

Cheetham and Moss Side. A war which will be catastrophic and a war that we will be brought slap bang in the middle of. What will that do for our reputation? We do not belong anywhere near this." JJ's words render McHay speechless as he understands, to a degree, some of what JJ is ranting on about but he doesn't want to question or denounce Hunter.

The two reach the park that's near Ace's apartment where they see Ace sitting on a nearby bench awaiting their arrival. Ace jumps into the back of the van.

"Morning, fellas."

"Well, if it isn't the man, the myth, the legend himself. How was date night then?" JJ's question slightly antagonises Ace as he hasn't told McHay about Ava yet.

"Date night? Something you want to tell me, Acey?" McHay contributes.

"The date was great. She's called Ava and she works as a comic book illustrator."

McHay turns to Ace and smiles. "I'm happy for you, Acey, well in, man."

"Thank you, McHay. It's nice, isn't it? A little bit of light in this world of darkness."

"Save the romance to Shakespeare kid," McHay laughs.

"Take no notice, Acey, he's just jealous because the last time he was touched by a woman was in 1971," JJ banters. Ace smiles.

"So, how far is this warehouse?" Ace diverts the conversation to business.

"About fifteen minutes from here."

"And the guy we are meeting. Can we trust him?" The always thinking Ace questions.

"Yes, Acey, he's an old friend of mine."

"How do you know him? Have you checked if he has any connections to Cheetham or Moss Side?"

"Acey, relax, I know him. He's not going to rat us out."

"It's important to check, JJ, especially with a job like this where the stakes are so high."

"Look, Acey, trust me, okay? This guy won't be a problem."

Fifteen minutes later, the three enter New Union Street and pull up outside of a grubby and aged warehouse with rusty steel shutters closing it from the outside world.

"Here we are, gentlemen," JJ announces as the three men stand at the fore of the shutters. JJ steps forward and bangs on the shutters three times. They slowly begin to ascend. The three silhouettes of Ace, JJ, and McHay breach the inside view of the warehouse as the shutter rises.

"Is it a bird? Is it a plane? Is it fuck? It's JJ Reeves!" The voice of Brian Bernard shouts out. Brian Bernard's appearance is rather chunky and a small crumb overweight. His brown hair is thinning each day, and his goatee is well overdue for a trim and the removal of several crisp crumbs it's collected over the past two days. His breath also wreaks as if a rat has just died inside his mouth.

Bernard is a friend of JJ's younger brother, AJ, and as JJ never made many friends at school, he would often spend his time with AJ and Brian. For the past five years, Brian has been running a small business selling supplies and doing the occasional mechanical job for anyone who would come to him. Among the area, Brian has the reputation of a scruffy and indolent man who is not well-liked.

"Brian Bernard, always a pleasure and never a chore. How are you, man?" JJ hugs his old-time friend.

"I'm all the better for seeing you, JJ."

"How's Nikki?" JJ asks referring to Brian's wife.

"She's gone. It was last month."

"Shit, Brian, I'm so sorry."

"It's fine, it was my fault. What was she supposed to do when she walked in on me and her sister in the bath."

Brian's words stun the three men. From the way he said it, Brian had implied that she'd died not broken up with him.

"Yeah, that will do it. Have you got our petrol?" Ace breaks the awkward silence.

"Yes. Yes, the petrol. Give me one second." Brian heads to his office in the back of the warehouse.

"Who is this clown, JJ?" McHay ponders.

"He's a little 'out there' I know but he's never done me wrong before."

"Well, there's always a first time for everything," Ace remarks.

Brian returns from his office with a trolley accommodating six containers of petrol.

"Here you are, gentlemen. That will be £40."

Ace reaches into his pocket and pulls out a fifty-pound note. "Keep the change."

"Yeah, there's a shop down the road. Maybe use that change to buy yourself some toothpaste," McHay insults Bernard.

With the purchase complete, the three men now must wait until nightfall to carry out the next step in the plan. To make the passage of time more entertaining they decide to head to 'The Blue Moon', where they sit in their usual booth and sip down some beers.

"Anyway, McHay, enough about me and Ava. H tells me you're interested in Amanda, Lizzy's sister," Ace brings McHay's love life to the attention of the group. JJ dramatically spits out some of his beer in shock.

"McHay, you dirty dog. Amanda? Does she know you're still a virgin?" JJ jokes.

"Lick a dick, JJ. I am interested in Amanda, yes. Big shock. Can we move on?"

"Don't be embarrassed, McHay, we've all had a crush on Amanda at one point in time. It would be impossible not to. Are you going to take her out?" JJ enquires.

"I'm thinking of doing, yes. Lizzy gave me her number and once we do the dance tonight, I'm going to call her. Now please can we change the subject?"

"Aw, look at McHay, Acey, he's all embarrassed because he's in love. It won't be long before I'll be standing at your wedding entertaining the masses with my best man speech. Bloody hell, that would make H your brother-in-law. That's the ultimate dream for you, right? Oh no, your ultimate dream would be if Hunter is the one that you're marrying." JJ's words have Ace slightly chuckling to himself.

"You're missing one key detail in there, JJ, to be the best man you actually have to be a man," McHay returns the banter. "Now, Acey, let's run through tonight's plan," he continues.

"The plan." Ace shuffles in his seat and gets comfy before leaning in to address the others. "At 11 pm, we arrive at the shop. Owens says that the alarm is in the back of the shop just before the entrance to the storage room. So, we break in that way and as fast as possible and we take out the alarm. Once we have the alarm disabled, we lay down the petrol and we set the joint blazing. We should be done by 11.20 pm."

"Should is the key word there, Acey," the wary JJ intervenes.

"Would you stop worrying, JJ? H wouldn't send us on the dance if he felt it was as dangerous as you are overthinking it to be," McHay stresses.

"McHay, for once will you realise that there is more to life than the smell of H's sweaty ass crack. This job has monumental stakes. One bad move and we find ourselves in the middle of a war."

"Fellas, enough. We can't do anything about our situation. H's mind is set. All we can do is play with the hand that is dealt. Now let's sit back and drink until the time comes." Ace raises his bottle of beer.

The time soon comes along. The three fellas arrive in Moss Side and park around the back of the betting shop owned by the 'Red Syndicate'. The shop is small-scale and is based on the corner of a craggy-looking street which last saw cleanliness back in the 60s.

JJ parks the van at the entrance of a back alley. Armed with two containers of petrol each, the three walk up the alley and reach the back of the betting shop. Not a single word is spoken.

After McHay breaks the back door using a nearby rock to bash the handle in, Ace realises that the alarm hasn't been triggered.

"Someone must be here. Keep sharp and keep alert. If someone comes and sees us, knock them out and we will drag them to the van and dump them somewhere on the way home," he orders.

McHay thinks to himself, *Wouldn't it be easier to just kill the person if they catch them?* But then he realises neither Ace nor JJ has attained their first kill yet.

"JJ, take the right side of the store. I'll take the left. McHay you take the basement." The three all separate to their locations where they begin to open the containers and pour down the petrol.

As the petrol flows down from Ace's container, he can't help but flicker his eyes over the store looking out for someone in the building. There is always the scenario that someone forgot to set the alarm before leaving but due to his paranoia and constant overthinking, Ace doesn't consider that scenario for a second.

BANG. Ace rapidly turns his head to his right side which is where the noise originated from. "Sorry, Acey, that was me. What a stupid place for a table!" The noise was caused by JJ accidentally backing up into a table as he was pouring down his petrol.

"Bloody hell, JJ, be careful."

"Hello?" The Irish voice of 'Red Syndicate' leader, Finn O'Sullivan, echoes through the store.

"Shit!" JJ exclaims as the sight of a slim, ginger, thin bearded, brown-eyed, and red trench coat-wearing Finn O'Sullivan entering the main floor haunts him.

O'Sullivan aims his silver Bren Ten handgun at Ace. "You move and I kill your buddy here, okay?" He threatens JJ.

"Now, tell me which frigging idiot sent you down here tonight?"

Ace refuses to answer, instead, he pulls his black SIG Sauer P226 handgun from his jacket and the two find themselves in a stand-off.

"Looks like we have ourselves a little western here, don't we, Clint Eastwood? Don't be a fool. You are no killer, you're just wasting my and your time."

Ace doesn't reply, he just looks into O'Sullivan's eyes. He doesn't want to pull the trigger. He only pulled his gun as it is the only thing on him that he can defend himself with. He stole the gun from a client he visited last year, only stealing it to look more intimidating on jobs. He never wants to actually use it. Hunter doesn't even know he has it.

"Okay. So, we're going to do this then? I haven't seen your faces before so you must have been sent here by someone. Who? That's all I want to know."

"Not a chance."

"Your loyalty is going to get you killed."

"Maybe one day, but that's not today."

Ace fires his gun up in the air only to the shock that it's not loaded. O'Sullivan laughs at Ace's revelation.

"Poor baby, all out of sweeties? I gave you a chance but it looks like you will be dying today." O'Sullivan cracks his neck before tightening his grip on his Bren Ten.

Ace throws down his gun and closes his eyes and accepts that this could be the end for him.

BASH. BANG.

Ace reopens his eyes to the sight of JJ tackling O'Sullivan. They crash into the side room. As O'Sullivan tumbles with JJ, he fires his gun, and it accidentally sparks the petrol causing a violent flame to ignite and follow the petrol trail. The main room is rising in flames. JJ and O'Sullivan are so focused on pummelling each other that they don't realise what's happening outside of the side room.

After hearing the commotion upstairs, McHay runs up where he witnesses the fire which is now beginning to engulf the room.

"McHay, leave! Get back to the van!" Ace shouts over. McHay observes his surroundings; tables collapsing, betting papers quickly turning to ash, and smoke overtaking the atmosphere. Realising there's nothing he can do as a wall of fire detaches him from Ace, he turns and escapes the building through the door they came in. He had no choice but to run.

"JJ. JJ, can you hear me?" Ace desperately hopes for a response but he doesn't get one. Ace knows that if he stays in the building any longer, he will perish as the flames will corner him. "JJ! JJ! Do you hear me, brother?" There is no answer. Ace must make a decision. The side room where O'Sullivan and JJ tumbled into is collapsing and is full of smoke. The chances of either of them surviving are very slim. He needs to get out of there and fast.

"I'm sorry, brother." A puddle of tears begin to form under Ace's eyes. He knows that if he attempts to help JJ, then there is a high chance that he won't make it out alive. He knows that he must act fast to get out of there. He quickly covers his mouth and nose and makes a run for the back door. Fighting his way through the vicious and vigorous flames shoulder first, he finally makes it out of the building and back into the van where McHay is sitting nervously waiting.

"JJ?" McHay asks.

Ace doesn't give a verbal response, he just looks up with a tear in his eye.

"Shit. We need to get out of here. JJ had the keys. We need to run, Acey."

Ace leans over and begins to hotwire the van which only takes him two minutes. McHay, in a rapid fashion, drives them out of the area.

V

'The First Meeting'

In the following weeks after the brutal burning of the betting shop, the police confirmed that JJ Reeves died from the fire and Finn O'Sullivan is currently in a coma following severe injuries from the collapsing building. Due to their leader being in a coma, 'Red Syndicate' is unable to identify who was responsible for the fire yet and thus a war between Cheetham and Moss Side hasn't started. Although, many members of 'Red Syndicate' are trying to find more details about JJ Reeves and whom he is connected to.

Grieving his best friend, Ace has turned to alcohol and has started on a downhill spiral. Ace has been drinking whisky every night torturing his liver and himself. He keeps reliving the night in his head over and over and over. He blames himself for JJ's death. He believes he could have done more and stayed in the building to help JJ rather than running free.

7 days after the fire

Heavy rain falls across the city as Ava enters Ace's apartment having just finished her shift. The apartment is dark with the only source of light coming from a lamp on the kitchen counter where Ace, now with a light yet scruffy-looking stubble of facial hair, stands with a glass of whisky in his hand.

"How are you today?" She asks as she takes off her coat and hangs up her umbrella.

Ace looks down at his whisky glass and then back up at her. "I have been standing at this spot staring out of that window since 3 pm. It is now 9 pm. The only movement I've had is to turn on this lamp when it got dark out." The smell of whisky from his breath is intoxicating. Ava puts her bag down on the couch, walks over to him, and takes away his whisky glass.

"Honey, you need to stop this. What happened to JJ was a tragic accident. It wasn't your fault."

A tear falls from Ace's eye. "It should have been me, Ava. He saved me and I couldn't do the same for him," Ace speaks as his eyes stare at the floor, almost as if he is ashamed of himself.

Ava puts her arms around him.

"Ace, it was an accident. JJ loved you. You were his brother, not by blood but by heart. Stop blaming yourself."

More tears begin to pour from Ace's eyes as Ava holds him tighter. JJ's death is the first time that Ava has seen Ace cry.

14 days after the fire

A small crowd of people are gathered in Saint Ann's Church for JJ's funeral. Hunter, Lizzy, McHay, Ace, and Ava are sitting in the front row when the doors spring open. Ace turns his head and sees JJ's younger, brown-haired, brown-eyed, 5' 11" brother, Alex-Joe Reeves, also known as AJ, walk in.

AJ sits on the front row allocated to the left of the aisle and to the opposite side of the row Ace is sitting on.

In preparation for the emotionally driven day, Ace drank five glasses of whisky this morning. He is slightly intoxicated. Ava has forced Ace to wear black sunglasses to prevent people from looking him in the eyes and realising that he is hammered.

A few speeches later and just after AJ's heartfelt speech, it is now time for Ace to make his. The speech which he spent three days working on and has written down on a piece of paper. As his name is called up to take to the front, he removes his speech from his blazer pocket and takes to the front. He sways a little but makes it to the front in one piece. No one notices that he is drunk.

He unravels his paper and irons it out with his hands. He then clears his throat and begins. "JJ Reeves, you were a brother to me…" He stops and begins to weep and wipes his tears under his glasses. He then scrunches up his paper and puts it into his trouser pocket. "It's all my fault, JJ. I failed you. You were my brother and I failed you. I didn't do enough that night. I failed. It should have been me, ladies and gentlemen. ME. Not you, JJ. I'm so sorry, brother. I'm so sorry." As Ace breaks down, Ava stands up to drag him back to his seat but Ace persists. "Why didn't you listen?"

Everyone sits and looks at Ace in confusion. They don't know to whom Ace is now directing his words. "Hunter, why didn't you listen? He warned you about that job. He warned us all. It's not just my fault he's gone, it's yours too. You didn't listen and now he's dead. How many people have to die for you to see that you are wrong?" At this point, Hunter rages up and drags Ace out of the church by his neck. He tells the people not to listen to Ace as he's drunk. Ava runs behind them.

Outside of the church, Hunter violently pins Ace up against the wall and removes his sunglasses. "Don't you ever run my name through the mud like that again! I expected better," he spits into Ace's face. "Take a look at yourself. I don't recognise the man in front of me. You're not my Ace."

Ava steps in and pulls Hunter off Ace. She holds her boyfriend's face.

Hunter realises that he may have overstepped a line. "Look, Ace, I'm sorry but you need to find yourself again. JJ is gone and there's nothing we can do to undo that. Whether you actually blame me or blame me because really you blame yourself, it doesn't matter. He's gone. You need to move on."

Hunter looks Ace up and down judging his untucked shirt, slight stubble, and erratic hair. "What have you let your man become, Ava? You are meant to pull him together. Come on, woman."

Hunter's words strike a nerve with Ace.

"Don't you speak to my woman like that!"

"Ace, relax! I'm just saying it's a woman's job to take care of her man, not feed him to be a deadbeat like you're becoming."

Ace marches forward with his fist clenched and takes a harsh swing at Hunter but he miscalculates his stepping and tumbles hard onto the ground.

Hunter walks over and stands over Ace's fallen body. "You are a joke, Acey. Man up." He then returns to Lizzy whilst Ava picks up her man and heads back to the car.

The thought of taking a swing at Hunter would have never flown through Ace's sober mind. It was the false confidence from alcohol he must thank for that one.

The scene that just transpired outside of the church has been tactically observed by three men standing in the far distance wearing long red trench coats; a brown-haired man with a 30cm scar down his face, a butch bald man, and a slim black-haired and long bearded man. These men are members of the 'Red Syndicate' and have been sent to JJ's funeral to take note of who's been in attendance so they can witness whom JJ was connected to in hopes of eventually getting answers to who sent JJ to start the fire.

In the aftermath of the inebriated state that Ace found himself in at JJ's funeral, Hunter decided to give Ace some time off from his jobs whilst he re-evaluated his behaviour and turned in the whisky for water. During this time, Ava became Ace's lifeline and she assisted Ace in processing his guilt and preventing his drinking. Taking slow steps day by day, Ava drove out Ace's desperate taste for whisky and gave Ace the idea to get in touch with JJ's younger brother, AJ, to help ease his guilt. Ava told Ace he could only contact AJ after he's proven he could stay off the booze.

This worked. He stopped drinking and even shaved off his stubble. With Ava being at Ace's side through it all, he knew that she was worth fighting each day for and he soon realised that if he wanted to keep her as an important part of his life then he needed to change his irresponsible antics, which he did. He didn't fight each day to better himself, he fought each day so he could keep her by his side.

Although Ace has re-taken control of his life again, he still isn't the same man he was before JJ died. His smile is gone and has been replaced with a crown of negativity that he has hung over his head every day, all stemming from the guilt he feels for JJ's death.

April 1st

An extremely important date in Ace's life.

As the clock strikes 10 am, Ace sits in his apartment at his dining table with a cup of hot coffee in front of him and his telephone to the left of him.

"How are you feeling, baby?" Ava asks as she enters the room.

"I'm fine. I need to do this, right? So, I'm fine." Any minute now, Ace is about to dial the number of AJ Reeves, JJ's younger brother. Ace feels he owes it to JJ to take care of his brother and give him work. The guilt of JJ's death will always hang over Ace but by doing this he will feel slightly better.

"You've got this, just don't overthink it. I'll be in the next room, I'll just go check if any letters have come." Ava heads into the hallway to check if any post has been posted through the door this morning. It has.

"Ace, wait." Ava returns to Ace with a letter opened in her hand. "Take a look at this. No need to call him, he's written to you." The letter is from AJ. She hands it over to Ace. It reads:

64

Dear Mr Johnson

My name is AJ Reeves and I believe you knew my brother, JJ, very well. I am writing to you in the hopes that you will meet me tomorrow at the park across from Carlton Apartments. I would just like to get to know you and hear stories about my brother. You were his best friend and I feel that I owe it to him to keep an eye on you. I hope this is okay. I will be at the park at 11 am.

Yours sincerely,
AJ Reeves

Ace sits back and lets the information settle into his brain. He reaches over and takes a sip of his coffee before saying, "I will meet him. I owe it to JJ."

The following day brings ghostly grey clouds hanging high above the waking city. Today is the day that history will be set in stone. Whether he knew it or not, this day will forever seal Ace's fate. The day that Tony 'Ace' Johnson meets AJ Reeves.

Ace stands in the empty park awaiting the arrival of AJ with a thousand thoughts racing through his mind. *What if this is a hit? A set up to have him killed out of an act of revenge for JJ. What if AJ gets cold feet and bails? What if this isn't AJ at all and is a member of 'Red Syndicate'? After all, anyone could have written that letter.* His heart begins to pump faster and he lets these irrational thoughts set up camp in his mind. He has nothing on him to defend himself with if it is a hit as he lost his gun in the fire. He stands alone.

He closes his eyes and takes several deep breaths to calm himself down before reopening them and surveying his surroundings.

Considering it is a Wednesday, the park is deserted and looks like a scene from an apocalypse film with no soul in sight, just the sight of the wind elegantly brushing the swing set of a million childhood memories and the old slide that has redecorated itself with the fallen leaves from the trees. Ace positions himself in the very heart of the park in front of an old stone fountain that is bubbling and shooting water rapidly out like there is a displacement from the inside or from the depth to the surface.

Ace then looks over to his left where he sees a figure approaching him. The figure is indeed AJ Reeves. Ace recognises the figure's build and matches it to AJ's having seen him once before at JJ's funeral.

"Mr Johnson?" AJ Reeves questions as he joins Ace.

"Yes."

"You also go by the name Ace, right?"

"I do." Ace can see that AJ has done his research.

"I'm AJ Reeves, it's a pleasure to meet you, Sir." AJ offers his hand, which Ace reluctantly and curiously shakes. He still doesn't know the purpose of AJ wanting to meet him and is hesitant whether to trust him yet.

"I know you and my brother have a history and were close, and I was just wondering if you could answer some questions that I have?"

"I can try. Let's walk."

The two begin to walk around the park as AJ asks Ace questions about JJ.

"At the funeral, I heard you call out a 'Hunter' and you told him that my brother had warned him about a job. I assume that job had something to do with the fire?"

"How much about his business did JJ tell you about?"

"He didn't talk about it much if any really. He always talked about you and a McHay but he never mentioned a Hunter or ever went into detail about the jobs. I just knew that he was a debt collector."

"I see. Your brother was a debt collector, yes, and the job he died on was an unfortunate accident. That's all there is to it." Ace doesn't wish to reveal too much about the job as he doesn't want to compromise Hunter by telling AJ that they were sent to blaze the betting shop on behalf of Bradley Owens. Ace's loyalty to Hunter and the gang is too strong to reveal information to a stranger, even if the stranger is the brother of his best friend.

"And I take it that this accident wouldn't have happened if Hunter had listened to JJ?"

Ace doesn't answer the question. "Why else did you want to meet me today, AJ? These questions you could have asked me through a phone call."

"You read people well, Ace. Two weeks ago, I was made redundant and if I don't make this month's rent, I will be homeless. I have applied everywhere and got nothing. I'm desperate for a job and I figured that you'd need a half-decent replacement to fill JJ's shoes and who better than his brother?"

Ace stops walking and eyes AJ from his shoes up to his eyes, where he stops and focuses. He wants to see that look that he once had when he first met Hunter those years ago. The twinkle of that desperate need and the willingness to do anything is present in JJ's eyes just like it was once present in his. That matched with his mounted guilt for JJ's death makes him feel that he owes this to JJ to look after his younger brother.

"Our business isn't for everyone. It can be a lot at times."

"I'm in no position to be picky. I will do anything. I really need this."

Ace takes a minute to think about this. Can he trust AJ? Would AJ just be another Flacco? But then again, this is JJ's brother. It doesn't take him long to answer. "Okay. Meet me at my place tomorrow morning and we will go to Hunter's meeting together. Hunter will make the decision, not me."

AJ smiles and shakes Ace's hand once more before leaving.

April 3rd

Hunter sits in his basement around his meeting table with McHay and Flacco. Today will mark Ace's return to the group from his short but needed hiatus.

The clock hits 10 am and the basement door can be heard opening. Down walks Ace dressed in his usual attire of a black shirt, dark leather jacket, and black fedora. Behind Ace walks AJ Reeves wearing a navy blue blazer and white shirt.

"Welcome home, Acey," Hunter greets his protégé with a hug.

"It's good to be back, fellas. I have someone I want you all to meet. This here is AJ Reeves, JJ's younger brother."

The group look over at AJ with slight confusion as to why Ace has brought him here.

Hunter approaches AJ and shakes his hand. "Your brother was a good man. His passing has left a dark hole in our organisation."

"That's why he's here. Depending on your approval, Hunter, I would like AJ to take JJ's place in our organisation. Who better to take JJ's spot other than his own blood?"

Hunter steps back for a short moment to think about the proposition.

"Acey, you and AJ leave us for a minute to discuss this matter. I will call you down when we are done." Ace and AJ head back upstairs to await the answer.

Hunter sits back down at the table and looks over to McHay. "So, what do you think?"

"Well, if Ace trusts him then we have no reason not to, right? Ace is like the most anxious man I know and if he puts his trust in the kid then we should, right?"

"True, very true. And we do need the extra hand at the minute."

67

"Why? You have me, boss. Let me back out there," Flacco adds.

"Fuck off, Flacco," Hunter sharply cuts him down. Ever since Flacco's incident with Andris, he has only been given small jobs such as coffee runs and other simple minor roles within the group.

"I say, if you are happy to, we take a chance on the kid. We owe it to JJ to look after his brother," McHay follows up.

"You're right, we do."

Hunter calls the two back down and announces that AJ can join the organisation but he's Ace's responsibility.

AJ takes a seat at the table.

The meeting commences and Hunter gives Ace a recap on all of the news that he has missed while he was on his hiatus. News of which includes Hunter and Lizzy's wedding taking place this June, Bradley Owens generously rewarding the group with £8000,000 for the burning of 'Red Syndicate's' betting shop, McHay and Amanda have started to date, and Finn O'Sullivan still being in a coma. He also details a new job that Bradley Owens has come to them about.

In four weeks, an old rival of Bradley Owens, Alec Ackhurst, will be released from prison. Owens and Ackhurst started Owens' protein company together ten years ago but Owens would betray Ackhurst and cut his shares in the company to gain sole control and final say. This would send Ackhurst down a dark downhill spiral as he turned to drugs and alcohol. Out of a stable income, he lost his home, and his wife took his little girl and left him.

Desperate to live, Ackhurst would then turn to dangerous men in the city and take on violent jobs gaining the nickname 'The Silencer' for his eccentric tactics which involved placing a metal bar, which he calls Sasha after his ex-wife, in the mouths of his victims and hitting it with a hammer hard enough that it would knock nearly all their teeth out. His victims would be nearly all males who owed money or who had done harm to these dangerous men he turned to. His status soon grew and he became like a free agent who would be hired out to carry out beatings across Manchester.

His actions have become a thing of legend around Manchester with children playing in the school playgrounds singing songs about him such as 'Oh, Mr Silencer, who have you silenced today?'.

Now that this monster is scheduled to be released from prison after serving a four-year sentence for assault, Owens fears he will come for him and wants protection from Hunter and his men.

"With all due respect, H, I think we've been here before and last time we lost. We lost big. We lost JJ," Ace reacts.

"I know this isn't a simple debt-collecting job but we are above all of that now. I told you this last time, we have evolved. Gone are the days of small simplistic jobs for boys. We are men with high reputations now. Owens pays well and he is well-connected. Jobs for him will take us places beyond our wildest imaginations. This city can be ours." Hunter's small-scale debt-collecting visions have vanished. His greed for more consumes him and Ace fears he is now flying too close to the sun, and it won't end well.

"He has a point, Ace. Owens can take us places. What happened to JJ was an accident that we won't let repeat itself," McHay chimes in.

"This is the way it's going, Acey, this is us now," Hunter states.

"You are asking us to kill a man," Ace emphasises.

"We must be able to do anything if we want to stay on top. We will be gods in this city of peasants," Hunter envisions.

"Look, H, you are the boss. I will follow the orders. Just make sure you think all of this through."

"Why do I feel that one day you will be the death of me, Acey? Of course, I have thought all of this through, it's me!" Hunter turns to McHay and laughs.

Your ego fails you, Ace thinks to himself.

AJ doesn't share his input, he just sits there and takes it all in. He feels that questioning Hunter so soon would be distrustful and he needs to earn his reputation before he can have an opinion.

"In four weeks, we will meet Alec Ackhurst in his safe house. The Silencer will be silenced. Owens has three suspected houses he has flagged that could be Ackhurst's. In the next couple of days, I and McHay will search these and find out which one belongs to him. In the meantime, Ace, I have a few jobs for you and AJ to get stuck into." Ace suspects that 'silencing the Silencer' will be a heavy challenge. Over the years, he has heard many stories about 'The Silencer' and the idea of ending this man sends shivers down his spine as he knows that many men before him have attempted the same feat only to fall and be silenced themselves.

Alec Ackhurst's first kill was as spine-chilling as you'd expect. A drug dealer under the name Andy Smithson had sent Ackhurst to pay a visit to a client of his who had been sleeping with Andy's wife. Armed with only 'Sasha' and his black ballpoint hammer, Ackhurst kicked his way into the man's apartment and hammered in his kneecaps grounding the man. Ackhurst would then tie the man's shaking hands behind his back and force open his mouth where he calmly slipped 'Sasha' in.

He then brutally closed the man's mouth so that his teeth were grinding on the metal before he stood to the side of the man and took a mighty swing smashing his hammer against the front of the bar several brutal times over and over. The man's teeth shattered instantly and he cried out in ultimate agony as he fell face down onto his floor. Ackhurst then stepped over the man and thumped his hammer into the back of his head, killing him. This is no man to be messed with or involved with.

VI

'The Proving Moment'

April 10th

Temperatures across Manchester are beginning to rise as summer is close approaching. This Thursday morning is sunny with some clouds scattered across the sky, as the threat of rain is slowly looming.

Today marks Ace's first job since that fatal night at the betting shop. He sits in his car with his hands firmly on the wheel. He is parked outside of AJ's apartment block.

Ace looks over to his left side at the empty passenger seat where JJ would often sit. Memories flood Ace as his longing and desperation to see his best friend one more time grows.

"I'll look after him, brother."

A few short moments later, AJ approaches and enters the car.

"Morning, Ace."

"Morning, you ready?"

"Is the sky blue? Let's rock and roll," AJ replies.

Spoken just like your brother, Ace thinks to himself. He starts the engine and embarks on the job.

Five miles south later, Ace and AJ are close in pursuit of their location.

"Since this is your first time on the job, H has given us what should be a simple debt collection," Ace informs AJ.

"Come on, man, throw me in at the deep end. I might just surprise you," the ever-confident AJ remarks.

"Listen, man, we don't know much about you or your previous line of work, so we need to break you into our world at a slow pace. Our world is dangerously different and constantly evolving."

"I assure you, Ace, I can handle myself. If I have to prove myself to you, fine gentlemen, then I will do so without fail."

"You have your brother's attitude I will give you that. But don't call us gentlemen. You will soon come to learn that we are no gentlemen. In this line of work, AJ, gentlemen don't exist. It's a long painful game of survival of the fittest and if you lose your way and take your eye off the ball in that game, then you end up in a hole in the ground."

"Understood. Anyway, I thought Hunter said that you guys are done with debt-collecting?"

"We still take on some debt-collecting jobs. If you forget what and where you came from then you run the risk of losing yourself," Ace educates.

"You're a wise man, Acey."

"I try."

Suddenly, Ace slams his brakes on.

"That's him! Our guy." Ace points over to a slim-looking man wearing a red beanie hat heading into the train station.

"Well, here is a good time to prove yourself, kid, get out after him. I'll park up and follow you."

AJ takes a quick deep breath to mentally prepare himself as he wants to impress Ace and prove his worth. He exits the car before sprinting after the man who, after noticing the charging AJ, begins to run. The chase is on!

Ace quickly and recklessly parks his car in a nearby taxi bay and soon follows AJ into the station.

The station is heavily populated today with people from all over the vast city of Manchester commuting to work. Men and women wearing suits holding important briefcases, young teenagers in school uniforms armed with their handbags and rucksacks, and small groups of elderly people anticipating their weekly morning trip out.

From the corner of his eye, Ace sees only two police officers monitoring the station. One of which has a chubby build and is fat-faced. Ace figures that if the job goes wrong, the fat officer will be easy to outrun. The other officer is much slimmer and has a serious scowling face. Ace believes that out of the two officers, this one will cause more problems for them.

Losing clear sight of AJ in the ever-rushing flock of people, Ace momentarily halts and scans his surroundings. Waves of people from his left to his right. Looking for AJ here is like looking for a needle in a haystack.

Suddenly, to Ace's left, he hears the two police officers yelling. Ace sharply turns and sees AJ jumping over the ticket barrier towards their target who is now boarding the train on platform two. The police officers are in hot pursuit of AJ. Ace walks towards the barriers but stops and watches the events unfold. *Okay, kid. Let's see what you've got*, he thinks to himself.

Sprinting at a post-haste rate, AJ jumps on board the train after the man. AJ sees him at the other end of the busy carriage through the sea of commuters. The two police officers have now entered the platform and seen AJ board the carriage. The heat is on. AJ now finds himself in that 'deep end' he so desired. Will he sink or will he swim?

An announcement repeats itself over the station's internal speaker system. "Train from platform two to Newcastle is set to depart in two minutes." A short amount of sweat begins to trickle down AJ's forehead. *I have to make my move.*

AJ wrestles his way through the standing commuters and heads towards the man who catches sight of him getting closer and closer. The man instantly panics and begins to frantically look around him and he weighs up his options; keep running down the train through the carriages or get off the train. He figures that if he keeps running, then so will AJ, and there are only four carriages on the train. Before he can even consider leaving the train, AJ dives through the crowd throwing himself in the man's direction and tackling him to the ground.

Chaos breaks loose in the carriage as AJ and the man are wrestling on the floor of the train throwing hefty punches at each other.

"Everybody stand back and clear the area," the chubby police officer, almost out of breath, yells at the top of his lungs as they board the carriage. The officers manage to pull AJ up and off the bleeding man. They escort him off the train and back through the barriers.

The officers stand at each side of AJ as they escort him out of the station. Ace closely, but not obvious to the eye, follows them with thoughts racing through his mind that AJ might be a liability and that taking him under his wing might have been a destructively poor decision. The officers position AJ against the brick wall outside of the station.

"Now, Sir, can you tell us what happened in there?" The slimmer officer asks.

"Yeah, I can. That guy just got battered."

"Sir, we ask that you take this seriously. You just assaulted that man in there and we want to know why," the chubby officer follows up.

"Please spare me the bullshit, officers. You guys don't want a motive. You want a name. That's all you care about. A name to pin the blame so you can go home and put your feet up. That guy could be a thief, a rapist, or a killer but you don't care. You just want the name of the guy who very publicly beat the crap out of him so that you can go back and tell your higher-ups that you dealt with it. A box ticked off. Case closed and daddy praises you. Well, with all due respect, officers, you are not getting any information out of me. I have no motive and as far as you are concerned, I have no name."

"You can't speak to us like that, you little runt." The slimmer officer loses his patience and pins AJ rigidly against the wall.

"You pigs are obsessed with this sense of power you think you have," AJ laughs. "You really don't possess a single slither of control in this city at all. Your only purpose here is to give the public false hope that they are safe, so they don't panic. In the grand scheme of things, you, my delusional friend, are irrelevant. You are not even a cog in the machine."

The officer kicks AJ in his genitals. "That's what you deserve."

After seeing the officers beginning to get physical, Ace finally steps in.

"Officers, your work here is done. He's one of Bradley Owens' men." Ace removes a fifty-pound note from his leather jacket and hands it to the slimmer officer.

"For god's sake!" The slimmer officer is almost ashamed to take the money and leave.

"Are you okay?" Ace asks the beaten AJ.

"You couldn't have done that earlier? You know before he punctured the crown jewels."

"I wanted to see how you reacted to the heat. You did well. You have a sharp tongue just like your brother."

"Yeah, sounds about right. Tell me, who is this Bradley Owens? I thought I was part of Hunter's organisation."

"You are. But Bradley Owens's name carries more weight around here. The police won't touch Owens. Now, since you got stopped, we will pay our man another visit tomorrow morning."

"I beg to differ, Acey." AJ pulls out the man's wallet and watch from his pants pocket. During their brawl on the carriage, AJ managed to steal his wallet and watch. "This should cover our costs, right?"

"You did good, kid. You did good." Ace pats AJ on his back; he is impressed with his apprentice.

The two of them get back into Ace's car.

"Where to now? Back to Hunter?"

"We have to make one last stop off at Flacco's place. H wants him to head to the tailor shop and pick up his new suit."

"Why don't we just do that?"

"It's a power move. He wants Flacco to know his place at the bottom of the ladder. He's the errand boy."

"That seems a bit harsh. What did he do to piss Hunter off?"

"He disobeyed orders. That's all you need to know."

Curtains drawn, stained clothes well overdue a wash scattered all over the floor, and the smell of weed infects the atmosphere. Flacco's bedroom would make even a pig disgusted. Flacco lives with his loving yet gullible mother, Dorothy.

Ace and AJ stand over the sight of Flacco lying face down asleep on top of his bed. Cocaine is all over the floor and in the carpets.

"What a dump," AJ remarks. The men are disgusted to be standing in the room. Ace heads over to Flacco and shakes his body to wake him. It doesn't work so he turns his body around and slaps him hard across his face. That works.

"Hey, man, not cool! What are you doing here?"

"Get up. Hunter's suits are ready to be picked up. Get your backside in gear."

Flacco sits up on his bed and feels around for his shirt to put on.

"How can you live like this?" AJ questions.

"Shut it, new boy. You don't know me to judge me," Flacco snaps.

"Take a look at yourself, man. Get a grip," Ace steps in.

"Do me a favour, Ace, and shut your mouth too!" Flacco stands and heads over to his desk which is covered in stains and more clothes. He opens his drawer and pulls out a small packet of cocaine. He pours some out and uses a ruler to line it up. Ace wipes it off the desk.

"What the hell, Acey!"

"You need to drive."

"I drive better after a line. It keeps me sharp."

"What has happened to you, Flacco? You are a disgrace."

"What has happened to me? Tell me, Ace, have you ever killed a man? Every time I close my eyes, I see his face. Everywhere I go, everything I do, he lingers in the back of my mind. Do you have any idea what that does to you?" The source of Flacco's fall from grace is the killing of Andris. Ever since he took Andris's life, he has been overcome with extreme guilt and depression.

Ace stays silent on the matter as he can't comment as he has never taken a life.

"Just get dressed. Hunter needs his suit before 12." Ace and AJ leave and get back into the car.

Before setting off, Ace turns to AJ. "Sorry about that," Ace apologises to AJ for taking him into the drug-infested pit which is Flacco's bedroom.

"It's fine. I went through a similar phase after my first kill."

Ace is surprised. "You've killed before?"

"Yeah. It was some time ago now. My mother was raped by a man who had come to repair our boiler. That day I had skipped school and was hiding out in my bedroom having forgotten the boiler man was coming that day and my mum needed to be home to let him in. Anyway, once he finished the job, he charged my mother way more than he said it would cost and when my mother told him she couldn't afford that much, he raped her. I heard it all go down. Sometimes I still hear her horrific scream." AJ pauses for a second to let his rising anger simmer. "I left my room armed with my action figure of 'One' from 'The Mighty Ten' comics. I hit the man over and over with little to no effect. He then hit me several times before turning his attention back to my mum to carry on raping her. But before he got to her, I opened the cutlery drawer and pulled out a steak knife. I lunged for the man and stabbed him several times until I killed him. Luckily for me, my mum's friend, Simon, was in town, and he came by and found us in the kitchen. He helped me get rid of the body and ever since that day, he took care of us."

"I'm so sorry to hear that, AJ. JJ never mentioned that to me."

"That's because we never told JJ. My mum didn't want him to find out what happened. The thing I took most from that whole day which stuck with me was how easy it was for the devil to walk right into our family. We opened our door and let him straight in. We let him straight in and he tore us apart."

"I'm sorry to hear that, AJ."

"Me too, Acey."

"How did Simon get rid of the body?"

"He never told me. He just came to our house the night after and told me that 'the weeds are gone'."

VII
'To Silence the Silencer'

May 1st

The sun begins to set and light soon retires to let the darkness take over the rainy city. Vince McHay sits alone in 'The Blue Moon' with a full pint of lager placed in front of him.

A few short moments later, Ace enters the pub and joins McHay in their usual booth.

"Evening, McHay, you not thirsty?" Ace notices that McHay hasn't touched his pint of lager.

"He's chosen me," McHay says with a sombre tone.

"Sorry?"

"Hunter wants me to put the bullet in Ackhurst's head tomorrow," McHay says softly as he stares lifelessly at his pint.

"I see. You've killed before though. This won't be any different to then. We keep it simple and fast."

"He promised me after the first one that I would never have to kill for him again. Why would he lie?" McHay looks up and asks Ace.

"Sometimes, McHay, you have to wise up and take these 'Gods' off the mantles you hold them so high upon."

"I've read some stories about Ackhurst. He's built from a different breed. He is unpredictable."

"Then let's match his crazy. Let's show him who we are and what we are capable of." Ace knows that there's no way out of the hit tomorrow and they are just going to have to follow Hunter's orders. "If you don't mind me asking, Vince, what actually went down on your first kill? You never talk about it."

McHay looks down at the table. "His name was Stark. I was twenty-five so it was around 1972 when it went down." He takes a short swig from his pint of lager before continuing. "I was sent to kill Stark face-to-face under orders to put a bullet in his skull. But I never signed up for that. How could I end another man's life and live with myself after? I couldn't bear that, so I took the easy way. I wasn't even man enough to look the man in his eyes and shoot him. I entered his home as he was sleeping and put a magazine into his toaster. Within half an hour, his home was set ablaze and he was dead," he drinks more. "I watched the whole thing happen from across the street. As soon as the sirens arrived, I headed back to the man who sent me to do the bidding. Hunter. I never talk about it, Ace, because I am ashamed. I killed a man I barely knew in the most cowardly way possible." He takes a larger swig of his lager.

Ace sits back having taken McHay's story in. He looks at McHay and sees that McHay has let the killing take over him and destroy his view of himself. Maybe this is why McHay idolises Hunter so much. Hunter, in McHay's eyes, is a man who is confident about himself and every decision he makes and never lets his regrets shape him.

"Why did Hunter want Stark dead?" Ace asks.

"Stark and Hunter had gone into business together debt-collecting over in Leeds. They knew each other from school. Anyway, they did well together for a few years, so I'm told. Then one day, Stark was made an offer from a local drug dealer who had more pull in the city. He offered Stark more money and sold him the dream only an idiot would refuse. So Stark left Hunter. Hunter couldn't take that. His close friend had walked out on him. Later in the year, Stark's new partner got nicked for fraud and Stark was left alone with sole control of the clients he and his partner had made in the past year." McHay finishes his pint off.

"So, Hunter was jealous?"

"Possibly. No one leaves Hunter Smith. He never got over it and he saw it as an insult. Hunter wanted to make an example. He wanted to build his name and reputation up and the only way he saw fit to do this was by having the man who walked out on him buried 6 feet under. Hunter came up with a plan and he got me to execute it. So, I did. After I did what I did, Hunter took on Stark's clients and we had a tight grip over Leeds until Hunter made the decision to move here to Manchester in 74' to capitalise on the larger interest here. Shortly after is when he took you on," McHay says before he calls over to the barmaid to pour him another pint of lager.

"I see."

"They say your first kill marries you to the game, and your last one divorces you. I hoped my first was my last. It's very rare to get out of the game once you make your first kill."

"Well, McHay, I am this game. I will kill Ackhurst." Ace has no desire to kill but he sees what Hunter's orders have done to McHay and doesn't want him to go through it all again after killing Ackhurst.

"No. I will kill Ackhurst. You're not ready for that. I hope that you never will be."

The barmaid comes with McHay's lager and Ace orders one too.

May 2nd

The day arrives. Alec 'The Silencer' Ackhurst's judgment day. The early morning sun peaks through the clouds as the clocks strike 5.30 am.

Ace has arrived at Flacco's mother's house to make sure Flacco is up and ready for the day ahead as he is the driver. Flacco's role for today is minor and is to deliver McHay to murder Ackhurst and to drive him away from the scene after it is done.

Dorothy comes to the door and lets Ace into her house.

"Good morning, Tony love, are you well?"

"As well as I can be Dorothy thank you. Is he up?"

"I think so, yes. He's really looking forward to the rollercoasters today. I haven't taken him to 'Paradise Park' since he was six."

Rollercoasters? Paradise Park? This must be Flacco's cover story to his mother, Ace thinks to himself. "Yes, it should be a fun day out."

Ace can smell the strong sense of weed from the hallway before entering Flacco's bedroom. *Dorothy really must be dizzy in the head if she can't smell this. Either that or the smell of it has gotten her high too.*

A sense of great relief overcomes Ace as he sees that Flacco is fully dressed in a shirt, jean shorts, and a white and red baseball cap. His room is still in complete and utter disarray though.

"You're ready."

"You look surprised," Flacco replies.

"Are you feeling up to it today? Or do we have to babysit you?"

"Shut it, Acey, I'm ready okay."

"Good. Come on, we have to go and get AJ and McHay."

Flacco kisses his mother goodbye and she gives him a pre-packed lunch box full of ham and cheese sandwiches for the gang. Once they enter the car, Flacco begins to bite down into one of the sandwiches.

"One thing before we set off, Flac. You shouldn't lie to your mother. She brought you into his world, you should never disrespect her."

"Acey, what was I meant to tell her? Oh, by the way, Mum, I'm off out today driving my friend to go and straight up murder a man," Flacco sarcastically strikes back, spitting small crumbs of ham out of his mouth as he does.

"Just tell her you are going out with your friends. Don't lie."

Flacco finishes his sandwich and sets off to pick up AJ and McHay.

Within fifteen minutes, they are a full car and are heading towards an old run-down strip club, 'Devil's Angel', where Ackhurst is rumoured to be hiding out.

'Devil's Angel' was an extremely popular strip club in Manchester but due to damage on the roof caused by a storm three years ago, it was forced to close its doors permanently for health and safety reasons.

"Here, Flacco, hand me a butty, would you? I need some food to ease my mind," McHay leans forward to the front and asks Flacco.

"In case you haven't noticed, McHay, I'm driving. Acey, throw tubby a butty."

Ace leans into his footwell and hands McHay a sandwich.

"Call me tubby again, kid, and I'll be committing two murders today. Don't get too confident just yet either, you're not out of the woods from your last big job," McHay reminds Flacco to not step out of line as he still hasn't gained the favour of the gang yet from his murderous mistake. Flacco remains silent.

"How far are we off?" AJ asks.

"It should be just around this corner to the left here," Ace responds.

"You're getting crumbs on me," AJ tells McHay as he is frantically eating, rushing the sandwich down his gullet.

"You want an apology? I don't know if you realise or not, but I have more important stuff going on right now, pal. Just wipe it off," McHay sharply says.

"There's no need to be a dick. I'm just saying slow down when you're eating. Are you some sort of dog?"

"Fellas, enough. Focus up, we are here," Ace interferes to diffuse the rising tension between McHay and AJ.

Blood stains the walls and floors. Tables are flipped, chairs are broken, and smashed bottles are scattered across the bar. The main floor of 'Devil's Angel' looks like something from a horror film. Ace, AJ, and McHay walk through the main room.

"What the hell." McHay points out to the stage where the strippers would once come out and perform on the poles. There is a body of a homeless squatter lying face down there.

"Is he dead?" AJ asks Ace who has gone over to check.

"Yeah."

McHay then sees another body lying in a private booth to the left of the stage. He heads over and turns the body and sees that the homeless man's teeth are missing. "It looks like these guys were squatting in here. And when Ackhurst came back, he took them out."

Suddenly, several male screams call out from the back of the building where the manager's office is.

"That's our man," AJ remarks.

"Stay tight, stay together," Ace orders as they slowly make their way into the back.

McHay cautiously leads them into the manager's office holding his AMT AutoMag V handgun tightly. He lightly pushes open the door with the nose of his gun to the sight of a butchered homeless man bleeding excessively from his mouth lying on the floor. The three men enter the room with Ackhurst nowhere in sight.

"This poor guy hasn't just been killed. He's been tortured. Made to suffer. What kind of animal are we dealing with here?" AJ rhetorically asks.

"A motherfucking silver back boy," Ackhurst's voice calls out as he enters from a side room in the office. His bulky 6ft 10" body and hardened and scarred face strikes fear into the three of them. His dark-skinned, bald head has several splats of blood on it from the man he has just slaughtered. He is armed with his blood-populated hammer.

"I saw you three grifters come in. Now, what can I do for you? I really hope for your sake that that gun isn't for me," his intimidatingly deep voice echoes.

McHay tightens his grip on his handgun and raises it to Ackhurst's head.

"You don't want to do that," Ackhurst says before smiling at McHay like he's teasing him to pull the trigger.

But before McHay can pull the trigger, Ackhurst hurdles his hammer at his genitals which floors him and makes him drop his gun in front of AJ's feet.

Ace dives over and brawls with the 6-foot goliath. Ackhurst throws Ace against the wall and beats him viscously in his groin. As this is happening, AJ is considering his options as he looks down at McHay's gun at his feet. He hasn't got much time to decide. He looks over and Ackhurst has now begun to strangle Ace with his humongous hands. Ace is losing his breath at an accelerated rate. AJ panics. Ace is now beginning to fade. AJ quickly reaches down for the gun and fires two shots, one to the back of Ackhurst's knee and the other into his torso.

Ackhurst's compacted grip on Ace's throat loosens and he slows drops to the floor. Ace falls straight away and holds his throat gasping for his breath to return.

AJ, who is too high on his adrenaline rush to contemplate what he has just done, heads over to the grounded Ackhurst. He stands over him and fires one last shot into his head which kills him.

AJ stares down at Ackhurst's lifeless body.

"You did it," Ace picks himself up. AJ has proven his worth here today. His trust has been gained.

"Good job, man," McHay adds as he begins to stand back up with one hand down his pants to check on his genitals. Ace assists McHay up.

"What do we do with the body?" AJ asks as the realisation begins to hit him.

"We leave it. No one will come in here and even if they do, we have left no traces. This animal had many enemies. We will be fine. Now come over here and help me get McHay back to the car," Ace says. AJ heads over to Ace and the two of them carry McHay out of the building together.

They lay McHay across the backseat and Ace orders Flacco to take him home and look after him.

"I'm taking you for a pint. Right now, you are high on adrenaline but that will wear off and that's when the shakes will start. That's why you need a drink," Ace informs AJ.

"Ace, it's only 6.30 in the morning. Where can we get a beer at 6.30 in the morning?"

"My place."

It's 7.15 am. Ace and AJ are sitting at Ace's small dining table in his apartment. AJ has a glass of wine placed in front of him. Since Ace has quit drinking, the only alcohol in the apartment is Ava's wine, and Ace has a cup of coffee in front of him.

"Here, kid, here's to the future and what it brings for us," Ace says as the two clink their drinks and sip.

"When you said you were taking me for a drink, I was under the assumption that you would be having one too," AJ comments.

"The last time alcohol touched my lips was the day of your brother's funeral. Alcohol is what the devil uses to get to you. I was destroying myself and I had to stop."

"Why do you keep wine here then?"

"Because I won't allow my weakness to dictate what my beautiful woman can enjoy. Anyway, I didn't know you were so comfortable with guns. Where did you learn to shoot like that?"

"Remember my mum's friend, Simon, I was telling you about? Well, he lived in a rough town not too far from Manchester. He had seen some heavy stuff. Anyway, he thought it was best to teach me how to look after myself, so he did. I learnt how to use and handle a gun. My mum never knew about this."

"This Simon sounds like a smart man. JJ never mentioned him."

"JJ never took to him. He fell out badly with Simon and my mum, so he moved out and cut all ties with the family apart from me."

"That he did mention," Ace says as he leans back in his chair for extra comfort.

"I'm just going to be honest with you, Ace, I want you to be able to trust me and we have no secrets. Simon is Simon Stark."

Ace leans forward in his chair. "Simon Stark? The man Hunter had business with over in Leeds?"

"Yes. The man that Hunter had killed. I just want you to know though that his business with Hunter came well after he left my mother. We cut our ties with him. I actually thought he was a bit of a prick. I didn't even go to his funeral."

"Thank you for being honest, AJ."

"I totally get it if you want to tell Hunter."

Ace takes a minute to think. "No. Look if anything, I trust you even more now for being honest with me. You have opened up and been straight with me about something that even your brother didn't tell me. This will stay between me and you."

"Thank you. It was a burden I have carried since I met you and I'm so glad to have told you."

"You are one of us, AJ, there is nothing we can't get over. Just don't mention it to McHay, he carries heavy baggage about Stark's murder."

AJ has gained more worthiness in Ace's eyes now. He believes that if he tells Hunter and McHay then they might unfairly distrust AJ which would be ludicrous. Ace has full trust in AJ and is grateful that he was truthful with him.

"You know, you did your brother proud today. You saved my life in there."

"It's what we do. It's what he would have done."

"It's what he did do." Ace looks down as the thought of JJ throwing himself at Finn O'Sullivan in the betting shop flashes into his mind. He quickly snaps out of it and looks back up at AJ. "You are a good man, AJ, a good man in this game of bad men." Ace sits back straight. "And that is very rare."

"What can I say, I am a special breed." AJ takes a swig of his bottle. "Are you a good man in this game, Ace?"

"In all honesty, I don't know anymore. When we were just collecting debts, I believed we were good, yeah. Everyone wants to believe that they are the good guys. The good guys doing bad things to bad people all in the name of the greater good. There's an honour to that. But since we've developed a relationship with Owens, I feel more and more each day that we have lost who we are. But that's not going to change so we must adapt, or we perish."

"Survival of the fittest."

"Survival of the fucking fittest."

"Have you been in this game long?"

"Long enough. I lost my parents in an accident and Hunter took care of me. He gave me a bed and a job. He took a chance on me when the world wouldn't. He saved me, and I've been with him ever since."

"Is that why you've never left to pursue a 'normal' life? You feel like you owe it to Hunter?"

Ace leans in. "Take a look around you, AJ. There is absolutely nothing about this world that is 'normal'. All I have ever known is this game and as much as I may disagree with his old-school ways or ego-driven decisions, Hunter is like a father to me."

"Well, I'll drink to that." AJ raises his bottle and drinks some more. Out of the corner of his left eye, on Ace's counter, he sees a framed photograph of his brother and Ace. They are posing in front of a museum. "How on Earth did you get him to a museum?"

"Sorry?" Ace looks over and realises what AJ is referring to. "Oh. Well, we never stepped inside, he just thought it would look 'cultural' if we took a photograph in front of it." Ace laughs as he reminisces.

AJ lets out a little laugh as well. "Sounds like him. I remember once when we were kids, my mother had taken us to an art museum and JJ hated the concept of walking around and staring at old paintings and sculptures all day. So, he turned to me and made me make a bet with him on how long it would take before he could get us kicked out of the museum. I bet two hours, he bet one. He did it in half an hour." AJ laughs some more.

"How did he pull it off?"

"He went around and pulled his pants down to show his ass to every sculpture he saw."

"Sounds like him." The two share a quiet moment as they reflect on their friend and brother.

"Did he ever talk about me?" AJ asks.

"All the time," Ace replies. "He told me all about what you both got up to. From sleepovers at your Nan's flat every Friday night to him taking you on your first night out and how he nearly brawled with a rugby player that night. He loved you very much."

Ace's words create a sensation of love and warmth in AJ.

"What was it Ackhurst called us earlier? Three Grifters? I like that."

"It has a good ring to it, doesn't it?"

A few moments later, Ava enters the room from the bedroom dressed in her work attire.

"Morning, you," Ace greets his girlfriend with a kiss. "This is AJ by the way. JJ's younger brother."

JJ stands and shakes Ava's hand. "It's a pleasure to finally meet you, Ava. Ace always talks about you," AJ charms her.

"I hope he does. It's nice to meet you, AJ. I hope you boys are playing nice."

"Always, ma'am," AJ laughs.

Ava grabs her handbag and kisses Ace goodbye as she heads out to work.

"You've got a good one there, Acey."

"I know. She is my light. If it wasn't for her, I have no idea how I would have gotten over your brother's death. Or if I would have at all."

AJ notices that Ace is extremely loyal to those who have saved him from experiences of hurt.

.

VIII
'Two Hearts as One'

June 4th

The wedding day. Today is the day that Hunter and Lizzy are set to finally tie the knot. The sun is out, the air is warming, and morale is high. Today will mark the last day that the gang will witness true and pure happiness, but you will come to see why that is later.

Ace and Ava arrive at the front of the church where they see several people waiting outside. The wedding isn't the most popular but it is also not a quiet one. Most members are from Lizzy's large family and the rest are close friends of Hunter's.

Ace and Ava head over to stand with AJ, who is standing with his hands in his pockets on his own as he doesn't know anyone in attendance.

"You brush up well," Ace remarks.

"So do you two. Well, you do, Ava, Ace could use some work on his hair," AJ banters.

"It's better than that mop you have attached to yours," Ace responds as AJ laughs.

From Ace's left, Vince McHay and Amanda rush over. McHay whispers into Ace's ear. "We have a problem. It's Flacco, he's as pissed as an alcoholic in a brewery."

"The kid is a joke. On today of all days! Where is he?"

"At the gate over there." McHay points over to the sight of an intoxicated Flacco leaning against the church gate heckling guests as they enter.

Ace and McHay head over to drunk and drugged-up Flacco. Ace grabs him and pulls him over to one side.

"What are you doing? Are you really going to act up today?" Ace slightly raises his voice.

"Give me a break, Ace. I'm trying to have some fun here."

"You're an embarrassment. Bradley Owens is standing over there, how do you think this is going to look to a man like that? A man we are in business with." Ace can easily tell from Flacco's dilated eyes that he's snorted at least a couple of lines of cocaine before coming here. "How are you this stupid?"

"I don't give a shit. Fuck Bradley Owens, fuck you two and fuck Hunter."

Flacco's drunken words begin to anger Ace and McHay notices this.

"Leave him, Acey, he's not worth it."

Flacco turns his attention to McHay. "Yeah, listen to the funky chunky, Acey." He pauses to laugh at his joke then continues, "You two are pathetic. You are so far up Hunter's ass, and you don't even know it."

Ace tightens his fist as if he's ready to flip at any given moment now. "McHay, take him away before I make a massacre of his face. It must be a sad little life you live, Flacco, if you must rely on drugs to have somewhat of a good time."

McHay grabs Flacco by his arm and escorts him away from the church.

As Ace makes his way back to Ava and AJ, he hears several cheers as Hunter pulls up and exits his car. Hunter has arrived for his big day.

He immediately goes over to Lizzy's family and greets them with excitement. Ace looks over and sees how calm and collected Hunter is on a day when most men's nerves take over them. Not only that but Ace admires how only a month ago Hunter had ordered a man's life to end and now here he is without a care in the world making happy families with people. Is it a facade? Or does Hunter genuinely have no remorse? Either way, Ace has an admiration for it.

After mingling with a few members of Lizzy's family, Hunter turns to the crowd of people. "Let's all make our way into the church. I hear that there's a big wedding today!"

Hunter leads the pack into the church and opens the doors letting them in. As Ace and Ava approach the doors, Hunter stops them and requests to talk to Ace alone.

What could this be about? Why on his biggest day does he wish to speak to me alone? Ace frantically thinks to himself.

The two begin to walk around the church premises. Ace is curious.

"Ah, Tony Johnson, my 'Ace'. Since I took you in that day those years ago, you have always been by my side. I've seen you grow, cry, and laugh. We have made quite the team me and you. I just wanted to take the time today to tell you that McHay might be my best man in there, but you, you are so much more than that. You are a son to me," Hunter speaks from the heart. His words leave Ace speechless for a few short moments. It's very rare that Hunter speaks from his heart. He is usually reserved when it comes to his emotions.

"Thank you, Hunter. You know I can never repay you enough for what you have done for me. You saved me in a time when I needed saving. I will always be by your side."

"Good. I just wanted to make that clear to you. I know I am tough on you at times but it's only because I care. And there's not a day that goes by since JJ died where I wish I had thought things more thoroughly through about that job. We could have done that job differently. Used Molotovs through the windows or just some way that didn't include you boys going inside."

Even in his half-arsed attempt at admitting regret, he still believes that burning the shop down and getting involved in a situation that didn't need us was the right call and the wrong call was how we burnt it down. What a joke. He is so far into his own delusion, it's not even worth responding to, Ace believes.

"It's fine, Hunter. Come on, it's your wedding day, go and get married," Ace simply says.

The exchanging of vows commences.

"Now, I believe you both have written your own vows. Hunter is first," the officiant directs Hunter.

"Thank you." Hunter looks over at his gorgeous wife-to-be's beautiful eyes as she stands in front of him in her long luxurious white wedding dress. "Lizzy, as you know, and probably most people here know, I'm not the best when it comes to remembering significant dates. But I still remember the very first time I saw you sitting on that train minding your own business reading the book *Love and Loss*, only to be interrupted by a bumbling idiot on his first week in this city asking you what the next stop was. I remember that even though you had every right to tell me to move on and go bother someone else, you gave me the time of day and would go on to tell me all about the city after hearing that I was new here. I remember that whilst you were talking, and I clearly wasn't listening, I looked up into your eyes and a warm sensation took over me just like it does now. It was like somehow I knew that I was listening to my future wife. I can't and never want to imagine my life without you. I love you. I promise to always, in every possible circumstance, make you feel the same love and warmth I have felt every day since meeting you that day on that train."

Some of the crowd have small tears in their eyes. Lizzy has a smile stretched across her face. Even if she didn't want to smile, she couldn't stop doing it after hearing that.

Ace looks over at Ava and smiles, almost to say that is how he feels about her. Hunter looks at the crowd and soaks it all in. A real wave of pride takes over him as he sees all the people in attendance gasping at each word he has spoken. The fact that Bradley Owens is sitting out there strokes his ego too. He's made it.

"And now Lizzy," the officiant says.

"Wow, I don't know how I'm going to follow that." She composes herself. "Hunter, before you, I never believed that I would be able to love and trust a man again in my life. But then you came along that day on that carriage and threw all of that out of the window for me. Your warmth, your care, and your terrible jokes are the most precious aspects of my life, and I wouldn't have it any other way. I hope every woman out there finds what I have found in you. I love you. I vow to always stand by your side through it all. All the hurt, all the laughs, all the joy. You are mine and I am yours. Forever." The crowd gets tearful again.

"Now the rings," the officiant declares.

After the rings are slowly and elegantly placed on, they both say I do, and the crowd erupts into cheers and claps.

"If you would all like to join the happy couple at the local cricket club for the celebrations," the officiant informs the crowd.

A quick ten-minute trip down the road and everyone reconvenes at the local cricket club where a scrumptious food buffet is spread and pints are flowing.

Music is blasting, people are dancing and having a great time, and free food is being devoured. Ace and Ava are sitting at a table with AJ, they don't like dancing, especially sober dancing.

Ace looks over to the dancefloor and sees McHay and Amanda embracing in a slow dance alongside Hunter and Lizzy.

"We can't be much worse than them. Come on." Ace takes Ava by the hand, and they take to the dancefloor. They break into a slow dance together. Ava looks up and smiles at her man.

"I never had you down as a slow dancer."

"I wouldn't call it dancing. It's more like a seizure really."

The DJ quickly switches the song to a more fast-paced one forcing the couples to switch up their routines.

"Yup. That's my time to leave," Ace says as he exits the dancefloor.

The wedding brought about high spirits to everyone involved. It was the happiest of all occasions. The last of its kind.

As the sun sets on the wedding celebrations, across the city in the hospital, 'Red Syndicate' leader Finn O'Sullivan abruptly wakes from his five-month coma.

'Red Syndicate' member Ryan Kelly is at his bedside and is suddenly stunned at the sight of his leader waking.

There would be a shift in the air tonight. A storm is brewing...

IX

'A Dark Night'

The night that changed it all forever.

June 8th

Moss Side. O'Sullivan's bar. Today marks the third day since Finn O'Sullivan got checked out of his hospital bed. Scarred on his face and now walking with a cane, he is hosting a meeting between the 'Red Syndicate' members in his bar. The bar is closed off to the public.

O'Sullivan stands at the front of the bar with the other members scattered at different tables in the room.

"Gentlemen, I have called this meeting here today to inform you all of a recent development. Thanks to a small group of you lads attending the funeral of that bastard who torched our shop, we have a few photographs." O'Sullivan passes around a small handful of photographs that the three members of the group who attended JJ's funeral took. The photographs show images of Ace, Hunter, and Bradley Owens.

"As you can see in those photographs, there is a fella with black hair standing with Hunter Smith. He was also in the betting shop that night. But more interestingly in the last photo, Bradley Owens is in attendance. This means only one thing, gentlemen; Bradley Owens is the one responsible and they have just started a war. Those rats have taken out a large source of our income. We must and will respond in a more catastrophic manner. Let it be known that the bloodiest of all drug wars has begun. AND WE TAKE NO PRISONERS!" O'Sullivan passionately rallies at the top of his lungs as he prepares his men for war. The members of 'Red Syndicate' cheer in agreement.

By 11 pm that very night, 'Red Syndicate' set ablaze all of Bradley Owens' garages and gyms with the clear message that war has begun. The city is burning.

Finn O'Sullivan and Ryan Kelly tracked down some of Owens' 'employees' who were selling drugs to clients. O'Sullivan and Kelly then robbed them at knifepoint taking their product to sell themselves. They plan to take Owens for everything he has got. Tonight marks a very dark night for Cheetham and Bradley Owens.

The aftermath of the night saw Bradley Owens lose an estimated £1.5 million in stock and damages; almost making him bankrupt. 40% of Owens's clients have cut all ties with him out of fear of being involved in the war with 'Red Syndicate'. More and more of Owens's workers dealing the narcotic products have been robbed by the 'Red Syndicate' and been heavily injured. The intense war between the 'Red Syndicate' and Bradley Owens has inspired many other gangs in Moss Side to take action and go to war with other gangs in Cheetham as well.

Ace, Vince McHay, and AJ are standing at the bar in 'The Blue Moon' and are watching the police press conference on the pub's television.

Chief Constable Mark Henderson takes to the podium as a field of press sits before him ready to listen and ask questions. The black-haired and muscle-toned Mark welcomes the press.

"Ladies and gentlemen, today marks a week since what has come to be known as 'the dark night' occurred. Today, I would like to enlighten you all on our progress to compress this rising and bloody drug war between the gangs of Moss Side and the gangs of Cheetham. Over this past week, we have made five arrests and shut down a warehouse on the outskirts of Moss Side that we came to learn was being run by the gang 'Red Syndicate'. I want to assure you, the great public of this city, that everything we can possibly do is being done to stop this war. We understand your frustrations. When we are done with our operations, no more will this city be controlled by drug dealers and gangsters. I thank you all for your patience. I would now like to open questions to the press."

"Hi, Sir, Pete from the 'Daily Dose'. Has there been any evidence to suggest that club owner and alleged gangster Paul Moonie is involved in this war?" A chubby and greasy-haired reporter stands up and asks.

"At this time, there is no evidence to suggest that, no."

A slim brown-haired lady stands. "Bianca from 'Your News Now'. With all due respect, why does it have to take a devastating night like last week for you to finally crack down on these gangs? These people have been operating in this city for well over a decade, so why now are you finally stepping in?" The blunt reporter asks.

"With all due respect, there is a lot more that goes into tracking down the operations of these gangs. A lot more behind-the-scenes work that can take up to several years to pin down. I assure you that we are doing everything we can. My men and women are working beyond their set hours to clean up this city. And I assure you, we will clean this city up."

McHay laughs at the TV before heading over to sit down in the gang's usual booth. Ace and AJ grab their pints and follow.

"What a load of bollocks that is," McHay says as he sips his lager.

"The only way this war is going to end is when one side is wiped out," AJ adds.

"At last, one thing we can agree on. Beasts can only be put down by beasts," McHay follows up.

"A beast can also be tamed," Ace chimes in.

"What are you suggesting, Acey?" A curious McHay asks.

"This war can't be good for anyone. Both sides will be losing income and profits. At one point, something will have to give. A truce between the two would be the most beneficial way out of it."

"Yeah okay, Ace, you try telling Bradley Owens that. That guy is as angry as an animal caged in a zoo at the moment," AJ shares his take.

"Forget Bradley Owens, he started this mess. This is what happens when egotistical men play god. People get hurt. All the time, every time. Change in this city needs to happen and happen fast," Ace states.

Little did they know that change was about to come in the form of a bald head and a black blazer…

Part II
'The Moonie Effect'

X

'Enter Paul Moonie'

June 25th

Something about today feels different to Ace. He wakes up early with a peculiar feeling eating away at his stomach. Something feels off but he can't tell what.

He kisses a sleeping Ava on her forehead and heads into the kitchen area of his apartment to make himself a nice warm morning coffee.

Two cautious sips of his coffee later, he hears someone banging on his door. He isn't expecting anyone and with the brutal nature of the rising drug war, he is even more on edge than normal. He rests his mug of coffee on his nearby dining table and reaches for a steak knife in his drawer. With the knife gripped tightly in his hand, he makes his way to the front door. The door bangs once more.

Ace stands before it. Who could be on the other side? Is this an overreaction? He takes one deep breath, holds the knife high and positions himself ready to lunge forward to do some harm with it. He opens the door.

"Jesus, Acey! Are you trying to give me a heart attack?" To Ace's relief, it's Vince McHay.

"It's you. Quick get in," Ace rushes McHay into his apartment.

"Who are you expecting?"

"It could be anyone these days. You must be prepared for anything."

"You could have killed me," McHay observes Ace's current attire of just his boxer shorts and nothing else. "Do you really sleep in just your boxers? Not even a shirt? Anyway, get dressed, I'm worried about H," McHay says to the almost-naked Ace.

"Why? What's happened with H?"

"He hasn't been answering my calls to the house. Amanda checked with Lizzy's work and she hasn't clocked in. I'm worried something might have happened."

Ace quickly heads back into his bedroom and gets dressed. He kisses Ava goodbye and heads out with McHay.

The sky over Manchester is darkening as heavy clouds hang over, looking like they are about to burst and pour out a flooding amount of rain at any given minute. Thunder suddenly and sharply breaks through. A storm is coming.

McHay and Ace pull up outside of Hunter and Lizzy's house. As they walk to the door, Ace notices that their plants are starting to die. They are slowly rotting away.

McHay knocks on the door to no answer. Ace tries the handle and the door opens. They enter.

Hunter and Lizzy are nowhere in sight.

"Hunter? Lizzy? It's Vince and Acey. Are you guys in?" McHay shouts.

"I'll check upstairs." Ace heads upstairs in hopes of finding them. This is very out of character for Hunter. Whenever he goes anywhere out of the vicinity of the city, he always notifies either McHay or Ace. And to Ace's knowledge, he and Lizzy are not scheduled to go on any vacation anytime soon. Ace heads straight to Hunter and Lizzy's bedroom. As he slowly opens the door, he doesn't expect to see anything on the other side. How he is mistaken.

Ace is met by the sight of a distraught Lizzy tied up on the bed with black duct tape across her mouth. He rushes over and sets her free. Crying, she thanks him and embraces him tightly. From the mascara marks on her face, Ace can tell that she has been crying heavily for a while.

"Lizzy, what happened? Did Hunter do this to you?"

Lizzy composes herself. "No, it wasn't Hunter. It was this man, he called here two nights ago. He had Hunter at gunpoint and took him to the basement after tying me up here. I don't know if he's killed him or not." Lizzy cries more. "Please help him, Ace."

It must be Red Syndicate, Ace thinks. "It's okay, Lizzy. Me and McHay are here now. You stay here, we will check the basement." Ace stands.

"Wait. Take this." Lizzy reaches over to Hunter's bedside cabinet and pulls out Hunter's silver Colt Python handgun. Ace has only ever fired a gun once and that was the blank one against O'Sullivan in the betting shop. He's always preferred not to use a gun as the idea of taking a life terrorises his conscience. However, he knows that the times are changing and he may have to use it for this situation.

Colt Python tightly in hand, Ace heads back downstairs to McHay. He motions over to McHay to get his attention and they make their way towards the basement.

They descend the basement stairs stealthy to avoid any attention. Each step down is a step closer to Ace possibly taking a life. He's too caught up in the moment for that to properly sink in yet. His only focus is making sure that Hunter is still alive.

To Ace's surprise, he doesn't see the 'Red Syndicate'. Instead, he sees a bald and early 40s-looking man dressed in an open black blazer and silk black shirt. The man is standing behind Hunter, who is in his dressing gown tied to a chair looking starved and deprived.

At first sight of this, Ace immediately points his gun at the bald man. The bald man smiles at this and gives Ace a look of respect.

"Well, well, look at what we have here." The man pats Hunter on his shoulders. "Your sheep have come. A little late mind you, but here they are, nonetheless. Live and in colour." The man's charismatic personality gleams through.

"Who is this guy, H?" McHay asks.

"Wow. So polite." The man smiles. "You seriously don't know me? You must be pulling my pisser. I'm Paul Moonie! The Paul Moonie." Paul Moonie's unapologetic charisma shines through as his words stun McHay and Ace, but Ace doesn't let it show, he refuses to be intimidated and remains calm.

Paul Moonie focuses his attention on Ace who is still pointing the gun at him.

"You. I like you. Not many people, if any, are brave enough to point guns at me. I respect you." Moonie nods at Ace. "But, my friend, I stopped fearing death a long time ago." Moonie looks at Ace's gun. "All that does to me now is excite me. But, for your boss's sake, I suggest you lower it. There is no need to fight here. In fact, there are only three reasons to fight in this world: for your family, for your woman, and for your country. And this fat fuck isn't any of them." Moonie pulls out his knife and holds it at Hunter's throat.

"Hunter is family," McHay says.

Looking down at his boss and father figure, Ace sees, for the first time, true fear in Hunter's eyes. Ace lowers the gun.

Paul Moonie reaches into his inside blazer pocket and pulls out a bright red handkerchief. He then wipes some sweat off Hunter's forehead.

"Close one, Hunter old boy. Now that I have everybody's attention, let's talk some business, shall we? Please slide that gun my way and take a seat." Moonie points at the table. Ace slides the gun over to Moonie across the table and he and McHay take a seat opposite Hunter and Moonie.

"What's all this about?" McHay frustratedly asks.

"Adrians Andris. Remember him?" Moonie replies. Ace remembers that name instantly, it's the man whom Flacco accidentally murdered. JJ always warned that it would come to this.

"Who? I haven't got a clue," McHay responds having forgotten the name of the man whom Flacco killed those months ago.

"Really? You are really going to sit there and lie to me when I have a knife to your boss's throat?"

"I remember him," Ace says.

"Ah. Jolly good. Well, Adrians was my head of security and earlier this year, he was butchered and murdered. An act that I imagine, from looking at the body, was carried out by a pack of fucking dogs."

"Yes, I remember him. I remember him crying like a bitch as he was stabbed to death," a firm-faced Ace follows on as he sits there staring Moonie dead in his eyes.

Moonie smiles. "I'm glad you remember. That's why I'm here. I know it was you lot that killed him, and I know you did it over that slag Eva. But you see, that whole incident has left me without a head of security and without the head of the one responsible. Now, I know it wasn't you because you seem too smart," Moonie says to Ace. He then looks over at McHay. "You. I don't think it was you because Adrians would have easily put your fat arse down. So, I want answers, or I will take your boss's head. I will either leave this room with a name, or a head."

"No one in this room killed Adrians that day," Ace informs Moonie.

"No? Then enlighten me, sweetheart, because I have a reliable witness on Eva's Street claiming to have seen three men leave Eva's house. One man carrying a bloodied sponge."

Ace looks over to Hunter not knowing what to do. He doesn't want to through Flacco under the bus and get him killed but at the same time, he knows that if he doesn't tell Moonie the truth then Hunter will be killed. Hunter motions a little nod at Ace, indicating to him to tell Moonie the truth.

Ace adjusts himself upright in his seat. "He's just a kid. He got carried away and made a mistake."

"Sorry, bell end, did I not make myself clear? I want his name," Moonie snaps back as he is beginning to run out of patience.

"His name is Flacco. He's one of us."

"Flacco? What a stupid name. Why did he do it?"

"He lost control. That's all there is to it."

"I appreciate your honesty. Now that is out of the way, it's time to brainstorm a plan."

"A plan? There is no plan. We told you what you want, now leave us be." McHay has had enough of Moonie's eccentric way of doing business.

"You. You like your voice to be heard, don't you? Does daddy here not give you enough attention? Or is it that you want him to think you are the man? Which one, tubby? Because the only man here in this basement is the sexy bald one who just happens to be holding a knife to your guy's throat. So, zip it, chubster! Believe it or not, I came here not to kill. I came here to propose." Moonie reaches over for the gun that Ace slid across earlier and empties out the bullets. He slides the gun and one bullet a little to the left of him and stands the other four bullets up on the right side of him. "The gun and bullet to the left of me here represent me and Adrians, my, now former, head of security. These four little pigs represent you pricks." He flicks the bullet representing Adrians down. "Adrians here is gone, thanks to your mate, 'fucko'. Now here is me, the lonely gun standing by himself. The gun needs its bullets. So, here is what I propose." He flicks one bullet from the four down. "Flacco goes and you all come to me." Moonie moves the three remaining bullets over to the gun and he loads them into it. "I have Flacco killed and you guys come to work for me as my protection. I have a club opening soon, you've probably read about it in the papers, it's big news. The biggest club in the UK and it will bring customers from all across the country. I need security. That's your 'option A'. Your 'option B' is not so romantic. 'Option B', you see, is I have you all killed for the murder of Adrians. What will your call be?" Moonie, armed with the gun, begins to circle the table.

Ace and McHay look over to Hunter for answers. What do they do? Flacco is just a kid.

"You all look confused. I suggest you way up 'option A' very carefully."

"I don't think we have much of a choice," Hunter declares.

"Hunter, he's just a kid," Ace quickly replies. Ace doesn't want Flacco to be killed. He's only young and he made a mistake. He is only human.

"Ace, Flacco caused this mess. Moonie will end us and everyone we love," McHay supports Hunter's thinking.

"Right on the money, fatty! Flacco's life or yours. I'm running out of patience," Moonie states.

"Option A," Hunter sharply answers.

Coward, Ace immediately thinks to himself.

"Ding. Ding. Ding. Looks like we have a brain in there after all. Very well. I want you to take this Flacco to my flat on Oxford Estate. You take him out in there," Moonie informs Ace.

"Me? You want me to kill him? I'm not killing Flacco," Ace responds as he shakes his head in refusal.

"Don't get all humble on me now. You pointed a gun at me, now you will pay the consequence. And compared to these two pricks, I like you. My flat is number 20. The place will smell because that's where I do all my killings. Have Flacco disposed of by midnight. You don't want to let me down." Moonie unties Hunter and gently strokes the blade of his knife down Hunter's sweaty cheek. "Gentlemen, it has been an absolute delight doing business with you all. Now please do not take my way of business here today personally, you see, the 'gang culture' is like that of the entertainment business, whoever makes the most noise wins."

Paul Moonie leaves the basement and makes his way out of the house. Lizzy soon runs down and hugs Hunter tightly and checks if he is okay. Ace sits in silence letting everything that has just transpired sink in. He knows that once he kills Flacco, he will always be married to this life whether he likes it or not. He will be forever trapped and tied to this life.

Before Ace leaves the house, Hunter talks to him privately in the living room.

"It's a shame what must happen next, Ace, but in reality, Flacco must take the consequences. We can't die at the hands of his error. Forming a relationship with Mr Moonie will establish us even further, especially in these times of war. We will be on top forever," Hunter informs Ace as he approaches his glass cabinet full of old artefacts that he has been collecting for decades. He bends down and opens a drawer at the bottom of the cabinet and pulls out his old Auto Mag pistol that he used when he was active in Leeds those years ago.

He turns and faces Ace. "Here, I want you to have this." He hands the gun to Ace. "This is your guardian angel. Judge, jury, and executioner. But most importantly, your protector. You are about to become a man, my boy."

Ace doesn't feel that he is ready. "Hunter, I'm not a killer. Flacco is one of us. We can't whack him. It's not right. It's not what we do," Ace stands his ground.

"Acey, I like Flacco, I do, but this is Paul Moonie, and if we don't kill Flacco then he will come for us and the people we love. Don't think of yourself, think of your Ava. Think of my Lizzy." Hunter's words begin to resonate with Ace. It's Flacco's life or theirs. Kill or be killed. He won't put Ava at risk.

"I don't think I'm ready to kill a man," Ace admits.

"We never are. It doesn't matter what you are, what you believe in or what you have done. When you fire this gun, all the answers are changed. Forever. When you aim that at another man's head, it either breaks or makes you. My tip is never to look them in the eye. Don't make it personal. You don't kill people over personal issues. You kill people for business. You must put business first. And for us right now, Flacco's death is best for business. It's time for you to step up, Ace."

Ace looks down at the gun in his hands then looks up at Hunter.

"I will do what has to be done," Ace says which puts Hunter's mind at ease.

"With us being Moonie's right-hand men, we will be untouchable."

"That's what I'm worried about," Ace mumbles as he puts the pistol into the inside pocket of his leather jacket and heads for the door.

Two hours removed from meeting Paul Moonie for the first time, Ace picks Flacco up from his mother's house and sets off driving towards Oxford Estate. Ace sits coldly and firmly in the driver's seat. Guilt is flowing through his veins. He doesn't want to do this but he has no choice.

"So, tell me again, what is this job?" Flacco vulnerably asks.

"Hunter thinks it's time to trust you again so he's giving you this job to see how you do," Ace lies.

"Cool. What is it exactly I need to do?"

"Simple job. You go into the flat with me and I kill whom I have to kill. Simple."

"So, I'm just there to watch?"

"Yes. Hunter wants you to learn from me. That's all there is to it, Flac."

Flacco relaxes a bit and pulls out a bag of cocaine. He uses his wallet and a small razor blade to rack up a line.

"Flac…" Ace stops mid-sentence and realises that if Flacco is full of coke when he kills him, it will be a better experience for Flacco. He will die high and somewhat happier than he would if not.

"What? It's just one-line, Acey, lighten up," Flacco replies.

"Have at it, kid. Have at it."

Flacco snorts up the line of cocaine. "So, who is it you are killing anyway? What did he do?"

"He made a mistake. A terrible mistake and now he must face the consequence."

"Sounds dramatic."

"That's definitely one way to put it, Flacco."

They arrive at the estate.

Ace tries the handle to flat number 20 but it's locked. Flacco checks under the welcome mat and the old, once shiny but now faded, silver key is there.

"Here. Always check the mat, Acey. Rookie move." Flacco hands Ace the key and they enter.

The stench of blood infests the empty flat. Stains of splattered guts drenched in thick dark red blood decorate the walls. There is no furniture in sight. The only item in there is an old vinyl player which Ace quickly puts on and raises the volume in order to compress the sound his gun will soon make. The sole purpose of this flat is to execute Moonie's killings. Killings he has been carrying out here since he bought the flat back in 1979.

"The place is empty. Where is this guy?" Flacco asks, slightly raising his voice over the loud music.

Ace stands behind Flacco and slowly raises his gun.

"Like seriously, Acey, where is this guy?"

"I'm sorry, Flacco. I had no choice." Ace tightens his grip to brace for the coming impact. Even though the music is blaring, Ace hears nothing but emptiness. He knows that he won't leave this flat the same person he was when he entered.

Ace figures that if he does this fast, it might reduce the emotional impact it will have on him. So, after one deep breath, he pulls the trigger. The vibrations race through his arm as the bullet enters the back of Flacco's young skull. His knees buckle and he slowly drops to the ground.

Ace lets out a gasp and slowly loosens his firm grip on the gun. He stands over Flacco's lifeless body. "I'm sorry, Flac." He looks up at one of the blood-stained walls. He stares aimlessly at a fresh patch of blood that has just been splattered from Flacco's demise. *What have I done?* he thinks to himself.

Here it is. Ace's first kill. His destiny is now forever forged into the life of a reluctant gangster.

Two hours after murdering Flacco for Paul Moonie, Ace returns to his apartment where Ava is sitting on the couch watching the local news on the television.

"Hey, hun, are you okay?" She asks noticing the bleak look on Ace's face. She watches as he heads straight into the kitchen area and removes a bottle of whiskey from the cupboard. "Ace, you told me you got rid of all the whiskey," she furiously says.

"I like to keep a bottle in the back of the cupboard to remind me of where I would be without you," Ace replies as he begins to pour the bottle down the sink. "But now I realise, Ava, my alcoholic demons are gone. But when one demon goes, a new one rises. Because I have you though, I will always be fine." He slumps down onto the couch next to her.

"Has something happened? What's this new demon?"

"I believe he goes by the name Paul Moonie."

The gang, with assistance from Paul Moonie, covered up Flacco's murder cleanly. They staged a car accident and informed Flacco's mother that he had died in the accident.

Moonie now holds Ace in great admiration and respect after undertaking the murder of Flacco, and Hunter and the gang are given the title of 'Head of Security' for Moonie's nightclubs across the city. This means that they now run the doors, acting as bouncers as well as any other protecting needs that Moonie requires. This further elevates the gang's rising reputation, and more people have begun to take them in high regard.

However, as summer rolls on, so does the heated drug war between Moss Side and Cheetham. Moonie fears that this war will affect him in a few ways; his right-hand men and heads of security are at risk, and he also fears that by associating with them, he will be roped into the war, and thus people won't want to do business with him or his nightclubs. Moonie needs this war to end before it gets taken too far.

Unfortunately, though, the war soon gets taken ruthlessly too far and no one sees it coming.

XI

'A Step Too Far'

Saturday, August 16th

Another dark day in Manchester. The time is 11 am and the world is about to forever change for the family of eight-year-old Martin Clements.

The sun is out and in full force today with only a few clouds in the sky. Spirits are high in Manchester as people are enjoying and making the most of the sunny Saturday knowing that summer will soon be in the rear-view mirror.

Young Martin Clements and his best friend, James Strong, are swinging on a set of swings at Smithsworth Park in Moss Side. Due to the ongoing drug war, their parents have warned them to keep an eye out for any trouble and if they come across any, they must run home immediately. But they are young, so they pay little to no attention to the warnings as their main concern is enjoying the sun and having a good time.

As the two boys swing on the swing set, they see two men dressed casually in dark hoodies enter the park and wait beside the slide. One of the men is carrying a small package wrapped in brown paper. Martin and James think nothing of it. Why would they? They are children after all.

A fact that is unknown to the boys is that these two men work for Bradley Owens and have been sent to sell a package of cocaine to a buyer. Owens dealing in Moss Side is nothing new, he has often operated on 'Red Syndicate's' turf for quite some time, even before the war.

The two dealers only wait a couple of minutes before a slim and acne-infested teenager strolls up to them dressed in a grey hoodie with his hood up.

"Aron Wyatt?" The dealer holding the package checks.

"Yes, that's me," the teenager replies.

"Could you have been followed here by anybody?" The other dealer questions.

"No, I took the long route."

The dealer hands over the package and in return receives an envelope of cash from the teenager. They begin to quickly count it to make sure they haven't been ripped off.

"It's all here. Get gone."

The teenager begins to walk away and looks to leave the park. However, one of the dealers realises that the teenager is waving over to a parked car. They see two men in long red trench coats exit the car and take the package from the teenager who then flees the scene.

"We've been set up. It's Red Syndicate!" One dealer panics to the other.

The two men in red trench coats throw the package into the car and begin to enter the park. They pull out two handguns with silencers equipped and approach Owens's men.

"Shit! What do we do?"

"We are Bradley Owens' men. We stand our ground." The dealers pull out their handguns and prepare for a gunfight.

"You lads better head home," one dealer informs Martin and James who are still swinging. The two boys jump off the swings but they don't leave the park. Instead, they are so intrigued, that they hide behind a purple climbing frame and watch the events unfold.

"We really should go home, James," a nervous Martin believes.

"It's like watching a real-life movie, we have to stay and watch," James replies.

Martin contemplates running home but he stops himself as he doesn't want to leave his friend behind in potential danger.

The Red Syndicate men are only steps away from Owens' men.

"Let's put them in the ground," a Red Syndicate man says. They open fire and shoot.

Owens men shoot back.

Red Syndicate pushes forward through the flying bullets that are failing to hit them.

"Fuck this," one of Owens's men drops his gun and runs, attempting to escape the park by mounting the fence. He is soon shot down and left to bleed out. One down.

Owens' man is rapidly firing shots, not having time to aim properly. "Shit!" He's out of ammunition. Thinking quickly, he sees Martin and James at the climbing frame and makes a run for them. He figures Red Syndicate will seize fire because of the children. How he will be mistaken.

Owens man lifts young Martin up in front of him.

"Using children for cover. All you men who work for Owens are all the same. Cowards. You are a plague and we are the cure," one of the Red Syndicate men declares as he raises his gun to fire.

"Shane, don't! There are kids there." The other Red Syndicate member is cautious as he doesn't want one of the children getting in the way of the bullet.

"I have a good aim."

The cautious Red Syndicate member disapproves and grabs hold of his partner.

"Shane, no. Don't fire. We don't want to hit a kid."

"I have a good aim. We need to get this mug, that is our job. Stop panicking, you fool."

As the two are arguing, Owens' man sees an opportunity. He puts Martin back down and charges at a heated pace to the Red Syndicate members. He dives straight at them and finds himself in a brawl with the one who wants to shoot.

They begin to wrestle each other around, punching one another in whatever body part they can get hold of. The cautious Red Syndicate member holds up his gun and is prepared to shoot Owens man. However, they are brawling and moving quickly around so the shot will have to be fast and accurate. They are now brawling in front of the climbing frame where Martin and James are hiding behind.

The 'Red Syndicate' member takes a deep breath, he believes he has a clear shot on Owens man and fires his gun.

"Shit!" Owens man sees this and quickly steps back, leaving Martin and James exposed in a clear view. Flying at an unforgivingly fast speed, the bullet accidentally enters the skull of young Martin.

The men suddenly stop fighting the minute they hear a screeching scream from James. They turn and see Martin face down on the floor with gallons of blood flowing from his head.

The Red Syndicate member who fired the gun falls to his knees in disbelief.

"You idiot! What have you done?" The other member picks up the gun he dropped when fighting and quickly shoots Owens' man dead in the head before picking up his partner. "I told you I had a good aim. Why didn't you just listen?

Look what you have done." He holds his partner's head and makes him look at Martin's body. He's horrified.

The people of Manchester are furious at the incident and are calling for an end to this devastating drug war. The murder of Martin Clements is immediately pinned to the Red Syndicate as Martin's friend, James, can describe the two Red Syndicate members.

Paul Moonie is sitting in his office in his new nightclub, 'The Rogue', which is still under construction but almost finished. A worker of his construction team enters and informs him of the murder of the young child, Martin Clements. His wife had just told him about it before coming to work.

Moonie sits back in his chair and is shocked at hearing of the death of the young child. *I need to end this war*, he believes.

This vile war has now taken the life of an innocent bystander. Not just any bystander, but an eight-year-old child. A young boy who had so much left to live for. A young life that had barely begun now deprived of the chance to live out his dreams all because of two grown men not having the ability to co-exist. A child has died in a war that he had no idea about.

XII

'The Truce'

Thursday, August 21st

The day the tide changed. The day the clouds cleared. The day peace was somewhat restored.

Paul Moonie has organised what will be a historic meeting that will be talked about for years to come. The meeting between Bradley Owens and Red Syndicate leader, Finn O'Sullivan. In this monumental meeting, Moonie hopes to achieve a truce between the two sides and bring an end to the war.

Moonie stands at the bar in the first pub he and his brothers ever owned, 'The Moonie'. This is where he has planned the meeting to take place. He stands at the bar and orders his chubby and ginger-haired bartender, Sam, to pour him a rum and coke.

"Are we expecting trouble today, Paulie?" Sam, making Moonie his drink, asks.

"Just pour me the drink treacle. I pay you to pour not to bore."

"Will I need to bring Peppa out?"

Peppa is Moonie's five-year-old Rottweiler. There is a rumour around Manchester that the Moonie brothers often have Peppa attack their enemies in the backroom. One story, the most vicious case of this, circulated last year that Paul poured dog food over a man's head in the backroom then had Peppa come out and literally eat chunks out of the man's face. Peppa is usually out sitting in the corner of the pub with her lead tied to a table leg, but over the past year she has gotten more aggressive, and Paul believes it's best for business to have her out of the way in the back.

"No, it's not one of them meetings. Sorry, Sam, I'm a little confused. Do I pay you to ask me questions or to pour me drinks?"

Nervous about what to say next, Sam looks up at Paul. "Sorry, boss. Here you go." He slides the rum across to him. Moonie finishes the glass in one swig.

"Gets the blood flowing. Make sure no one else enters this establishment apart from Bradley Owens and Finn O'Sullivan. I'm taking a quick shit."

Bradley Owens and Finn O'Sullivan sit at opposite ends of a table placed in the centre of the pub. Both Owens and O'Sullivan have entered the building wearing bulletproof vests for protection from one another.

"How long is he going to be?" Owens, referring to Paul Moonie's whereabouts, asks Sam.

"He will be out any minute now."

"Where did he say he was going?" O'Sullivan wonders.

"He told me he was going for a shit."

"Charming," O'Sullivan responds.

The doors spring open and in walks Paul Moonie with his hands in the air. Moonie never needed to go to the bathroom, he wanted the men to wait for him to make his entrance, showing that he held more power over them. He wants them to keep their egos in check.

"Gentlemen. Gentlemen. Rejoice, for I am here. I hope sugar tits behind the bar there has been looking after you," Moonie says. He notices that they don't have drinks on the table. "Sam! Where are your manners? Where are the drinks?"

Sam doesn't know if Moonie is messing with him or is serious. "They never ordered any, boss."

"Well, pour them a fucking water then. Sorry for him, gentlemen."

"With all due respect, Mr Moonie, I would like to get straight to business here," O'Sullivan attempts to move the purpose of the meeting forward.

"Let's make one thing clear, O'Sullivan, you don't ever talk to me about respect. We are not on the same level. Your men murdered a child. An eight-year-old boy." Moonie has a serious attitude adjustment.

"That wasn't my order. It was an accident."

"A young child lies in the ground because of the actions of your men. Your men, your responsibility." Moonie's words have O'Sullivan speechless. "Now, to business. I called you fine gentlemen here today..." He stops mid-sentence. "Sam, what are you doing? Give these men a glass of water and fuck off into the back room. Bloody amateur."

Sam places two glasses of water down on the table and heads into the backroom.

"As you know, I called you fine gentlemen here today to discuss an end to this unnecessarily bloody war. This war is not only affecting business and reputation but is now costing the lives of innocent people. It is in everybody's best interest for it to end."

Owens and O'Sullivan stare at each other stubbornly. These men have torn each other and Manchester apart these past few months and share a true and pure hatred for each other.

"Look, there's a reason you both showed up here today. You both know that this pissing contest must end. You two have waged war against each other and beaten and killed many men from the other's side. And for what? Your business is falling and your men are dying. You are killing yourselves while trying to kill each other. You are killing this great city!" Moonie exclaims.

"This war never had to begin. It was Owens who sent those men to set alight our shop. He woke the sleeping lion." O'Sullivan tries to justify Red Syndicate's actions.

"Red Syndicate have come for me ever since I came to this city. I lost men. Good men. Way more men than you. I watched them die." Owens leans over the table. "I had to look their families, their children, in the eyes and tell them that daddy wasn't coming home. Red Syndicate didn't just want war with us, they wanted nuclear war." Owens' words come from a passionate and sensitive place.

SLAM! Moonie smacks down on the centre of the table with an aggressive force. He's frustrated at each side's stubbornness.

"Enough with the back and forth. You have both waged this war. I don't care about the why, the how, or even the fucking smell. What I care about is the end to this carnival of bloodshed. So today, right here and right now, it ends."

"I'm willing to co-exist for a price," O'Sullivan announces, acknowledging that Moonie's words hold truth. Business from both sides has been severely gut-punched by this war.

"Nope. No prices. No pay-outs. This is done with honour. How it should always be done," Moonie shuts him down. "I have a proposition but before I do so, I need you both to confirm that you are willing to end this madness and co-exist once more. This is the only way your profits will rise again and peace will resume in this city."

Bradley Owens looks over to O'Sullivan. They both reluctantly nod in approval as if both men's egos have been tainted by agreeing with each other.

"Finally. Okay, gentlemen, my proposition is as follows, I and my brothers bring in the most profits in Ordswall and Beswick through our dealings, nightclubs and other hustles. Today, if you both shake hands and end this war, I will set Red Syndicate up with clientele in Beswick and Owens' organisation with clients in Ordswall," Moonie declares.

Both O'Sullivan and Owens like the sound of this as clients in these areas will help make up profits that they lost in the war.

"However, if I hear or see that you are still waging war and hits on each other, then this deal will be called off and I will make sure that you both will never get another penny from any client again. Are we understood?" Moonie looks down at both men. Both men realise that this arrangement will benefit them greatly as it will expand their reach across the city as well as assist them in rebuilding their profits.

Bradley Owens nods in agreement.

"And you, O'Sullivan?" Moonie prompts.

O'Sullivan drinks a sip of his water. "Understood, Mr Moonie," he says making direct eye contact with Bradley Owens before offering out his hand for a handshake. Owens obliges and thus the war has ended.

"Peace has been achieved! Sam, you chubby bastard, bring out the champers!" Moonie is pleased as he shouts into the backroom for Sam.

"With negotiation like that, you should run for prime minister, Paulie," Sam says as he goes to get a bottle of champagne.

"All politics is poetry written by blind men, Sam my boy."

This truce is pivotal for the future of Manchester. Less violence on the streets increases public safety and in turn, will attract more customers to the nightlife and thus Moonie's pockets will remain wealthy, and Manchester can thrive and transform into the nightlife spectacle that Moonie is aiming to achieve.

XIII
'Two Pints and an Orange Juice'

December 1986

It has been several months now since the end of the Moss Side vs Cheetham drug war and one month since Alex Ferguson was appointed the manager of Manchester United; just like the end of the drug war, this has brought about a sense of great hope for the city. It has also been several months since Hunter's organisation acquired the role of 'head of security' for Paul Moonie's nightclubs across the city. Moonie owns a collection of clubs all over Manchester including but not limited to 'Moon Treasure', 'Galaxy UK', 'Thrust and Lust', 'Paradise Lounge', 'Loco Lounge', and 'Infinity 80'. Club life in Manchester is Moonie's monopoly with his crown jewel, 'The Rogue', set to open this coming February.

Moonie's high maintenance ambitions for 'The Rogue' is to design it to be the epicentre of the UK's rising and extremely lucrative electronic dance music scene. He wants 'The Rogue' to stand out and attract people from all over the country, bringing in business from everywhere. Moonie hopes to help rebrand the city from the recession-populated industrial backwater into an Ibiza-inspired dreamland and believes that with the 90s soon approaching, now is the perfect time to make Manchester stand out and eclipse other cities. Moonie views himself as the 'saviour of the city' and the face of the wind of change that will blow Manchester into the party-heavy 1990s.

During the several months since Hunter and his men have been working for Moonie and running the doors at his nightclubs, Hunter and Lizzy have welcomed into the world their firstborn baby boy, Tommy. Ace has been made godfather to Tommy and Amanda as godmother. However, the birth of Tommy has not stalled the gang's momentum as Hunter keeps working whilst Lizzy is at home caring for him.

Hunter and his gang's role for Moonie is to run the doors to his nightclubs as bouncers and kick out anyone attempting to start any trouble and only let in those formally dressed and not intoxicated. Since the months that Hunter and his men have taken over as security, everything has run smoothly with only one time where the boys have had to get physical.

It was a chilly Friday night in October. October 10th to be specific. Ace and AJ were on the doors for 'Infinity 80'. The night was busy as usual for a Friday night and Ace and AJ were hoping for a bit of trouble to warm themselves up from the cold night.

At around midnight, a couple of young and clearly underage lads approached the entrance of the club where Ace stopped them.

"Any ID, lads?" He asked them.

One of the lads, a curly-haired lanky boy, reached into his wallet and claimed to have left his ID at home. The other lad, a chubby-looking fella, didn't even attempt to reach for his.

"Sorry, guys, no ID means no entrance tonight," AJ said.

"Come on, man, I've left it at home," the lanky lad pleaded.

"I must not speak English me, Acey. I'm pretty sure I just said no ID, no entrance," AJ snapped back.

"No need to be a prick, we are in here all of the time," the chubby boy rebelled.

"Oh, I'm sure that you and all of your pre-adolescence pimples are locals to this fine establishment but as I said, NO ID, NO ENTRANCE." AJ raised his voice which gained the attention of the queue of party seekers waiting behind the lads to get in.

"Listen, lads, do us a favour we have a big line of people behind you so just leave. We are not letting you in," Ace attempted to calm the situation.

The chubby lad spat down on AJ's shoes. Without a second's hesitation, AJ right-hooked the chubby lad which knocked him off his feet. AJ then turned to face Ace who had an almost disappointed look on his face.

"Acey, they were new shoes," AJ justified.

"Fair enough," Ace replied as he then right-hooked the lanky lad which also knocked him off his feet.

It's mid-morning and inside 'Moon Treasure', several bar staff are decorating the nightclub with Christmas decorations; snowflake banners, a few small Christmas trees, and scattering Santa hats all over the bar for partygoers to wear for free.

Moonie has called Hunter and his men into the club for a quick meeting at 1 pm. The time is currently 12.55 pm.

Moonie arrives at the club and waits in the main room where the decorations are being put up.

"Good job, guys," he tells his workers as he goes behind the bar and pours himself a tequila. He downs the glass of tequila in fast fashion. "The best breakfast anyone can have in the morning." He chuckles to himself as he makes his way over to one of his premiere booths which he charges £50 for people to hire out for the night.

The clock hits 1 pm and Hunter, Ace, AJ, and McHay arrive and join Moonie in his booth. Hunter shakes Moonie's hand as they all take a seat. Every time that Hunter sees Moonie, he always shakes his hand. This slightly irritates Moonie each time he does it. At first, Moonie liked it as it fed his ego but ever since the time that Hunter did it in the toilets after Moonie had just evacuated his bladder in the urinals, it began to bug him.

"Right on time, gentlemen, if you were any later, I'd have thought you were pulling my pisser," Moonie opens the meeting.

"Traffic is awful out there, Paulie, I apologise," Hunter worms.

"Never apologise, Hunter, never. It's not a good look for you. Anyway, I digress; in the short number of months that you boys have been working for me, my clubs have never run smoother. That's why I would like to present you all with the opportunity to allow me to rest more responsibility on all your shoulders."

Hunter is excited at the opportunity to carry out more jobs for Moonie as it will benefit his gang greatly; they will become almost untouchable in the city. No one will ever challenge them if it is known that Paul Moonie has put his trust in them.

"What would that consist of?" A curious and always thinking Ace ponders.

"Does it matter what it consists of, Acey? That's Paul fucking Moonie," Hunter sucks up to Moonie.

"No, no, I like it. You, Acey, have a voice for yourself and I respect that," Moonie shows admiration for Ace yet again. "However, you don't really have a choice here. I can make you or break you so I highly recommend that you take this opportunity that so many in this city would kill for. Well, an opportunity you did kill for."

"Well, I'm in," McHay says.

"Of course, you're in. What will it be, Acey? A few extra jobs to oversee some deals and chores or sleeping with the homeless on the mean streets of Manchester?" Moonie looks directly at Ace.

"I'm the boss here and I say that we are in, Mr Moonie," Hunter states.

"Shush, Hunter. I'm asking Ace here." Moonie doesn't hold much respect for Hunter. He is of the belief that you can never trust a leader who doesn't fight alongside his soldiers. He sees an untouched rising fire inside Ace and he desperately wants to pour petrol on and see his full potential burn through, as he believes that by having a man like Ace by his side, he is ensured the best enforcing security and right-hand man possible.

"I'm in," Ace replies.

Moonie smiles and rests back in the booth before turning his attention to AJ. "And you, you are a quiet one, aren't you?"

"I like to take everything in," AJ defends his silence.

"Well, I don't trust a man who has no voice. Having no voice doesn't mean you can't whistle. But whistle in which direction, are we yet to find out?"

AJ sees this as Moonie challenging him. He is taken slightly by surprise here. He edges forward in his seat and leans in. "Oh, don't get it mistaken, Mr Moonie, I assure you I do have a voice. That voice is loud and can be very disturbing."

"Mmm. Well from my experience, the only reason that a man in this game is quiet is if he's hiding something or has done something." Moonie slightly squints at AJ as he assesses his body language trying to figure him out. "Let's hope that I'm wrong because where there is one rat, there is always more."

"You are wrong." AJ won't back down or be disrespected.

Moonie tilts his head a little and smiles at AJ. AJ can't figure out if Moonie is taunting him and messing with him, or if he is assessing him, so he does the same back to Moonie and tilts his head smiling.

"AJ is one of us, Paulie. Through and through," Ace defends AJ.

"Good." Moonie now shifts his attention off AJ. "Anyway, gentlemen, tomorrow night there will be a deal taking place at the abandoned 'Greatman

Factory' and I want a few of you there to oversee that it goes smoothly. The deal is between a local dealer who is buying some of my product and one of my guys. My guy will meet the buyer at the factory yard at 9 pm," Moonie explains.

"Do you not trust the buyer?" Ace questions why their presence is needed there.

"In the past, he has been known to be dodgy but he pays well. So, you guys will watch in the shadows and if he tries anything, I want you to step in and do what you have to do, but don't kill him."

"So, we show up and if things go wrong, we bust a few heads?" McHay checks with Moonie.

"You catch on fast, Mr McHay. Now since Hunter is your boss, I will leave it to his wisdom to decide who does the job. I just want you all to understand that I am putting my trust in you, so do not let me down," Moonie stands up. "Please help yourself to a drink, I have other business to attend to." Moonie leaves the booth and heads into the back to where his office is located.

"So, who does the job, H?" AJ asks Hunter.

"All three of you. This is the first job that Moonie has put us on so we can't afford to mess this one up," Hunter decides.

"We won't let you down, H," McHay chimes in.

It's Moonie we can't afford to let down, you kiss ass, Ace thinks to himself.

"Good, now that is all for today, so go and rest up for tomorrow night." Hunter stands and leaves the club.

"Forget that. Does anyone fancy a drink tonight?" AJ raises the question.

"I can do with a drink, sure," McHay replies.

"Are you sure Amanda is going to let you off the lead?" AJ pokes fun.

"Get fucked."

"Acey, you in? Obviously for an orange juice," AJ asks.

"Sure, I'll come down for an orange juice."

"Perfect, let's say 8 pm."

"8 pm it is," Ace replies.

"Oh, and McHay, if you are late again then the first round is on you," AJ declares.

"You will never get a pint from me. I'd rather die than buy you anything," McHay jokes.

On the drive back to his apartment, Ace takes the longer route that passes by Flacco's mother's house. Ace pulls up outside of the house. He wants to do this.

Waves of guilt flood him and he takes a deep breath before exiting the car and approaching the doorstep.

'It's only right that I do this', Ace says to himself. He knocks on the door.

Guilt. Anxiety. Fear. All feelings electrify Ace's body as he waits in anticipation for Dorothy to answer the door. He thinks about what to say when she opens the door but he can't pick the right words, so he decides to just say what comes to him in the moment.

A few short moments that feel like a lifetime to Ace later, Dorothy opens the front door and is met with the sight of Ace.

"Tony, what a nice surprise," she says.

"Hi, Dorothy, I was just passing by and thought I would check up on you. How are you doing?"

"What a lovely thought, Tony. Please do come in, it's freezing out here."

"No, no, it's okay, Dorothy, honestly."

"I won't have it, Tony, I insist, come in."

Ace reluctantly enters the house.

Dorothy walks Ace into her clean and well-kept living room. The first thing that Ace sees is young photos of Flacco on the windowsill and on top of the TV.

"Can I get you a cup of tea or something?" Dorothy, in her caring nature, asks.

"No, thank you, I'm fine. I only swung by to see if there is anything I can do for you," Ace says as Dorothy sits down.

"Please do sit."

Ace slowly and hesitantly sits down. He doesn't like how nice Dorothy is treating him. He knows that he doesn't deserve to be welcomed so warmly. Not after what he did and all the pain that he has put her through.

"Is there anything I can do for you?" He asks again.

"You have done so much already. You were a genuine friend to my Flacco and cared for him greatly. That's enough in my book. He admired you a lot, Tony."

"Well, I don't know about that, Dorothy. I wasn't always the best friend to him."

"You were and he knew it. He always used to tell me about you looking out for him. And out of all his friends, you are the only one who has come to check up on me."

Ace struggles to look her in her eyes as she speaks to him.

"Are you sure there is nothing I can get you?" Dorothy asks Ace.

"Could I please use your bathroom?" Ace asks.

"Of course, you know which room it is."

Ace ascends the stairs but he doesn't go to the bathroom. Instead, he heads into Flacco's bedroom.

He stands in the room and stares at Flacco's bed which Dorothy has neatly made and rested some of his clothes on with a framed photo of him placed on top of the clothes.

"I'm so sorry, Flacco. I had to do it." A small tear falls from Ace's eye.

All of a sudden, Ace feels a lump of vomit rise in his throat. He rushes downstairs and out of the front door where he vomits all over Dorothy's garden.

Dorothy hurries out behind Ace and sees the mess splattered over her grass.

"Oh, Tony, let me get you a towel."

"No. Dorothy, no. Please do not help me. Coming here was a mistake." Ace readjusts himself and heads towards his car. Before entering his car, he turns to face Dorothy and says, "Nobody calls me Tony anymore, I'm called Ace. Tony is gone. He went a long, long time ago." He swings open his car door and slams it aggressively behind him so hard that the car shakes a little on the impact. He has treated her this way as he doesn't want her to view him as a good person. Ace also truly believes that after murdering Flacco, his old life as the innocent Tony Johnson, a man who had morals and self-respect, is over and any traces of the man he once was, are fading.

He is only surviving and being able to live with himself for what he's done because he has Ava. His light and his lifeline.

The night soon comes, and Ace enters 'The Blue Moon' where he orders an orange juice from the barmaid, Eden. He then heads over to McHay and AJ who are sitting in the gang's reserved booth.

"Hey, McHay, do you know what arsehole in Italian is?" AJ randomly asks out of the blue.

"How would I know that, you shit sniffer?" McHay, looking puzzled, replies.

"It would be you if you ever went to Italy." AJ laughs at his own joke before sipping more of his beer as McHay sits on shaking his head.

"You are a disease, AJ. I guess you were saving that one so Ace could hear it."

"At least I don't lick Ace's arse clean. 'Yes, Hunter, I'll jump. How high, Hunter? Are you watching me, Hunter? Look at me, I'm just like you. I love you,

Daddy, I mean Hunter'," AJ ridicules McHay's desperate need for Hunter's approval, he finds it self-degrading on McHay's part.

"Piss off, you little runt."

McHay and AJ have always had a rocky relationship. McHay doesn't like AJ's sarcastic attitude and believes his ego is bigger than his head. As for AJ, he takes a slight dislike to McHay due to his efforts to apple-polish up to Hunter.

"Gentlemen, ease off. It's been a rough day as it is, I don't need to babysit your arses too." Ace brings the boiling, yet playful, tension to a close.

"Why what's happened?" AJ asks.

"I went to see Dorothy," Ace replies in a sombre tone of regret.

"Who's Dorothy?" McHay quizzes.

"You know Dorothy. She is Flacco's mother."

"Why on earth did you go and see her, Ace?" McHay stresses. "That's not going to help you get rid of your guilt. You have to live with it and move on."

"I didn't go to clear my conscience. I went to check on her. She's alone because of me. I went to see if she needed any help."

"Any help? Ace, you killed her son. The only help you could possibly bring her is bringing her son back from the dead," AJ remarks.

"I, unfortunately, must agree with the schmuck here, Ace. No good could have ever come from that."

"I just wanted to give something back to her."

"The only thing you could give back to her is your death, and don't do that because we need your fedora-wearing ass," McHay says in an attempt to brighten the darkened mood. "Anyway, have you seen what the papers have been calling us?" McHay picks up the newspaper that he brought in and turns to page five. He holds it up to Ace.

The article in question reads: *MOONIE'S THREE GRIFTERS ATTACK DRUNK PUNTERS*. The article is referring to an incident that occurred last weekend.

McHay and AJ were running the doors to 'Moon Treasure' and Ace was circling the inside of the club keeping an eye out for anyone who needed throwing out. It was around 1 pm when he saw one lad harassing a young lady on the dancefloor. After the lady rejected the man, he forced himself on her and began to grind on her. Ace didn't stand for this so he stormed over and got the man in a headlock before escorting him out of the club to where McHay and AJ were standing. The outside of the club was quiet with no soul in sight as it was nearly closing time.

However, two of the man's friends were in fast pursuit and followed Ace outside.

"What have we got here, Acey?" McHay asked.

"A prick who thinks it's okay to harass women." Ace forcefully threw the man down as AJ went over and kicked him several times in his stomach.

"Hey, hey, what the hell man!" One of the man's friends shouted as the two rushed over to their grounded friend.

"Get your boy here and hit the road," AJ ordered them.

"Oh yeah and what are you going to do if we don't?" One friend snapped back and got in AJ's face.

"I was really hoping you asked me that," AJ said before he violently headbutted the friend, which sent him flying backwards into the road. At the sight of this, the other friend began to rush over to AJ grinding his teeth and clenching his fists but before he could get there, Ace strook him hard in the face. After shaking off the impactful blow, the man immediately lunged his body forward at Ace and pinned him against the wall. McHay and AJ dove in and tackled the man to the ground where they began to pound him several times over before they hurdled him into the road.

"Here, fellas, there's one for each of us," Ace pointed out as the three of them walked into the road and beat senselessly the three fallen men. They didn't stop until they drew blood.

"Who are you?" One of the men asked as he lay in a puddle of his own blood.

Ace, McHay, and AJ began to walk out of the road leaving them behind.

"We are the three fucking grifters," AJ answered as he spat down on the floor.

Ace smiles after reading the headline. "You were right, AJ, it does have a good ring to it."

"It sure is a better name than 'Hunter and his merry men'," AJ laughs.

"Well, fellas, cheers to us. The Three Grifters." McHay puts down the paper and raises his pint for a toast. "We might have our occasional differences," McHay looks at AJ before continuing, "But we are brothers. Brothers in arms. And let me tell you both, we will be remembered in this city."

"I'll drink to that," AJ says.

"Me too." Ace raises his orange juice.

The three men take several gulps of their drinks and finish them in a fast fashion.

"I heard this next round is on Vino. Hey, Eden, we will have two tequila shots, two lagers, and one orange juice, please. Put it on McHay's tab," AJ calls over to the barmaid. "And you know what, I think he is feeling generous so pour yourself one."

"In your fucking dreams, AJ," McHay says.

"What's that? Oh, wait up Eden, pour yourself two. He's in a wonderful mood this evening."

"I swear, one of these days I'm going to kill you," McHay says.

XIV
'Dog Food'

The night air is chilly with a slight breeze passing by. The Three Grifters have arrived at 'Greatman Factory' and are positioned out of sight behind some large wooden crates in the yard which is a short distance from where the deal is set to go down.

Moonie's two men, Butch and Billy, two largely framed ex-army men, are waiting in the yard for the buyer to arrive. They are holding a briefcase containing Moonie's narcotics. Butch and Billy fought in the army alongside each other but since they came home, finding work had been extremely difficult for the two, so in their hour of need, they turned to their old friend, Paul Moonie, who set them up working for him. They have been with Moonie for a few years now.

From where the Grifters are, they can see Butch and Billy in clear sight.

"It's bloody freezing," AJ complains as he shivers holding his handgun.

"Cry me a river! It's December, it's not meant to be warm," McHay snaps back.

"Well observed, McHay. I'm glad you know your months because I wasn't sure what month we are in," AJ sarcastically responds.

"There you go again with the sarcasm. One of these days I'm going to plant you in the ground."

"Oh yeah, my brother in arms, well make it today, big boy, come on."

"Knock it off, you two, we have a job to do here," Ace breaks it up.

A black van soon pulls up in the yard opposite Butch and Billy.

"This must be the buyer," McHay states.

"Another solid observation," AJ mumbles.

A short, 5ft tall Chinese man exits the van dressed in a light brown bomber jacket. He holds a briefcase full of cash.

"Good evening, Mr Li," Billy greets him.

Mr Li steps forward to Butch and Billy. "Good evening, gentlemen. Shall we exchange?" Mr Li holds out his briefcase. Butch raises his and both parties exchange.

Billy opens Mr Li's briefcase and begins to count the amount of money inside. It's all there. Mr Li then opens the one Butch handed to him and begins to check the 'product'. That too is all there.

"Everything looks in order," a satisfied Mr Li announces.

"Our product is the best of the best, Mr Li, I assure you," Butch says.

"That I don't doubt. Mr Moonie is a highly driven man. But not as highly driven as me. BOYS!" Mr Li calls out and the back doors of his van open. Out come two of Li's men holding shotguns. This is an ambush.

Butch and Billy pull out their handguns in an attempt to retaliate but it's too late. The two men from the van open fire and blast Billy down dead and clip the side of Butch's leg. Mr Li heads behind the van for cover as his men continue firing at Butch, who is now in cover with the Grifters after he crawled himself over to them.

"Those fuckers!" McHay says.

"You stay here, we will sort this," Ace orders Butch to stay in cover.

"My leg. I'm losing a lot of blood here," Butch cries out.

"McHay, give me your blazer," Ace demands.

"It's an expensi…" McHay stops himself as he realises that he is being selfish. He quickly removes his blazer and hands it over to Ace who then ties it tight around Butch's wounded leg to compress the bleeding.

"Put pressure on it and you should be okay," Ace tells Butch.

The Grifters then step out from behind the crate and open fire on Li's men. Their sudden emergence takes Li's men by surprise. Bullets fly everywhere.

Before they can even comprehend and sink in the appearance of the Grifters, AJ has shot one in the face. One down.

The other shotgun-wielding man calls out in a rage as he continues to fire. As he focuses his attention and aims at AJ, Ace shoots him in his torso. He drops his shotgun and falls to the ground.

AJ smugly walks over to the grounded man. "Any final remarks?" He asks.

"Fuck you, and fuck Paul Moonie."

AJ finishes him off with a shot to his head. "Don't bring a handgun to a shotgun fight they said. More fool them," he remarks.

After hearing the sudden silence, Mr Li peaks his head around from the back of the van, only to be immediately met by a right hook from Ace which knocks him cleanly out.

"What do we do with him?" AJ asks as the Grifters stand over the fallen Mr Li.

"Should we kill him?" McHay wonders.

"We bring him to Moonie," Ace announces.

Within the space of an hour, the Grifters have brought Mr Li to Moonie's pub, stripped him naked, and tied him to a chair in the basement.

Ace enters the basement having just spoken to Paul Moonie on the telephone.

"He will be here in ten minutes he said," Ace tells AJ and McHay who are standing and staring at the tied-up Mr Li.

"I can't wait to see what he does to you." AJ spits on Mr Li's exposed feet.

"Fuck you," Mr Li says. AJ hits him across the face.

"I've heard stories of what he does to people down here," McHay tells Ace and AJ. "Apparently, he has a dog." After McHay says this, Mr Li's face becomes overwhelmed with fear.

"I don't get it, Mr Li, why would you try to do over a man like Paul Moonie? You must be aware of the man's reputation," Ace questions.

"A man is only powerful until he is shot in the face."

"And are you that man who shoots him in the face? Because from where I'm stood, you're a bit tied up, pal."

"If not me, then someone else will. A man like Mr Moonie has a very short life expectancy. One day, he will bite off more than he can chew. It's the food chain. Everyone has a predator."

"Yeah, and Moonie is yours," AJ remarks.

"Maybe that is the case, but who is yours?"

"Shut your mouth. You talk crap." McHay slaps Mr Li across his face.

"You don't put two fighter fish in the same tank. They simply cannot co-exist," Mr Li says. "It's only a matter of time before one eats the other."

"You talk bollocks," AJ tells him.

Ten minutes soon pass and Paul Moonie storms down the stairs into the basement holding his crowbar in one hand and holding 'Peppa' by her lead in the other.

"Sorry for the delay, gentlemen, I was making sweet, sweet love to a young lady," Moonie says before he takes a look at Mr Li on the chair. "Well, well, Mr

127

Li, you have messed up royally this time, Sir." Moonie places Peppa's lead in Ace's hand. "My Billy lies dead because of you. Not only that but in his dying breath, your man said 'fuck Paul Moonie'. Nobody in this city says 'fuck Paul Moonie'!" Moonie swings the crowbar around in the air several times before bashing it down on Mr Li's crotch which soon turns blood red.

Mr Li cries out in pain.

"Tears of a clown," Moonie says as he then proceeds to kick Mr Li brutally in his chest which sends him and the chair flying backwards and crashing down onto the floor. "Hand me that bag of 'Tail Wagger's Delight' please, McHay."

McHay scans the room and sees a bag of 'Tail Wagger's Delight' dog food on the shelf to his right. He quickly hands it to Moonie.

Moonie then splits open the bag of dog food and pours it over Mr Li's face. "What you are about to witness, gentlemen, is art at its finest. Acey, drop the lead," Moonie demands.

Ace drops the lead and 'Peppa' runs over and begins to indulge in Mr Li's face. Her shark-like teeth pierce through his flesh. She rocks her head aggressively side to side as she chews the chunks of meat that she has just violently tugged off Mr Li's face.

AJ turns to the side, looking away to prevent himself from vomiting at the sight of the malicious mauling.

Mr Li's cries can be heard from the bar.

"Do we have to stay to watch this?" A disgusted McHay asks Moonie. His face now a ghostly pale white.

"Does my business method make you feel uncomfortable, McHay?" Moonie, laughing at McHay's face of pending vomit, asks.

"A little."

"Good. You can leave if you want to, McHay, I won't make you stay. I'm not a monster. Go on, you and AJ leave but, Ace, you stay."

McHay and AJ leave quickly and rush up to the bar to drink away the images of the gruesome murder they have just witnessed.

"Acey, my boy, I have a job that requires your service," Moonie says to Ace.

"Sure. What do you need me to do?"

Moonie and Ace step to one side to dilute the noise of Mr Li's cries.

"Tomorrow morning, my brothers will be released from prison and I need you to go and pick them up. I have other business to attend to."

"That shouldn't be a problem, Paulie."

"Good, good. On their way back here, they need to make a quick stop off at my apartment. My, let's call it, 'spare' apartment. My 'murderpartment'."

"I see. Are they going to 'whack' someone?"

"They are. It's the man responsible for putting them behind bars. I will make sure he is already in there waiting for them. You don't have to enter with them, just keep the engine running outside."

"Okay. What time shall I head to the prison?"

"8 am. Oh, and invite the rest of the gang here at night. I'm hosting a little welcome home party for them both."

"I will."

"AHHHHHHHHHHHH!" Mr Li uncontrollably bellows some more in the background.

"Such a noisy prick," Moonie remarks.

XV

'A Brothers Reunion'

After a long night trying desperately to sleep but not being able to due to the horrifying visuals of Mr Li's face being mauled plaguing his mind, Ace starts his drive towards the prison to pick up Paul's younger brothers.

Ace hasn't met Jack and John Moonie yet. He has only ever seen photos of them in Moonie's pub. The stories he has heard about the two twins are just as intimidating as the ones he heard about Paul.

One story of this is when the erratic and mentally unstable Jack pinned down a drug dealer and carved his initials onto the man's forehead with a butter knife, whilst John hit the man several times in his genitals with knuckle dusters.

To some locals of Manchester, well, those brave enough to speak out against them, often refer to the three brothers as 'The Terrible Trio'.

Both Jack and John were sentenced to two years in prison back in 1984 after assaulting and crippling a plumber who attempted to rip the brothers off for a job in 'The Moonie' pub.

The plumber, Derrick Riley, charged the brothers double the amount he should have for repairing the pub's water system. Derrick just happened to catch Jack and John on a day when they woke up on the wrong side of the bed.

After asking for his ridiculous amount of money, Derrick and John got into a heated argument. The shouting soon gained Jack's attention, who then smashed a pint glass over Derrick's head as John began to kick him whilst he was down.

The brothers then halted the attack and gave Derrick a chance to reconsider his price.

To which Derrick responded, "I now want triple that amount, you stupid pricks." He shouldn't have said that.

John then began to harshly kick him in his ribs, shattering two.

Not one to be outdone, Jack then took a piece of shattered glass that was from the pint glass he bashed over Derrick's head earlier and slowly stabbed it into Derrick's eye which blinded him in that eye. Derrick was never the same after his experience with the two brothers, and he even quit plumbing after that day. In Spring 1985, his wife would go on to take her own life after suffering from severe mental health issues following her husband's encounter with the two brothers. She grew fearful that Paul would come after them for sending his brothers down. So fearful that she refused to even leave her house. Her paranoia drove Derrick insane but he too felt the same way. Paul never did attempt to come after them though. She killed herself for nothing.

Due to Paul Moonie's friendly relationship with the judge, Jack and John were only given two years for the assault.

Jack Moonie, the mentally unstable and spiky-haired brother, is extremely short-tempered with the littlest of things that can trigger a manic episode. He used to beat his ex-girlfriend excessively until she left him in 1983. Before he was sent down for assaulting Derrick, Jack was addicted to alcohol and even tried to go to rehab, which worked for a short while until he came back home and relapsed. He never attempted rehab again. He always preached that if you take an alcoholic out of the environment that caused him to drink in the first place and then place him back into that environment after the rehab, they are just going to fall back into their old habits. It's the environment that needs to change and since he never saw himself leaving his brothers, he never ventured into rehab again. Jack also believes that someone who has an unstable and unhinged mind can never change that. It is too deeply rooted in them and there is nothing anyone can do to fix it.

He wears his unhinged mindset as a badge of honour. For example, in 1982, he found himself in a vicious bar fight where he was cut on the right side of his head after being thrown head-first through the pub window. It left him with a 35cm long jiggered and crooked scar running down the right side of his face. Upon noticing it, Jack took his silver pocketknife and made adjustments to the scar, turning the rickety scar line into the letter 'J'. He wore the scar like a medal.

Jack's partner in crime, his brother John, is not much different to him. The muscular, buzz-cut and equally as violent John Moonie, was once married to a dancer named Rosie for three years. However, after Rosie came to the realisation that John was a gangster and not the businessman that he proclaimed himself to be, she left him and took their daughter, Amy, with her. John has never seen them since.

After Rosie's departure, John signed up for the navy as a distraction and ended up fighting in the Falklands War. When he returned home, it soon became apparent to everyone that knew him that John had changed as he became increasingly more aggressive on his jobs and in his day to day life. He has also never been with or loved another woman since Rosie.

Although his violence usually matches Jack's, John is more approachable than his twin. People can reason with John as his temper is not as short as Jack's. For example, when Jack starts, no one can stop him. Whereas John will think before he acts and knows when to draw a line. To Jack, that line doesn't exist. It never has.

Even as a child, Jack's lust for violence shone through. At age five, Jack got into a fight with a school bully and ended up paralysing the other child after the fight.

Make no mistake about it, these brothers are ruthless and not to be crossed.

What am I getting myself into here? I wonder what they are like? Will they trust me like Paul does? Ace's overthinking kicks in as he nears the prison. His overthinking and paranoia grow whenever he is anxious about a situation.

Ace arrives at the prison gates where he sees Jack and John waiting with a couple of security guards at the side of them. Both Jack and John are dressed in their discharge clothes, grey jumper and jogger bottoms, and holding duffel bags containing their personal belongings.

"It's been a pleasure, gentlemen," Jack sarcastically waves goodbye to the prison guards as he and John enter Ace's car.

"So, you must be Ace right?" John asks as Ace begins the drive to Paul's murder apartment.

"Yeah, that's me. It's nice to meet you, gentlemen. Paul has a lot of affection for you both," a still-anxious Ace responds, hoping that the brothers will take a liking to him.

"Paul has a lot of affection for you as well." John can sense Ace's anxiety, so he attempts to ease him.

"That's him though. You are still yet to prove yourself to us," Jack shakes Ace's anxiety.

"You don't need to worry about that," Ace courageously says.

"Good. Now, I take it Paul has given you our guns?" Jack asks.

"Here." Ace takes his left hand off the steering wheel, grabs a small black bag that's sitting in the passenger seat and throws it to the two brothers sitting in the back.

Jack takes out his handgun and smells it before saying, "Oh baby, daddy is home."

"It sure does feel good to be back, brother." John smiles.

"I can't wait to put a bullet in the head of that plumber. A bit of justice," an excited Jack claims.

"Hey, Ace, did Paul tell you who we are whacking today?" John asks.

"He told me that it's the man responsible for putting you in jail. From what I hear, he was a plumber, right? Tried to rip you off?"

"Yup. The little bitch went crying to the pigs when we gave him a little beating. But today is his judgment day," a now serious Jack answers.

"He cost us two years of our lives. Two years we can never get back. Today he pays," John says.

As the drive continues, Jack asks Ace to turn on the car's radio, which he does. When on a job, Ace prefers to have the radio off as he is normally too anxious and focused on the job at hand to listen to and enjoy music. However, he doesn't want to anger the brothers on his first introduction to them so he obliges this time.

"I love this shit," Jack states as a popular song from the early 80s begins to play. He sings along to it.

It's at this moment that Ace thinks to himself, *How can a man who is about to take the life of another man be so calm and sing on his way to do the murder? These brothers aren't human. They must be beyond saving.*

Ace pulls up to the apartment block. The apartment block is all too familiar to him. Images of Flacco's limp body invade his head as he stares at the building. He can feel a small lump of vomit begin to rise in his throat but he manages to settle it.

"This won't take long, Ace," John says as he and Jack exit the car with their handguns shoved down the front of their pants.

Ace can't take his eyes off the building. He can't help but think about Flacco. Visuals of Flacco's innocent smile, childlike naivety, and his voice populate Ace's harrowing mind. He closes his eyes tight to stop it but it fails to work. He switches the car's radio back on to distract his mind which works only for a few seconds. Slamming his hands down on the steering wheel and hanging his head

133

low, Ace can't shake the guilt he feels for Flacco's murder. It is eating him alive. *What am I becoming?* He feels as though his ankles have been tied to a heavy weight and he has been thrown into the deep sea. No escape and destined to drown.

Ace reaches into the passenger side glove compartment, grabs his white and brick-like 1985 mobile phone and calls Ava. The only person who can snap his head out of the madness it puts itself in.

"Hey, you," Ace greets her.

"Hey, Ace, are you okay?"

"I am now that I hear your voice."

"Why, what's happened?"

"Nothing. I just needed to hear your voice. Hey, how about we go out for a meal tonight, me and you?"

"Erm…sure yeah, we can do. Shall we say 8 pm?"

"That works for me. How's your day going?"

"It's barely just started, Ace. Are you sure everything is okay?" A concerned Ava checks.

"I'm sure, Ava. Fuck! I've just remembered we can't do the meal tonight, there is a party at Moonie's bar. Come with me to that." Ace is so riddled with guilt that his mind is all over the place. He suddenly hears laughter and he looks up to see Jack and John leaving the apartment building. Jack's hands are dripping with blood. "Okay, baby, I have to go. I'll meet you at mine tonight and we will head to the party. I love you, bye." Ace hangs up the phone and Jack and John get back into the car.

"We are done here," John tells Ace who starts up the engine.

Jack takes a deep breath in. "That was art. We have still got it, man. Did you see his stupid face when I put the pliers on his balls?" He asks with great pride.

"I sure did, brother, just what that piece of crap deserved. IT FEELS FUCKING ELECTRIC, BABY!" John shouts out with great pleasure.

After fifteen minutes of listening to Jack and John go over several excruciating details about the murder they have just committed, Ace arrives at 'The Moonie' pub.

Jack leads the way and barges the pub doors wide open. "Oh honey, I'm home!" He exclaims to Sam behind the bar and Paul who is standing at the bar drinking a bottle of beer.

The three brothers embrace.

"Sam, get these men a drink on the house. Today is a good day!" Paul says.

"What will it be, gentlemen?" Sam asks.

"A beer please, Sam," John replies. "How I've missed the taste of beer."

"Surprise me, darling," Jack responds.

"And you, Ace?"

"I'm good, thanks, Sam," Ace politely declines.

"Are you not a drinker Ace?" Jack questions.

"I've stopped drinking. All alcohol does is plague the mind."

"Oh, are you some sort of poet now?" Jack laughs.

"Hey, Ace is a good man. He is one of us so respect him," Paul defends his favourite member of the Three Grifters. "Anyway, don't drink too much too soon, boys, tonight is the party," Paul informs his brothers.

"Fuck yeah!" An excited Jack exclaims.

"The papers have already had a field day on us," John says as he reads the newspaper resting on the side of the bar. The headline reads: *The Terrible Trio Reunited.*

"Forget them. All that matters is that we are back as one again," a prideful Paul responds.

"What's this about Henderson hiring a private investigator to look into claims of fraud? Paulie, we just got out of the nick, we don't want to go straight back in," John says as he continues to read the article.

"Yeah, give us a week at least," Jack laughs.

"It's all talk. Look at us, we are the Moonie brothers. Nobody can take us. This city is ours, boys." Paul walks over and takes the paper out of John's hands. "Enough of the bullshit they print in here and charge extortionate money for. No claims, no blame, and no other crimes can be proved. They frankly don't have the balls to come for us, so let's ignore them and party!"

It's 8 pm and the 'welcome home' party for Jack and John is well underway. Friends of the Moonie brothers and regulars to the pub are in attendance along with Hunter, Vince McHay, Amanda, and AJ. There are around thirty people here. The pub is decorated with 'welcome home' banners and balloons. Music is blasting from the jukebox and good vibes are being had all around.

Paul Moonie, after shaking several hands, makes his way over to Hunter, McHay, Amanda, and AJ who are standing together with drinks in their hands.

"Gentlemen, gentlemen, and lady, I'm so glad you made it. Have you had the pleasure of meeting the men of the hour?" He asks them.

"We have, Paulie, great men," Hunter worms.

"Of course, they are great men, they are related to me!"

"Hey, Paulie, who's the schmuck over there with the notepad?" McHay points over to a man sitting at a table with a glass of lemonade and making notes on a notepad.

"That, my eagle-eyed friend, is reporter Mr Harry Watkins from the 'Daily Dose'. I invited him here tonight to take notes and report on the fireworks."

"Fireworks?" AJ curiously asks.

"Indeedy, young AJ. The fireworks will begin shortly. Trust me, you won't miss them."

Suddenly, Ace and Ava enter the pub and are greeted by Paul straight away as he hurries over to them.

"Acey, you made it!" Paul hugs Ace before turning his attention to the beautiful Ava. "My oh my, Acey, this must be Ava." Paul holds out her hand and kisses it.

"That it is. Ava, this is Paul Moonie."

"Ah, Mr Moonie, I have heard so much about you," Ava, slightly nervously, says to Paul.

"I hope you've not heard it from the papers." Moonie laughs before continuing, "Now make yourselves at home and mingle around, there are a few important people here tonight. For example, over there, the guy in the blue suit, that's the mayor's son." Paul points over to a twenty-nine-year-old man in a blue suit flirting with a blonde lady at the bar. "We're in bed with them all, Acey."

Paul leaves Ace and Ava to it and continues to go around the pub greeting people.

"You head over to Hunter over there, I'll get your drink in, love," Ace says to Ava who heads over to Hunter, McHay, Amanda, and AJ.

"You've got a looker there, Acey," John Moonie, sitting at the bar, says as Ace waits to get served.

"I know, John, she's one of the good ones."

"Look after her. Never let her go. Trust me, you lose her, and your life will never be the same again," John preaches.

"I will do everything I can not to," Ace cautiously says knowing about John's past with his ex-wife and how the end of that marriage destroyed him.

"How much does she know about what you do?"

"She knows what she needs to."

"Paulie tells me that you killed a boy for us. Does she know about that?"

"No."

"Keep it that way. After what we do, we all need that someone who keeps us sane. That someone who brings us in from the rain and dries us off."

"Manchester is a big place, John. Get yourself out there."

John smacks down on the bar so hard that a few punters turn their heads his way to see what's going on. "I loved once. I won't go through that again," he says with a heavy tone of regret in his voice.

"Fair enough. I'm sorry, John."

"Me and you both," He says before he takes a swig of his drink. "HMS Sheffield."

"Sorry?"

John takes another swig of his drink and then places it down slowly and softly. "HMS Sheffield. May 4th, 1982. I was on board."

"The Falklands?"

"As soon as that missile hit, I knew that good men were about to die that day. The panic and fear overcame us. We knew that there was nothing we could do. I held my friend as the ship began to go under. He was trapped under some debris from the hit, his legs were split in two. There was no way he could be saved. But I didn't care. No man should die alone. Sometimes, when I close my eyes, I can still hear his cries." John stops for a moment and he stares down at his pint glass as he reflects on the horrifying experience. "I held on tight as we went down, and on the way down, I must have hit something hard as the last thing I remember is his helpless face looking up at me for answers that I didn't have. I woke up on a nearby shore. They said I was one of the lucky ones. It sure as shit doesn't feel like that. But all of that, losing twenty great naval brothers, is nothing compared to the pain of lost love."

Ace doesn't react as he can tell that John is a few pints deep, so he is even more temperamental than he would be if he were sober. It can be difficult to read any one of the Moonie brothers. The slightest thing you say can trigger them into a massacre if they are in a bad mood. But if they are in a positive mood, then you can laugh with them till the sun goes down.

Ace heads back and hands Ava a glass of white wine as he joins the group.

"Who's the guy with the glasses sat on his own over there?" Ace questions them, referring to Harry Watkins.

"Some reporter. Paulie says he invited him," AJ answers.

"Nothing wrong with getting publicity, gentlemen," Hunter adds, wanting to seize any opportunity he can to let them know that he supports Moonie.

"I think something is going to go down. He said something about fireworks," McHay informs Ace.

"Surely he would have told us first? We are his security. Did he mention anything to you, H?" Ace asks.

"No, he said nothing to me. Look, Paulie has a way with words, he could have meant anything. Let's just sit back, enjoy the night, and deal with anything that happens when it happens."

"Why does it always have to be a danger with you men? He could have meant literal fireworks," Ava attempts to ease the speculation.

"Ava, nothing in our world is ever that simple," Ace's reply has AJ and McHay chuckling.

As the night carries on, the party remains in full swing. Vince McHay heads to the bar with Ace for refills, or in Ace's case, Ava's refill.

"It's been good so far tonight. Better than I expected," McHay says as they wait for Sam to finish serving the couple next to them.

"Yeah, there will definitely be some sore heads in the morning. I don't miss them days."

"Tell me, Ace, is everything okay?"

Ace looks a little confused. "Of course, McHay. Why do you ask?"

"Ava has been talking with Amanda, you know just usual women talk normally. But when they went out for lunch last week, you got brought up. Ava tells Amanda that you haven't been sleeping all that well. She says you wake up during the night in sweats and then you can't switch back off."

"I'm fine, McHay."

"Acey, I have known you for years. Talk to me. Is it about JJ? It's soon coming up to a year since his death."

"It's not JJ, no."

"Acey, we are the Grifters. We are a band of brothers remember? Talk to me."

"Look around you, McHay. Gangsters, politicians, murderers. This was never what we were meant to be."

"Is this about Flacco?"

"Flacco is a part of it, yes. Ever since I pulled that trigger, a part of me has shut off. I don't feel the same. Standing over his body, staring into that dark hole in the back of his head. It was like my own spirit had left my body and I knew that nothing would ever be the same again. I feel like I'm sitting on a timebomb and when it goes off, everything will come crashing down with it."

"Ace, you need to get what happened with Flacco out of your head. That punk had it coming long before you put the bullet in his head. We are all in this together and whether we like it or not, this around us is what we are now. Like H said, we adapt or we perish. It's as simple as that. Kill or be killed."

"Does it ever get easier? The guilt?"

"No, you just have to keep your mind occupied and focus on the things you don't want to lose. Like Ava. You have an amazing girl there, Acey. Focus your mind on her and make her the happiest woman in this city."

Ace turns his head around and looks over at Ava who is conversing with AJ and Amanda at the table.

"I know. If it weren't for her, I'd have destroyed myself by now."

"Don't look at the past, look at the now. Now for that expert advice, this round is on you."

As Ace and McHay return to the table, Ace, out of the corner of his eye, sees Paul approach Jack and whisper something into his ear. Jack then quickly downs his pint of lager and heads over to John to whisper in his ear.

Jack and John begin to make their way over to the mayor's son who is dancing with the same blonde lady he was flirting with earlier. Without hesitation, Jack kicks the back of his knees and John hits him in the back of the head. Let the fireworks commence.

The crowd of dancing punters soon clear the makeshift dancefloor. Reporter Harry Watkins' attention is soon perked. He stands with his notepad and watches on.

The two twins have the mayor's son floored and they are drilling their fists into him relentlessly. Ace feels that this is unfair to the man as he is outnumbered and Ace believes never to harm a man who is already grounded. It's cowardly. He quickly stands and is about to make his way over to break it up but Ava stops him by reaching out her hand.

"This isn't your fight, Ace. Leave it," she says to him.

A few short, but what feels like excoriating moments to the mayor's son later, Paul Moonie superiorly walks over and calls his brothers off the man.

Jack looks down at his hand and realises that some of the man's blood has rubbed off on him. He wipes the blood down his cheek and lets out a roar to the people all standing in shock at what they have just witnessed. Silence fills the pub. No one dares to say a single word or move a muscle.

Paul then stands over the grounded man and spits in his face before focusing his attention on the punters. "What you have just witnessed here is what happens when you disrespect, drunkenly or sober, any one of the Moonie brothers. It doesn't matter who you are, what gender you are, what race you are." He looks back down at the man. "Or who your daddy is. The Moonie brothers are back as one and are as bad as ever. This city will always be ours!" Paul then turns to Harry Watkins. "Write that in your fucking paper."

Ace now realises why Paul invited Watkins here tonight. It is to make a statement to the city that the Moonie brothers are back and they are still a dangerous force in Manchester. Their presence is unrivalled.

XVI
'The First Dance'

February 1987

Tonight is the night. There has been something in the air all day today. A feeling of wonder, a feeling of excitement, a feeling that something important is happening. We are on the brink of a change. Tonight 'The Rogue' opens.

A line of around two hundred people all line up at the grand entrance of the new, oval-shaped, super nightclub. These people have come from every avenue of the country and some have even come from abroad. A group of five young men have travelled all the way from Las Vegas to celebrate a stag do here. This is a big deal for Manchester and will hopefully help bring the city out of the industrial age and into the new world of the 1990s, really putting Manchester on the map with Paul Moonie acting as the foreman for that change. Hopefully, this club will inspire change within the city.

Press and paparazzi flock to the entrance doors of the club like out-of-control sheep determined not to be rounded up by the shepherd.

Manchester hasn't had this many eyes on it since 1917 when Ernest Rutherford split the atom at The University of Manchester, and the streets haven't been this flooded by press and paparazzi since 1976 when local MP Jerome Hanson was found guilty of fraud. That dampened the city's reputation which is the opposite of what Moonie aims to achieve tonight. Moonie's ambition for 'The Rogue' is to rebrand Manchester from the recession-ravaged industrial age into the age of prosperity and wealth.

This has been four years in the making for Paul Moonie and many of his close associates have doubted the success and longevity of the project. However, as he stands at the entrance doors looking out at the sea of people, he smiles and laughs at their doubts. A shepherd doesn't listen to his sheep, he rules them.

The second he exits the club and stands out with the people, holding a small glass of whisky, the press bombards questions left, right and centre at him.

"Mr Moonie, is it true that during the construction here, a painter had a seizure and fell off a scaffolding only to climb right back up and finish when he came round?" One asks.

Moonie sees a shiny black limo pull up in the distance. "I'm not here to answer any questions, enjoy your night."

To Moonie's delight, Ace and Ava exit the limo smartly dressed. Ace is in an expensive black tuxedo and Ava is wearing a silver silk dress. They begin walking through the press to meet Moonie at the entrance.

"Wow, there are so many people here," Ava, astonished at what she sees, says.

"Tonight is a big deal for people," Ace replies. They look over and see Moonie standing at the entrance admiring the mass of people whilst enjoying his whisky.

"Look at Paul, it's like he's a celebrity," Ava remarks.

"He might as well be. To most people here, he's the uncrowned king of Manchester."

"Here they are! Manchester's sexiest power couple!" Paul Moonie animatedly exclaims as he hugs them both. "Are you both ready for the big night?"

"Of course, Paulie. You didn't have to send us a limo by the way. Thank you though," Ace says.

"The limo is the least I can do for my right-hand man and his beautiful girlfriend."

"Are we expecting any fireworks tonight?" Ace replies with some concern.

Moonie smiles. "Acey, when you are me, you can't afford to not expect trouble. But tonight isn't the night for that. Get in my club and get your dance on, sunshine. Tonight is going to be a good night. If anything is to happen, Jack and John will handle it." Moonie pats Ace on his back and gestures for them to enter the club.

The impressive interior of the club consists of one large main room and two separate side rooms with their own dance floors which are based to the right of the main room. The main room has a stage to the far left for hired entertainers to perform, an angled bar on the opposite side of the room, and a dancefloor around the size of half a football pitch. Several booths also populate the room.

As the night continues, Hunter, McHay, and AJ arrive at the venue. AJ joins Ace and Ava who are sitting in a booth on the outskirts of the room.

"What a spectacle," AJ remarks as the disco lights turn on and highlight areas of the dancefloor.

"Welcome to the new age, AJ." Ace raises his glass of water. "Where's the other two?"

"They've gone to the bar." AJ observes the room. "There's no press in here. I thought they would be all over this place. Especially since Kevin Kelly and Ruth Kelly are over there." Kevin Kelly and Ruth Kelly are stars of a popular soap opera called 'The Nation's Row'.

"Moonie has paid the press off. The only access they have is the outside of the club. He doesn't want any photos printed in the papers."

"Why? Surely that's good for business," Ava questions.

"He says he wants to create an enigma around the place, so it feels like more of an experience than a nightclub. That's why at every side of the main room, you find something there, whether it's the bar, the stage, or the other rooms. He wants spectacle and people to feel immersed in the whole experience."

"He really does want to change the world with this thing, doesn't he?" AJ says.

Over at the bar, Hunter and McHay are waiting as their cocktails are being made.

"What a night this will be, H," McHay claims.

"Too right, McHay. Look how far we have come." Hunter pats McHay's back as he looks around the club gleaming with joy. "All those years in Leeds to this. We are fucking giants, McHay."

The bartender slides McHay his cocktail. McHay reaches into his pocket but the bartender waves him off. "They are on the house tonight for you gentlemen, Mr Moonie's orders."

"What a night." McHay smiles. He suddenly gets jolted forward as a young, greasy-haired man nudges him in the back accidentally.

"Hey, watch it, punk!"

The young man is fired up by McHay's comments and he looks up. "Don't call me a punk, you…" He stops as soon as he realises that he is talking to Vince McHay. "Shit, I'm sorry, man. I didn't mean to offend you."

McHay pats his hand on the young man's shoulder. His ego has been stroked by the apology. "Don't worry, kid. Enjoy your night."

Near the stage area, Jack and John Moonie are conversing with a small, middle-aged overweight man. Grooving on the dancefloor, Paul Moonie sees this interaction and he heads over to them.

The overweight man hands the two Moonie twins two packets of cocaine. In exchange, they hand him an envelope full of cash.

Fuelled by rage, Paul storms over and smacks the envelope of cash out of the man's hand. "What in the sweet fuck do you three think you are doing?"

"I was making a sale," the snarky overweight man replies.

"Not in my establishment you aren't. I told you two I do not want any of this shit in here. This is a place of class. I want people to feel safe, not dirty," Paul states.

"Paulie, it is a small deal. No one has even seen it happen," Jack responds.

"I saw it happen. Get your heads out of your arses, gentlemen. A place like this will not survive if this kind of behaviour goes on. Take it outside." Paul reaches down and picks up the envelope of cash. He takes a handful of cash out for himself. "For compensation for your stupidity," he justifies to the overweight man before handing him back the envelope.

"Preach all that to those fellas over there then." John turns Paul's attention to a group of young men all looking in their early twenties and dressed in tracksuits talking to several people near the dancefloor.

"I've never seen a bigger set of wank stains in my life." Paul instantly knows who these young men are. They are local, small-time drug dealers. Paul begins to make his way over to them.

"You sure you don't need backup, brother? They look an aggressive little bunch," Jack jokes. Paul continues to look on and walk in the direction of the young men and raises his hand sticking his middle finger up back at his brother.

Moonie confidently approaches the group of small-time drug dealers who are on their way to the bar. Moonie whistles at their small but well-chiselled ringleader, Philip Timmings, who stops in his tracks.

Philip Timmings and his gang run a small drug dealing organisation around Manchester. They also branch out to car theft as well from time to time. They steal the cars and sell them on.

Timmings is originally from Leeds. However, at the young age of twelve, he ran away from his abusive parents and fled to Manchester to set up a new life for himself.

After being kicked out of school several times and rejected from jobs, Timmings realised that there is more money in dealing drugs. Thus, it wasn't long before he befriended a local dealer under the name, Trevor Wyatt. Trevor took Philip under his wing and morphed him into the dealer he is today. Trevor and Philip became inseparable, as close as brothers. Until one cold winter night when Trevor was found dead in the canal. No one was ever charged with Trevor's murder, although Philip was questioned by the police. Many people in the city believe Philip was responsible for Trevor's murder and that Philip used Trevor to teach him the business and make the connections with the right people, and after Trevor did this, he then became useless to Philip, so Phillip cut his ties. This could never be proven though.

Timming's gang all stare Moonie in his eyes as he approaches them. They aren't phased.

"Gentlemen, welcome to my club," Moonie politely says. "I hope tonight you are not here for business but rather pleasure."

Timmings looks Moonie up and down. "What if we are here for both, 'Mr Baldy'?" He asks.

"Well, no business is permitted on my premises to anyone, 'Mr Shortarse'."

"I am here for both business and pleasure."

"As I said, no business is permitted here."

Timmings slides a knife down from the inside of his sleeve, revealing the tip which peaks out of the bottom of his jacket's arm like a shark fin. "As I said, I am here for business and pleasure."

"That's real cute. Listen, you punch-able prick, I've been hit harder by a lot lower men than you. Let's have a quick lesson here children, do you know who I am?" Moonie asks. The gang stay silent and Moonie leans in closer. "I thought not. I am Paul Moonie. Many knives have been pointed in front and behind me in my time. Let me tell you, it is going to take more than one cheap blade to take me down. I'm talking the whole fucking army, kid. Now take your knife, hand it in at the bar, and buy yourself a drink. Tonight will be a good night."

"Or what?"

"My words go far in this city, child. I will make sure you never make a single penny again in Manchester. Oh, and I will kick your skinny little ass out of my building. I'm more gangster than you will ever be. So, what will it be, business or pleasure?"

Timmings takes a long look at Paul, considering his options. He slowly raises his knife back up his sleeve. "Pleasure." He leads his gang to the bar.

Upon success, Paul returns to his brothers.

"They hassle you?" Jack asks.

"Fuck me, these kids carry knives now. What kind of world is this?" Paul remarks.

"Do you want us to kick them out?" John questions.

"No, they are small-time. We don't deal with small-time. We are big-time, let's not feed their little delusional egos. Big fish should never mix with small fish. If small fish mix with big fish, they falsely believe they too are the big fish." Moonie suspects that Timmings and his gang are here tonight to 'stakeout' the place and see if they can get viable custom here.

As the night progresses, Hunter and the intoxicated McHay, who has had far too many cocktails, join Ace, Ava, and AJ at their booth.

"So, how's the parent life treating you, Hunter?" Ava asks.

"It's going swell you know. I can just see in his little blue eyes that one day he will grow up just like me. He's already got my temper," Hunter laughs.

Shouldn't you want more than this way of life we live for your child? Ace thinks to himself.

"It will be you next, McHay. Let's hope that a kid of yours doesn't inherit your looks though," AJ pokes fun.

"Piss off, virgin."

"I am no virgin, McHay, just ask your Amanda," AJ quickly fires back.

"Seriously though, AJ, have you not got your eye on a woman?" Ava diffuses the banter and hostility between McHay and AJ.

AJ laughs. "There isn't a woman on this Earth that could handle me, Ava."

McHay rolls his eyes at AJ's see-through attempt at trying to hide his insecurities through humour and takes a swig of his drink.

"What about the barmaid over there?" Ace points AJ's direction to the brunette with sparkling green eyes behind the bar.

"Bloody hell, Acey, AJ couldn't pull her in his dreams. She must be a model," Hunter admires.

"Easy, tiger, you have a kid now. She's not bad, Acey, but I don't want to settle down."

"Why not?" Ava wonders.

"Because, Ava, nothing in this life is guaranteed to last, especially love. You can think you really know someone, then, all of a sudden, BOOM! You are stabbed in the back and left alone."

"That's a lonely life to live, AJ," Ava says.

"It's the life I'm used to."

McHay rolls his eyes again.

"Would you ever want to meet someone? Start a family?" Ava is persistent.

"Maybe someday, but I don't see that day on the horizon anytime soon. I mean, ideally, ever since I was a kid, I've wanted to move out of this country and move to California. Why die in the rain when you can die in the sun, right?"

"Is that where you see yourself settling down?" Ava asks.

"Yeah. One day."

"Why California? Apart from the sun of course."

"Why not California? The city of the stars. The city where anyone can become someone in the country where anyone can become someone."

"It sounds like a fresh start."

"There is very little in this country. Even the sun doesn't think we are worth it," AJ says.

"Enough of your morbid shit. I'm going to talk to her." Hunter finishes his drink and stands up.

"You have a wife, H. And a kid," AJ reminds Hunter.

"What happens in 'The Rogue', stays in 'The Rogue', AJ." Hunter laughs as he begins to make his way over to the barmaid.

Pig, Ace thinks to himself.

"Vince, you are dating his wife's sister, aren't you going to do something?" Ava calls out McHay.

"Listen, darling, Hunter is a man who gets what he wants, and nothing can stop him. It is admirable really," McHay condescends.

"Don't patronise my girl, McHay. Hunter is out of line there," Ace defends Ava.

McHay realises that he might have overstepped a line. "Sorry, Ava. There isn't anything we can do though. Hunter does what he wants."

"It doesn't make it right," Ace replies.

AJ doesn't comment on the situation, he just sits and observes.

"Who is it to say what's right or wrong, Acey? None of us are perfect."

"Enough now, McHay, you've had enough to drink." Ace can tell that the booze has begun to hit and take over McHay, his lips are getting loose.

"I haven't had enough at all, I'm just saying we shouldn't sit here and judge. Hunter has done a lot for us you know."

"There's no disputing that. I'm just saying that cheating on his wife isn't right."

"What happened to Flacco wasn't right either. What happened to the mayor's son wasn't right. Life isn't right."

"McHay, enough!" Ace is ripping with outrage that McHay has brought Flacco up.

"What happened to Flacco?" Ava asks Ace. "You said he went travelling."

"Oh, do you not know? Well, I'm sure 'Mr Perfecto' over here will tell you." McHay leans in closer to Ace. "No one here is perfect, Acey."

"You are drunk and pathetic, McHay. Go home."

Suddenly, Hunter returns to the booth all flustered and irritated and holding his face.

"What's up, H? Is she not into pensioners?" AJ mocks.

"Get up. We have trouble."

Ace looks up at Hunter. "Who and where?"

"Those lads over there. That one just hit me in front of the barmaid. Nobody makes a mockery out of me. Get him outside and beat him so bad that he wishes he was dead." Hunter is embarrassed and furious that he has been made to look inferior. The lad he is referring to is Philip Timmings.

Paul Moonie, who has just seen everything unfold, races over fearing that Hunter will want retaliation.

"Hunter, Hunter, relax. Leave it," Paul tries to calm him.

"Leave it? Not a chance, Paulie. I will not be made a fool out of."

"There will be no drama here tonight, Hunter. They are kids, leave it."

"Paulie, I will not stand for disrespect."

"You start something and the whole place will go up. I will not stand for that. Tonight is my fucking night."

Hunter looks down and takes a deep breath. "Okay."

"Good. Now sit back down and forget about it." Paul guides Hunter back down into his seat. "Right, I'm going to the bar. Can I trust that you will not retaliate?"

Hunter looks up at Paul. "Yes."

"Good man." Paul leaves them and heads to the bar.

"I want you three to watch and follow that bastard out when he leaves. There's an alley to the right of this place. Get him in there," Hunter orders the Three Grifters.

AJ looks over at Ace and then McHay. "Hunter, Paulie just said leave it."

"I don't care. I want that moron to pay."

"We can't disobey Paulie, H," Ace speaks up.

"Sorry? Who do you owe your loyalty to? I'm your boss, you will do as I ask."

Ace reluctantly agrees knowing that Hunter won't let this go.

Over at the stage area of the club, a young and aspiring comedian, the handsome Jerry Stewart is preparing to perform. Paul has ordered the DJ to halt his set and direct everyone's attention to the comedian.

Stewart is on edge and extremely nervous to perform as he doesn't want to disappoint the Moonie brothers. When he first accepted the gig here tonight, his friends had warned him not to get on the wrong side of the brothers as their reputation travels in waves in the city. To say Stewart is intimidated would be an understatement.

In an attempt to settle his nerves, Stewart is four double vodkas deep. Feeling slightly unbalanced and seeing double vision, Stewart takes to the stage after a stellar introduction from Paul Moonie.

"Thank you, Mr Moonie. What a great honour it is to be here tonight performing for all of you," Stewart shouts down the microphone.

"Hey, kid, you been drinking?" Paul, who can smell the booze on Stewart's breath, whispers into his ear.

"Have I been drinking? Ladies and gentlemen, Mr Moonie isn't thinking straight. I'm from Manchester, of course I've been drinking." Stewart has the crowd in laughter. Paul says nothing and instead, he silently walks off the stage and joins his brothers in a nearby booth to observe the performance.

"Is he drunk?" John asks.

"Drunk as a Goddam skunk."

"Do you want us to escort him out?"

"Let's just see how good he is."

"This guy is great, Paulie, I've seen him before," Jack, eating pork scratchings, pitches in.

Palms sweating, Stewart grips the microphone tightly. He tries to settle his head from swaying and clears his throat loudly before beginning his act.

"Ladies and gentlemen, I hope you are all having a wonderful time here tonight. I want to quickly thank the Moonie brothers for inviting me here tonight. I always preferred them to their cousins, the Sunny brothers," Stewart's first joke only has a very small percentage of the crowd, and Jack Moonie, laughing. "Tough crowd, huh? Well, get this one. Which Knight invented King Arthur's Round Table?" He pauses for a moment before answering, "It was Sir Cumference." Stewart laughs at his own joke. Which is a good job because no one else did.

"Tell us something funny," someone from the audience heckles.

Paul watches Stewart closely to see how he will react.

"Okay, okay. You know I have always felt bad for calendars, their days are numbered."

"Your jokes are shit!" Someone else from the audience heckles.

"Yeah, just get the music back on and let us dance!" Someone else calls out.

"You think this is easy, you prick? Do you really think that I need your approval, you fat degenerate? Look at you, you disgust me," Stewart snaps. Jack laughs.

Paul signals his brothers to remove Stewart from the stage immediately.

"Shit," Stewart says as he sees the menacing figures of John and Jack Moonie heading his way. Out of sheer panic, Stewart jumps off the stage and tries to run but people in the audience hold him still for the brothers to grab him and throw him out of the venue. John and Jack beat him down outside the back of the club.

"Sincere apologies, ladies and gentlemen. DJ take it away," Paul orders the DJ to resume his set.

"I'd make a better comedian than that goon. Isn't that right, Hunter?" McHay says as he nudges Hunter who has a face of thunder. Hunter can't let go of the humiliation he has experienced at the hands of Timmings.

"Don't let it get to you, H, he's a nobody," AJ attempts to calm Hunter as he notices his silent demeanour.

"Everyone is a nobody until they are somebody," Hunter replies.

"On that note, I need a piss." McHay breaks the tension and heads for the toilets.

McHay is zipping back up his pants after just finishing urinating in the urinal when two young-looking lads enter dressed in tracksuits. They both pull out a knife and stare at McHay. They are members of Timmings' gang.

"Are you sure you want to do this, fellas?" McHay says. "You kill me and you will just gain more enemies I assure you."

"We will kill all our enemies if we have to," one lad responds.

"You really think you can take out men like Hunter Smith? Men like Paul Moonie?"

"We will kill them all. Starting with you, fatty," the other lad says.

"You are young and stupid."

"And you are dead."

McHay laughs but he doesn't see a clear way out of this. He's outnumbered. "Well, if this is how I go, let's fucking dance," he says as he rolls up his blazer's sleeves. He realises at this point, the booze is doing most of the talking, and he likes the attitude.

The two lads put their knives back in their pockets and lunge forward. It's a two-on-one attack. McHay holds his ground for a short few seconds as he lands several punches on each lad, however, the numbers game catches up and he is tripped to the floor in no time.

Pinned down by one of the lads, the other one mounts McHay and removes his knife from his pocket. "Where to cut first, fatty," he says as he waves his knife over McHay's body. "Any preference?"

"You do this and you and your whole gang will regret it," McHay claims.

"I don't think you are as important as you think you are."

BOOM! The bathroom door smacks wide open and in walks a familiar face with a scar on his nose.

The lad holding the knife jumps up off McHay and turns his attention to the interrupter. "If you know what is good for you, you will leave and say nothing to no one."

"That's hard to do when you've got my friend down there."

"Don't be stupid. You don't want to die for this man."

"Oh, child, I don't intend to die."

Before the lad can get another word out, the scarred intruder kicks the knife out of his hand and bashes his head against the bathroom sink knocking him unconscious and falling to the floor.

Shocked and slightly startled, the other lad lets go of McHay and pulls his knife out. He stands opposite the intruder. The two lock eyes in a tense stand-off.

Without hesitation, McHay quietly rises to his feet behind the knife-wielding teenager and kicks him in his genitals. He drops the knife and McHay holds him up as the familiar interrupter tightens his fists and drills him over and over, drawing an immense amount of blood from his face.

McHay then throws the teenager down onto the floor before looking up at his saviour. "I don't believe it, Darren Swade!" The same man who helped McHay out in 'Big Stu's Gym' last year.

"You did say you hoped we meet again."

McHay laughs and shakes Darren's hand. "I had them you know."

"I'm sure you did."

"Thank you, again."

"I'm starting to get good at saving your ass."

"What even brings you here?"

"Opening night of the biggest club in the city. Only a fool would miss this," Darren says. "I was on the dancefloor and I saw you come in here and these pricks follow you in. And when no one left after a while, I assumed trouble."

"Come on, I owe you a round," McHay says.

"Before that, we need to hide these fuckers." Darren and McHay hide the unconscious teenagers inside a cubicle and jam the door shut so no one can find them.

An Hour Has Passed

Philip Timmings and his gang have just left the nightclub. Ace sees this and alerts AJ and the now water-drinking McHay. The Three Grifters are in pursuit of Timmings and his gang.

Once outside, Timmings and his gang turn right near the alleyway as they embark on their way home.

The 'Grifters', storming out with a purpose, run up behind the gang and kick their knees in. A brawl breaks out. Fists are flying blindly, spit is getting spat in faces, knuckles are getting bloody, and legs are getting kicked in. They all end up in the middle of the alleyway in a heated skirmish.

The 'Grifters' have managed to ground most of Timmings' gang. McHay has helped this massively by bashing their heads against the cold brick wall which has instantly busted them open and knocked them unconscious.

Ace, AJ, and McHay stand over a floored Philip Timmings who has blood and gashes all over his face. He spits a spat of blood on Ace's shoe.

"Now that wasn't friendly, was it?" Ace spits back down in Timmings' eyes.

"You fuckers have no idea how dangerous I am."

"That's cute." AJ laughs before kicking Timmings in his genitals several times over and over. Timmings cries out in agony. Ace then kneels and punches Timmings across his face several times. As Ace stands back up, he sees McHay arming himself with a brick and is about to bash Timming's head in with it. His adrenaline has taken a hold of him.

"McHay, no." Ace stands in front of McHay and prevents him from possibly committing murder. "He's just a kid. He gets the message now."

McHay drops the brick down and Timmings, even though it physically pains him, laughs. "You can't even finish the job. Pathetic."

Out of frustration, McHay boots Timmings in his ribs with the intense intention of obliterating them into tiny pieces.

"Enough," Ace tells McHay before kneeling back down to Timmings. "You don't ever disrespect the Grifters again and when your friends come around, you tell them they have joined the long list of people who have had their arses kicked by the Three Grifters." Ace pats Timmings' face and stands back up. The three begin to walk out of the alleyway but before they do, Ace pulls McHay to one side and slaps him across the face.

"Acey, what was that?" AJ says as he witnesses the slap.

"Keep walking, AJ, we will be with you in a minute," Ace coldly replies.

"Acey, come on, we are all on the same side here," AJ responds.

"AJ, just keep walking," McHay says. AJ obliges.

"You don't ever talk about Flacco or any of our business to my girl again or you will join Flacco in the ground, okay?" A stern Ace orders, referring to McHay drunkenly blurting to Ava about Flacco earlier in the club.

"I know, Acey. I'm sorry. I am just drunk, that's all it is."

"Good. I can't lose her, McHay. I can't lose her."

XVII
'The Light Diffused'

Like a dagger to the chest, the alarm clock violently strikes 8 am. Ace, still tired from last night's opening of 'The Rogue', rolls over to his side and admires the beauty that is Ava sleeping.

"I know you are looking at me," she says smiling.

"I just can't help myself."

"My head is in agony." Ava is feeling the effects of last night's drinking.

"Lightweight." Ace gets out of bed and stretches. "Do you want a coffee?"

Ava moans and buries herself under the duvet. Ace begins to get dressed.

"Where are you going?" Ava muffles under the covers.

"Some of us have work to do today. I'm heading to H's, I should be back around 6ish." Ace mounts the bed and pulls down some of the duvet which reveals Ava's face. "I'll see you later." Ace kisses her forehead and makes his way to the bedroom door.

"I love you," Ava tells him.

Ace turns and faces her. "Hell yeah, you do." Ace leaves and heads over to Hunter's house.

Little does he know that someone has been watching the apartment and waiting for him to leave this whole time...

6 pm. Clouds all full of rain burst open and pour heavily from the sky, bringing darkness over the city. Drenched wet through, Ace makes his way up the steep apartment stairs and reaches his door. He's grateful to be out of the rain.

He finds the door open a crack. *That's strange*, he thinks to himself. He pushes open the door and steps in.

"Ava?" He calls out to no answer. "Ava?" The living room and kitchen area are empty. Ace then turns his attention to the bedroom door and opens it. *Surely she's not still in bed.*

A feeling of numbness overtakes him. He is knocked sick. To his absolute horror, the room is wrecked. Chairs flipped, the bedside drawers tipped over, and the window shattered. These are signs of a struggle. In the bed, the duvet is raised looking like someone is underneath the sheets.

"Ava? Please. Ava?" Ace approaches the bed with great caution. He has a nauseous gut wrenching feeling that he can't shake. He slowly peals back the duvet. And just like that, his heart is shattered into a million pieces. His life is over. Ava's blooded body lays before him pale and dead. Her chest and stomach is covered in several deep slashes. She has clearly been stabbed in a savage and ruthless manner.

Ace's knees give way and he falls down. Hands shaking and heart racing. His light has been put out. He stares intently at the bed not knowing how to think or what to do. He is lost. Lost in a nightmare come true.

After a few moments of kneeling in silence and tears rolling aimlessly from his eyes, Ace slowly stands and takes one last look at his love. "I am so sorry," he sobs. A wave of aggression then overcomes him. His upset is now raging anger. He turns and swings at the wall punching a hole right through it. He then cries out and falls back to the floor.

The reason he got out of bed every morning, the reason he kept going in times when he didn't want to, and the reason why he never lost himself has been stolen from him in the most gruesome of ways. At this moment, Ace knows that nothing will ever be the same again.

7.30 pm. Paul Moonie, with his brothers, is sitting in a booth in 'The Rogue'. The venue is packed. The brothers are enjoying a round of shots when Paul's attention is turned to a commotion coming from the dancefloor. People are getting shoved out of the way by a raging Ace who is making his way towards Moonie's booth. Moonie can see a tremendous fury in Ace's war-torn eyes.

Soaked wet through, Ace reaches the brothers, tears still pouring down his face. Paul looks down and sees blood on Ace's fist from where he punched his bedroom wall.

"Jack, John, give us a minute," Paul orders his brothers to leave which they do. "Ace, what's happened?"

Ace's face stays cold and serious. Paul can see pent-up frustration matched with hurt in his eyes. "The lad we did a number on for Hunter last night, what's his name?" He sternly spits out.

"Lad you did a number on? Fuck's sake, the lad I told Hunter to leave?"

Ace stares at Paul looking like he is ready to kill. "His name, Paul. I want his fucking name."

"He's called Philip Timmings, why?"

"Where can I find him?"

"Acey, why? What's happened?" Paul's concern grows now.

"Where can I find him?"

"I'm not telling you where until you tell me what is going on."

"Ava."

"What about Ava?"

"She's dead."

Paul is stunned. He stands up immediately and hugs Ace. "Acey, I am so sorry, mate. That is heart-breaking."

"Where can I find Philip Timmings?"

"Is he responsible?"

"Where can I find him?"

"How do you know it's him?"

Ace reaches into the pocket of his leather jacket and hands Paul a note that reads:

When your wife comes around, tell her she has joined the long list of people who have suffered for their partner's actions.

"I don't get it," Paul states.

"I said something similar to him last night after we beat him."

Paul puts the note down on the table. "Acey, I am so sorry this has happened." Paul then reaches into the inside pocket of his blazer for a pen and writes Timmings' address on the back of the note before handing it back over to Ace. "That's where I'm told he lives."

"I let him live. Last night, I stopped McHay from bashing his skull in with a brick. I let him live."

"Then go and make him wish you didn't." Paul looks at Ace and sees that nothing is going to get in his way to stop him from raining hell on Timmings tonight. Moonie reaches into his pocket and hands Ace his car keys. "Take my car. If anyone sees you leave the address and makes a note of the car, the police will know to ignore it. 'Sandy' is in the boot." 'Sandy' is what Moonie names his shotgun.

Ace nods at Paul indicating his gratefulness.

As Ace leaves, Paul sits back, strokes his chin, and embarks on a deep chain of thinking. He thinks that if Hunter had listened to him and left Timmings alone, then Ava would still be alive. Paul now sees that Hunter is the problem that he always feared he was. Hunter is a liability to the organisation.

The rain is still blasting down hard. Ace parks Moonie's car outside a three-story house on New Terrace Street. It only took him ten minutes to get here as he was driving at 50 mph and skipping red lights the entire way.

Ace slowly exits the vehicle and cracks open the boot. 'Sandy', looking battered and used, stares up at him. As well as grabbing 'Sandy', he also takes with him a small container of petrol that was resting to the side of 'Sandy'. It's time.

Armed with 'Sandy' over his shoulder and the petrol in his left hand, Ace approaches the entrance of the house looking like he means serious business. He doesn't hesitate before kicking in the front door like an uncontrollable bull in a China shop.

He immediately enters the house's living room where he finds Timmings and two of his friends sitting at a table playing a game of cards. Without saying a word, Ace drops the container of petrol to his side and quickly blasts the two friends with two shots each, sending them flying backwards out of their chairs.

"Are you fucking crazy?" Timmings shouts out as he stands upright in a fast fashion petrified.

Ace looks him dead in the eyes and, with his nose twitching in fury, he throws the shotgun to the floor. He then reaches into the inside of his leather jacket and pulls out a knife. "You. You will suffer how she did," he says and then spits onto the floor.

"You need to leave now, or you will regret it."

Ace looks down at the knife in his hand, then back up at Timmings. "I will not regret any part of this." Ace grabs the knife by the blade and throws it towards Timmings. It directly hits him in his throat which hinders his breathing as he looks at Ace in shock. Ace begins to slowly walk up to Timmings, who is now falling to his knees desperately gasping for breath as the knife is solidly lodged into his throat, piercing it critically.

Admiring his crime, Ace grabs Timmings' chin and perks his head up. He then spits in his face before retrieving the knife from his throat and slicing it into the side of his head, hoping it goes straight to his brain. Timmings falls face-first onto the floor dead.

Standing back, Ace takes in a deep breath and lets out a sigh of relief. Like a weight has just been lifted from his heartbroken shoulders. He looks over his left shoulder and sees the petrol container. Without hesitation, he begins to pour it all over the living room and over Timmings' body.

As the small flame from his match ignites, he stands at the door staring at Timmings' body. A small, but short, wave of joy flows through him before he drops the match.

A blaze erupts across the path of petrol and Timmings' body begins to burn.

XVIII
'An Ego's End'

Three weeks have passed since Ava's brutal demise. Today is her funeral. Ace, who is now once again sporting a stubble and finding himself returning to the depressive state that Ava rescued him from, sits in his living room on his couch looking down at the floor. Ace's living room is in a state. A pig wouldn't even sleep there. Clothes on the floor, bins overflowing, and food stains on the chairs. He has been sleeping on the couch ever since Ava's murder. Just the thought of going back to that bedroom brings him too much harrowing pain.

The clock strikes 3 pm. Ace looks up and realises the time. The funeral would have ended now. Ace chose not to attend. He feels responsible for Ava's death, having been the one who brought her into this way of life. He believes that if he never met her, then she would be still among the living today. His mind is infecting him with the notion that everyone he gets close to suffers because of him. After noticing the time, he stands and heads over to his kitchen area where he opens his cupboard door and stares at a bottle of whiskey. As he looks down, a tear comes from his eye. He knows now that the rest of his life will never be the same as it once was. He knows that he's returning to the life that Ava saved him from. His lifeline has gone, forever.

The candle that burns the flame of happiness has been extinguished, by himself. He takes the bottle and begins to drink, breaking his sobriety. He heads back over to his couch and slumps back down drinking more and more. It feels like he has just re-connected with an ex-lover.

A few moments later, he hears a knock on his door. The handle turns and someone steps in. He jumps straight up to his feet and pulls his gun from his pocket. Moving as stealthy as possible, he positions himself behind his living room door. He can hear footsteps approach him. The door opens. Ace aims the gun at the perpetrator.

"Holy shit! At ease, soldier!" A startled Paul Moonie calls out.

Ace lowers his gun at the realisation that it's Moonie who has entered the apartment.

"Who are you expecting?" Moonie says. He is almost blinded by the state of disarray that Ace's apartment is in. "Acey, this isn't good, man. How can you sleep in this mess?"

"I don't get much sleep."

"I can tell." Moonie sits down at the small table opposite Ace's couch which Ace sits back down on.

Ace sees that Moonie is dressed in a black suit and tie. "How was the funeral?"

"It was a good send-off, Acey. You should have been there."

"No, I never deserved her, Paulie. I am the reason she is gone. She saved me and I couldn't save her. Just like JJ."

"You can't seriously blame yourself, Ace. Ava was a wonderful soul who was too pure for this world and her fate was beyond unfair and undeserving. But she is gone. You are still here, and we still need you. I need you."

Ace looks up at Moonie. "Why did you come here, Paulie?"

"I came here to check on you. We haven't heard from you in three weeks and I was concerned."

"I'm fine."

"The bottle of whisky beside your foot there would beg to differ, but hey, each to their own."

"If I want to drink, then I will drink."

Paul sighs. "Do you know why I am the way I am, Acey? Cold, ruthless, and not trusting of many people."

Ace doesn't answer.

Paul continues, "Because a long, long time ago, I lost someone very close to me. Her name was Sandy Hutters. She was a friend of mine since we were toddlers all the way until we were eighteen. I fell in love with Sandy. Head over heels. And one night, we had both been invited to this house party. It was here where I planned to finally confess my love to her. And in my mind, she would follow suit and we would live happily ever after. So, at the party, after a few poorly homemade cocktails, I went to find her. After searching high and low for her, I was told she was upstairs. So, I went looking upstairs and I found her in the spare room under the covers with one Ben Rogers. My heart sank. Later that night, Sandy got a lift home with her best friend, Amelia. Amelia was way too intoxicated to even stand, let alone drive. Someone at the party had seen the state that Amelia was in and took her car keys from her but Amelia snuck them back after they were left on the kitchen counter. Amelia got Sandy and they hurried outside and entered the car. I was the only one who saw this but rather than stop Sandy from getting into the car, I wanted her to suffer for the pain she had just caused me." Paul's voice takes on a more sombre tone. A tone that Ace hasn't heard him in before. "I stood by and watched them both get into the car. Amelia and Sandy didn't make it home that night. They made it ten minutes before Amelia spun out and they crashed into a wall at 80mph. I could have stopped that from happening but I wanted Sandy to suffer. I had the chance to warn her about getting into Amelia's car but I wanted her to suffer. Sandy didn't even do anything wrong, I let my hurt take over and it cost her her life. I knew right then and there that nothing would ever be the same again. I had reached the point of no return. Every day since her death, I have lived with that guilt and regret. Don't reach that point, Ace. Be better. Ava's death was not on you."

"I'm sorry for your loss."

"So I am, every single day. But I can't change the past. I have to live with it."

"And how's that going?"

"It will always be a work in progress. After hearing of her death, I attempted to take my own life but I failed. The rope snapped. That's when I knew that I had to keep going. Even the Devil in hell didn't want me." Paul pauses for a minute as he flicks his eyes down and bites the inside of his bottom lip. "But it does get better, Acey."

"Why did you come here, Paulie?"

"I came here today to offer you a proposition. Things need to change."

"Like what?"

"We need to do something about Hunter."

"What about Hunter?"

"He needs to go. He is a threat to the future of our business and I can no longer allow him to be."

Ace flicks his eyes down and looks at the floor. He understands what Moonie is saying here. He always knew that Hunter's hubris ways would be the death of him.

"I know that this might be hard for you to hear as he has treated you like a son, but you need to think about the bigger picture here, Ace. If he would have listened to you, then your friend JJ would still be with you, and if he would have listened to me, then Ava would still be with you. The man is a dint in our armour, a stain on our shirt and I need that stain gone."

"You want him killed?"

"There's no want. He will be killed. I want you to be the one who gets it done. Once done, you will take his position in my organisation."

"That's a lot to take in."

"Look, Hunter has got you far, there's no argument there. But he's reached his limit to how far he can get you, especially with his ego. At this rate, the fall is as inevitable as the rise was."

Ace flicks his eyes back up at Moonie who leans in closer.

"Who do you owe your loyalty to? Your girl or the man who killed her?"

Ace understands what has to be done. After all, Ace knows that if Hunter had just put his ego to the side and listened to Paul that night, then Ava would still be here.

"I will get it done."

"Good. I will let you decide the how and the where but make sure it is in the next few days and is airtight. There is a new commissioner in the city and I have been tipped off that he is cracking down on me and my brothers. So, make it like a condom and keep this clean." Moonie puts his hand on Ace's shoulder and says, "The times, they are changing. For the better, Ace."

Twenty-nine hours later

8 pm. The night air is clear and slightly chilly as Ace waits in his car which is parked outside of Hunter's home.

"Goodnight, son, I'll see you in the morning," Hunter shouts back as he leaves his house and locks his door. He then turns and looks at Ace waiting in the car. This is the first time that Hunter has seen Ace since the night before Ava was murdered. Hunter doesn't know what to feel upon the sight of Ace. He's not good with his words in these types of situations. He feels sadness for what Ace has been through but he doesn't feel any responsibility towards what has happened. He makes his way towards Ace and gets in the car.

"Sorry, I'm a little late, Acey. Tommy kept me playing before bed, the little bugger," Hunter laughs.

Ace's face is stone-cold and emotionless as he starts up the engine. Impossible to read.

"So, where are we burying this schmuck?"

"The body is in the boot. McHay and AJ have dug a hole for us in a forest not too far out of the city," Ace lies. It's all part of his plan. To get Hunter out in the forest, he needed a reason. So earlier in the day he called Hunter and told him that Moonie had him whack a guy who owed him money and he needed help burying the body. Hunter blindly obliged thinking that Moonie would be grateful he helped in the cover-up.

"You know, Acey, I haven't had the chance to properly see you since, well you know, and I just want to say how sorry I am for your loss. There are some cold bastards out there and I want you to know that me and Lizzy will always be here for you," Hunter says.

"I don't want to talk about her. We have a job to do."

"Yes, yes, sorry." Hunter pauses before he tries to ease the mood. "I see you have copied my style." Hunter strokes his beard comparing Ace's stubble to his.

"I don't have time to shave."

Hunter can sense a little hostility but disregards that he could be the reason and puts it down to Ace still being in a state of mourning for Ava. He leans forward and switches on the car's radio.

Forty minutes later.

Ace and Hunter have arrived in the forest. The forest is three acres in size and is mostly unused by the public with only a handful of people that occupy it mid-day when walking their dogs. Ace stops the car and turns off the engine.

"The hole is up there." Ace points at a small heap of dirt in the distance.

"Then let's go bury this prick." Hunter exits the car with Ace not far behind.

Hunter stands looking at a shovel in the heap of dirt and he calls out to Ace, who he believes is heading to the car's boot to remove the body.

"I'll go ahead and grab the shovel, Acey," Hunter calls back.

Ace doesn't answer.

"Acey?" He calls again.

"You won't be needing the shovel," Ace says in a short dead and cold tone.

A wave of fear and realisation suddenly overcomes Hunter. "You motherfucker." He turns around and sees an aggrieved Ace aiming his gun at him. A small tear forms in Hunter's right eye. "I always feared that my demise would come from the end of an enemy's barrel. But I never thought that it would come from the end of yours."

"I have to do this, Hunter."

"Oh, save me the bullshit, Ace. I raised you like a son. LIKE A SON!" He pauses for a few moments and lets his emotions settle before continuing. "This is Moonie, isn't it? He's behind this, isn't he?"

"This is me, Hunter."

"How are you going to look Lizzy in the eye after this? How are you going to look my son in his eyes? You are the boy's godfather!" He shouts as his heart breaks. "Your mind is fogged up with grief. You aren't thinking clearly."

"You are out of time, Hunter."

"Acey, what is this? What have I ever done to deserve this? After all of these years, is this really going to be how it all ends?"

"JJ. Ava. That's what you did."

"What? Are you serious? Do you really blame me for their deaths? I put food on your plate, I put a roof over your head, and I gave you the opportunity to work yet you blame me. JJ's death wasn't on me, he did what he did that night for you. YOU! And let's face it, Ace, you only blame me for Ava's death because you can't face the reality that Timmings outplayed you. And if you had just locked the door behind you when you left that morning, then she wouldn't be six feet under with her body mangled. Don't you dare blame me!"

"How dare you. Your own ego has failed you. You are so delusional that even now, in the eye of your demise, you fail to see the pain you have caused."

"I know you, Ace, you fire that bullet and you will not be able to live with yourself."

"I died when she died."

"You don't have it in you to fire that bullet."

"There's no way out of this, Hunter. You die tonight."

"Acey, please. I love you. I can see in your eyes that you are conflicted, or you would have done it by now. Please, Acey, think about this." Hunter begins to break down in tears. He doesn't know what to do.

"I have thought about this. You mean nothing to me now."

"You don't mean that. You need me, Acey. If this is Moonie, we can take him on. Me and you."

"No."

"It can't end like this. Let me fake my death and move away with my family. That's the least you owe me."

"I owe you fucking nothing. You are out of time." Ace shoots two bullets which directly hit Hunter's stomach. His body drops to the cold ground. He slowly reaches forward and digs one of his hands into the soil to drag his fallen body forward, his other hand rests over the gun wound on his stomach as blood flows through his shirt. He soon stops after realising he is getting nowhere.

Ace stands over his scared and belittled leader.

Hunter, crying, looks up at his 'Ace' for one last time.

"Please, Ace."

"Goodbye, Hunter." Ace fires the killing bullet into Hunter's skull. A single tear drops from Ace's eye as he lets out an aching sigh. A weight has been heartbrokenly lifted.

As Ace takes a moment to recollect himself, he observes his surroundings. On one of the trees, he notices a dangling rope in the shape of a noose. He stares at it and closes his eyes as more tears roll from his eyes.

Realising that there is still work to be done, he soon snaps out of his observation. He carries Hunter's heavy body over his right shoulder and dumps him in the hole. He takes one last look at his mentor, his father figure, and his friend before he spits down on his lifeless body and begins to shovel the dirt over him.

The drive back into the city is a very quiet one for Ace, thoughts of JJ and Ava filter through his mind. He has no doubt that killing Hunter was the right thing to do.

Ace pulls up outside of 'The Blue Moon', which is the place where he arranged to meet AJ and McHay. AJ and McHay are unaware of what has just transpired. All they know is that Ace called them this morning and told them to meet him here.

The pub doors open and Ace walks in expressionless. He sees that AJ and McHay are sitting in their booth with a pint each.

"A whiskey please, Eden," Ace calls over to the barmaid as he approaches the booth. Ace doesn't sit down, instead, he stands at the end of the booth.

"Whisky? You drink now?" McHay questions.

"I do."

"It's been a good few weeks, Acey, how are you?" AJ asks.

"I'm fine."

Eden comes over and hands Ace his glass of whisky.

"Thank you." He necks the glass in one and places it down on the table. He then rests his hands in his pockets.

"Take it easy, Acey," a concerned McHay says.

"Gentlemen, I called you both here today to inform you that Hunter is gone. Paulie has appointed me in his position, meaning I now run our side of his organisation."

AJ and McHay look at each with a sense of great confusion and wonder.

"Gone? As in sacked or dead?" AJ ponders.

"What do you mean gone?" A worried McHay asks fearing the worst.

"Nothing in Moonie's organisation changes, it just means that I now call the shots over us three and the club security."

"Ace, is he dead?" A persistent McHay is desperate to know.

"It's the way Moonie wanted it, McHay. Hunter is gone."

"Well, who whacked him? Was it you?" McHay questions.

AJ looks up at Ace, who flicks his left eye over at him for a short moment then flicks it back. Without saying a word, AJ then understands what has happened. He sits back and drinks his pint of lager silently.

"That information is irrelevant to you," Ace coldly responds.

"It couldn't be more fucking relevant. He was my friend and he was yours!."

"It is the way Moonie wanted it. Hunter became a weakness to us. His ego made him irrational and he put us all at risk."

"I can't believe this. So, Moonie had him whacked? At least tell me if he is fucking dead, Ace. That's the least you owe me."

"I owe you nothing, McHay. But yes, he is dead."

McHay sits back and he begins to cry a little.

"So, what happens now?" AJ asks Ace.

"Business as usual." Ace pulls out a ten-pound note and places it on the table. "Get a few rounds on me. I will see you both at the club tomorrow," Ace says.

"Who killed him, Ace?" A distraught McHay asks.

"Moonie made the call. This is the way it is, McHay. I'll see you both tomorrow." Ace leaves the pub. The soldier is now the general.

AJ looks at the tearful McHay with fear in his eyes. No one is safe anymore. There are no limits. "Welcome to the cold new world."

Part III
'The Fall'

XIX
'Facing the Truth'

June 10th

We are now just over three months into Ace's reign as leader of the 'Three Grifters'. A lot has changed in the three months since Ace murdered Hunter. McHay didn't handle Hunter's death well at all and being so close to Hunter's wife and in love with her sister, they had questions about his disappearance that McHay simply couldn't answer. They pressed and pressed and McHay could no longer take it. One night, he came home drunk and Amanda began to ask more questions again. McHay reached his boiling point and hit her.

As a result, she left him that same night. McHay has been ashamed of himself ever since and has never tried to reach out to Amanda for forgiveness as he now feels unworthy of her love.

As well as this, a new commissioner, the blonde and brash Cody Kenyon, has been appointed in the city and has made it his personal mission to take down the Moonie brothers. He has been working long hours with the private investigator that Constable Henderson hired to look into claims of fraud against the Moonie brothers. Paul welcomes it and is excited that there is finally a challenge for him to take on.

Regarding Ace, he is truly lost, yet he doesn't acknowledge it. He has become dependent on alcohol, drinking four bottles of whisky a week. His attitude towards those who oppose him, or Paul, is relentless and aggressive as his anxiety and paranoia have worsened considerably. His eyes always look to have deep sadness and regret in them. He now takes no prisoners and will inflict as much violence and harm as possible. AJ believes this is the result of all the built-up guilt and rage he has over JJ, Flacco, Ava, and Hunter's deaths. With the old Ace, you could reason with him and he would have some humanity.

Nowadays, Ace doesn't know humanity and is a former shell of the man he once was.

As the sun begins to set and after a short drive home from working at 'The Rogue', Ace, who is now sporting a small black beard that he started growing out in the weeks following Ava's death, arrives back at his apartment. He mounts the block's stairs and ascends to his floor where he can hear the voices of a male and a female as he nears his hallway.

Frozen and not knowing what to do, Ace sees Ava's parents standing at his door. Ace has only ever met Ava's parents twice before this; once at Ava's cousin's twenty-first birthday party, and the other time was when Ava's mother, Sydney, had invited the two over for a Sunday dinner. He has no idea how they have found where he lives.

The grey-haired, brown-eyed, and stumpy sixty-two-year-old Alfie Sutton stands beside his wife, the brown-haired and brown-eyed, sixty-year-old Sydney Sutton, as they glare at the stunned Ace.

"Tony, can we head in for a chat?" Alfie asks.

Ace can't comprehend what to say or do, so he simply says, "Yes." He removes his door keys from his pants pocket and unlocks his door.

As they enter, Alfie and Sydney look appalled at the appearance and stench of the place. They sit on Ace's couch.

"Would you like a drink?" Ace asks them.

"No, thank you. Sit with us," Sydney says.

Ace takes a seat at his table opposite the couch.

"I bet you are curious as to why we are here, Tony," Alfie opens.

"Not curious. Surprised."

"Well, we are here as we just want to know what you know about our daughter's death."

"And we are here to check up on you," Sydney softly speaks.

"Of course, to check up on you also," a stern-faced Alfie says. Ace can't detect Alfie's tone. He feels like he is on trial. Alfie has never liked Ace. He always thought that he was too secretive and lacking ambition to be something in this world.

"I loved your daughter very much."

"We know you did, Tony. We just want to know more about why she was attacked," Sydney states.

"It was a random attack by a local drug gang. That's all there is to it."

"You see, with all due respect, Tony, I fail to see why a drug gang would come to this apartment block and try all the doors until one was open and then just slaughter whoever was behind it. Make it make sense to us." Alfie's patience is running thin and his anger is boiling.

"That's a job for the police to figure out."

"Stop trying to protect us and tell us the truth," Sydney says.

"You can't trust the police in this city, everyone with a brain knows this. Something happened which caused my little girl to get caught up in the backlash. I want to know what." Alfie's voice slightly rises in volume as he loses grip of his rage. Ace can hear the pain of his words.

"We all do, Mr Sutton."

"Bullshit. The gang leader who they suspect is responsible was found dead within hours after my Ava's death."

"I don't understand what you are getting at, Mr Sutton."

"Just tell us the truth. The truth, which is my Ava, my innocent Ava, fell victim over the actions of you getting involved with someone you shouldn't have!"

"The police have proven no involvement between me and Philip Timmings."

"That doesn't mean shit. I'm not stupid. Paul Moonie sleeps with the fucking police." Alfie spits out as he leans in closer to Ace.

"Alfie, please don't swear," Sydney tries to calm her husband. "What Alfie is trying to say, is that we just need your help figuring out what really caused our daughter's death."

"Your daughter died in a tragic and random attack by a drug dealer who was coked up."

"Say her name," Alfie says.

"Eh?"

"This whole time you've not said her name. That's guilt is that," Alfie stresses.

"Alfie, come on. He is grieving."

"No, Sydney, we are grieving. He is guilty. You caused this, didn't you? It should be you lying in the ground, not her!"

"It should."

"Do you not think that you owe it to us to tell us the truth, Tony? We know this wasn't a random attack. You are too closely associated with Paul Moonie for it to be a random attack," Sydney voices.

Ace knows that Alfie and Sydney deserve better than to be lied to about their daughter's death. They are good people. They need that closure to move on, or for the rest of their lives they will always be wondering about what led to their daughter's death.

Ace lets out a deepening and painful sigh. "There was an altercation in 'The Rogue' between my boss at the time and Timmings." Ace pauses for a moment. Reliving these events is like pouring sanitiser into an open wound. "We were ordered to jump Timmings and his gang outside. Which, after some reluctance, we did. I believe Timmings murdered your daughter in a way to get back at me."

"So, you are to blame," Alfie blurts out.

"Was it you who killed Timmings?"

"There is no evidence to suggest that."

"But was it?"

"Yes."

Alfie and Sydney sit back on the couch letting the information settle in.

"I wish my daughter never met you," Alfie says, after resisting the urge to hit Ace.

"Me too, Mr Sutton. Me too."

"Come on, Syd, let's get out of here." Alfie and Sydney stand up to leave.

Alfie storms out of the apartment but Sydney stops and turns around to face Ace. "Thank you."

"You shouldn't be thanking me."

"You told us what the police didn't have the balls to tell us. And you brought justice to Timmings."

Ace doesn't reply to Sydney, instead, he sits in silence waiting for her to leave.

Sydney rests her hand on Ace's shoulder. "Look after yourself, Tony."

One Day Later

Ace sits in his newly acquired office which is located in the basement of 'The Rogue'. He has made no attempts to keep the office looking in a professional appearance with the dark red carpet stained, dust-covering the shelves, a dim flickering light bulb as the room's only source of light, papers and documents scattered over his desk as well as a four-day-old half-eaten ham and cheese sandwich resting next to an open bottle of whisky.

Ace sits at his desk with his head hung low as last night's hangover has kicked in. He gets a knock on his door before AJ enters with two full bottles of whisky. He places them down on Ace's desk.

"Morning, Acey, Lizzy is banging on the doors with her kid. She wants to see you," he says.

Ace looks up at AJ in confusion. "Hunter's Lizzy?"

"Yeah. Do you want me to let her in?"

"Is she causing a commotion?"

"A fair bit, yeah. She is screaming out there."

"Let her in."

AJ quickly heads out to let Lizzy in. Within a few short moments, she bursts into Ace's office holding Tommy in her arms.

For fucks sake, thinks Ace.

Lizzy stands hysterically with a look of pure fury in her eyes. Ace can see from looking at her face that she hasn't been getting much sleep.

"Lizzy, what can I help…"

"The only help I want, no, the only help I need from you is answers, Ace! It has been months since you reached out to me. You are keeping me in the dark and it's not fair!" Lizzy says infuriated.

What a mess, Ace thinks to himself.

He stays silent and takes a swig of his whisky.

"It's 10 in the morning, Ace!" Lizzy screams which prompts her son to begin to cry. "Do you have any leads on Hunter? We need him, Ace. Help me understand what has happened."

Ace refuses to answer again. He sits there in silence hoping that Lizzy will just leave.

"Ace, you are like a son to us. He thinks the world of you, so why can't you help us?" She questions.

Ace has had enough. He doesn't see this conversation going anywhere so he stands and approaches his coat rack where he puts on his leather jacket before walking up to Lizzy and getting in her face.

"Shut that fucking kid up," he says as he leaves the office. Lizzy begins to follow him screaming abuse at him. Ace sighs. He turns to face Lizzy. "Hunter is dead." Ace then turns back around and leaves.

Lizzy erupts in vexation and wants more answers. She goes to follow Ace up the stairs which leads up to the club but AJ intercepts and takes her to the side to calm her down. Ace leaves the club. There is only one place he feels that he needs to go…

After a short drive, Ace pulls up outside of a house that is all too familiar yet foreign to him. He approaches the house belonging to Dorothy, Flacco's mother. After witnessing and experiencing the emotional state that he has inflicted on Ava's parents and Lizzy, he feels that it is only fair to Dorothy that she gets the closure that she deserves. He also has another intention of coming here. Ace does not intend to leave this house alive…

After being welcomed in by the always warm and caring Dorothy, Ace enters the kitchen and tells Dorothy to sit down at the table. Ace stands before her.

"What is it? I didn't expect to see you back here after last time."

"A lot has changed since then, Dorothy. Nothing about what I am going to say is going to be comfortable for you to hear, but I believe it's only fair that you hear it."

Dorothy senses a great sadness in Ace's tone. A sense of depression and guilt. "Before you continue, can I get you something? A cup of coffee maybe? You look so tired."

"No. Dorothy, I came here today to tell you that…" Ace can't bring himself to tell Dorothy that he is the one who murdered her son. *You coward!* he calls himself internally.

"What is it? I'm getting concerned now, come sit with me."

Ace shakes his head. "Don't treat me with kindness, Dorothy."

"I just want to help you. You look like you need it. What did you come here to tell me?"

"I came here to tell you that." Ace pauses for a short moment as he looks into Dorothy's eyes. He knows that what he is about to admit will shatter her soul but also help her in the long run, giving her peace of mind and closure. "I came here to tell you that I am the man who is responsible for your son's death. Dorothy, I murdered your son."

Dorothy doesn't know what to think. She sits baffled and hurt. All the sadness and grief she had buried for her son has suddenly resurfaced and hit her hard across the face.

"I don't understand. You told me he died in a car accident," she says with her voice cracking under all the emotions that are piling up inside her.

"I lied. The car accident was a cover. I took him to a spot and put a bullet in the back of his head." He goes into his pocket and reveals his gun. "I used this."

Dorothy sits back and begins to uncontrollably weep. Ace stands and watches her grieve. He observes the pain he has caused and feels shame.

"Why come here and tell me this?"

"You had to know the truth, Dorothy." He watches her cry. "I need you to do something for me."

"I will do nothing for you, you monster. MONSTER! Why would you kill him? My boy never hurt anyone."

"I did what I had to do. He gave us no choice."

"Don't you dare! My son was a better man than you!"

"That I don't doubt, Dorothy. Now, I need you to do something for me."

"Never."

Ace walks over and softly stands the heartbroken Dorothy up. She attempts to resist Ace's grip but she is too weak. They are now face-to-face.

"I want you to take this gun, point it at my head, and pull the trigger." Ace places the gun in Dorothy's shaking hands and rests the gun's nose against his forehead. "Give me what I deserve. I took your world from you."

Heavily sobbing, Dorothy really does want to pull the trigger. She feels an immense rage of vengeance towards Ace right now. *How could his own friend betray and kill him? What a cruel and evil man*, she thinks. Her hands shake as she seriously contemplates pulling the trigger.

Ultimately though, she lowers the gun and launches it across to the other side of the kitchen. "You will never know how close I came to doing it, but if I pulled that trigger, then I would be no different to you and that is not me. Killing you won't bring my son back but you living and remembering each day, feeling the guilt and pain, will bring me satisfaction."

Ace hangs his head low. "You should have fired that bullet and stopped me from hurting more people."

"I heard what happened to your girlfriend. Tell me, do you think she would be proud?"

"No. No, I do not, Dorothy." Ace heads over and picks up his gun. "I'm so sorry for what I have put you through. Deep down, Flacco was a good kid."

"You no longer have the right to say my boy's name. Now get out of my house!"

"Just think of all the lives you could have just saved by putting a bullet into my head." Ace leaves the house.

Later that night at 'The Rogue', McHay, on his break from monitoring the club doors, heads down to the basement to call into Ace's office. As he enters, he sees Ace drinking from a whisky bottle. This is a normal sight. An opened pack of cards lay down in front of him on his desk.

"McHay, how can I help you?"

"I just wanted to check in, Acey, that's all. You been playing?" McHay notices the cards.

"Jack and John use my office for some downtime when Paulie isn't around," Ace replies as he swipes the cards to the side.

McHay gets a strong aroma of whisky from Ace's breath. "How much have you had to drink?"

"Not enough. How's business upstairs?"

"Booming. The place is packed again. Listen, Ace, is it true that you went to Dorothy's today?"

Ace stops drinking and places the bottle back down on his desk. "Who told you that? Did they follow me?" The anxiety fuelled Ace asks.

"No, nobody followed you. Dorothy left a message on my answering machine. She said you went over and told her about Flacco."

"My business is my business, McHay," Ace bluntly responds.

"It is your business until you start to compromise me, Acey. What were you thinking? You admitted to murder! I know recently there has been a bit of friction between us ever since Hunter's death but I'm still here, Acey. We are the 'Three Grifters'. Talk to me. I don't understand what is going on with you at the moment."

"Just leave me in peace, McHay."

"There you go again. You don't listen. You are acting way out of line. Just look at you, I don't even recognise you anymore. You are a shell of the person you once were. You are no man." McHay hopes that his harsh words will make Ace realise just how lost he has become and help him break out of the pit of despair that he is holding himself captive in.

"A man, like you? Me and you are not men, McHay. We cause all this harm in a world already diseased by it. I'm tired, McHay. I'm tired of all the shit but I'm too far gone now."

"You can't keep blaming yourself for JJ and Ava. It's fogging up your head. I mean let's be honest, the only reason you took on AJ was out of guilt for JJ. AJ doesn't belong to this life but you brought him into it because you blamed yourself for JJ's death."

McHay's words cut Ace deep. "Do not ever talk to me about JJ or Ava again."

"Do you know what I think, Ace? I think the only reason you keep AJ close is because he is the only link to the person that you used to be. A time when you were happy and life was simple. And I think you hope that one day you will come back to who you were. So why not let that be now? Bin the booze, clear your head, and come back, Acey. Guilt has consumed you and you hate who you have become. You are lost in a world that you never belonged in."

McHay's words take Ace back. McHay, for a short, small moment in time, sees a glimpse of the old Ace in his eyes as he sees a small tear forming. Ace brushes it to one side and lets out a fake cough.

"It's too late for that, McHay. What more do I have to lose? I've lost so much. I can't lose anymore."

McHay can see the pain in Ace's eyes. "No. No, it's not, Ace. This isn't you. Get out of your head. Stop living in the sewers and live up in the real world with us. Do not be the man who kills the 'Three Grifters', let alone himself."

"I am already dead."

"Then guilt has become you." McHay puts his head down and leaves the office.

Ace sits there alone lingering and thinking deeply about everything McHay has just said and knowing it holds truth. Sudden intrusive thoughts and images of Ava begin to force their way into his head. He smacks down on his desk which causes his knuckles to bleed. He begins to cry, not from physical pain but from mental. He holds his hands in his head. The truth hurts. Ace has lost touch with who he used to be. He feels trapped. Trapped in a life that he never belonged in. The path you chose really does matter.

XX

'To Kill a Rat'

Twelve hours have passed since Ace and McHay's conversation last night. After yet another heavy night on the whisky, a hungover Ace enters his office to the sight of Paul Moonie sitting behind his desk spinning around an empty whisky bottle. *What's all this about? What have I done?* Ace thinks.

"Here he is. My right-hand man, right on time."

"Morning, Paulie. Everything okay?" A curious Ace asks.

"It will be, Acey, my good man, it will be. Please take your seat." Paul stands and guides Ace down into his chair as he goes to stand at the opposite side of the desk. "Acey, we have a problem. A problem that I hope you can sort out."

"That's what I do. What's the problem?"

"Before I get into that, I have a gift for you." Paul approaches Ace's wardrobe which is located at the back of the office. On the wardrobe hangs a long bag which Ace guesses a suit lays rest in. Paul takes it off the door and lies it across Ace's desk.

"A suit?" Ace asks.

Paul unzips the bag revealing a fresh-smelling, neatly ironed navy-blue three-piece suit. "With the police sniffing around, I need my men to look as professional as possible. McHay and AJ have been gifted black blazers and trousers, as for you, well you have been given the most expensive suit in the city. My right-hand man must look classy."

Ace isn't sure how to react as he has never been overly fond of suits, he prefers his casual attire of a leather jacket over a black shirt and tie. However, he figures he must show gratitude to Paul just to keep him satisfied. "Thank you, Paulie."

"No more of this." Paul points at Ace's top half. "It's time for this. Times are changing in this city and we need to change with them. That means no more fedoras too. We are men of serious business."

"That we are, Paulie. Now, what is this problem?"

"Straight back to business. That's why I like you, Acey. Dan Smithson is my problem." Paul drags a chair from behind him, wipes off the cobwebs, and sits down. "Smithson used to work for me a couple of years ago. We grew close but then a few months later, he wanted to leave my organisation as one of his daughters fell ill and he needed to take care of her. Now, Smithson saw some shit and did some shit for me, but I trusted him to keep his mouth shut so I let him leave and left him be. Unfortunately, earlier last year his eldest daughter sadly passed away. Heart-breaking stuff. But now, I have been informed by an associate down at the police station that Smithson has been supplying information about me and my organisation to the commissioner. I need a cap putting on that Acey and quick."

"I will handle it, Paulie."

"That I do not doubt, Acey. But do not kill him, we do not need that unnecessary heat. Scare him into silence, okay?"

"Okay."

Paul smiles and stands. "I am very grateful, Ace. Now his youngest daughter might be at the house when you pay the visit but she shouldn't cause any problems."

"She won't be an issue for us."

"Good man. Enjoy the suit, sugar." Paul leaves the office.

Ace sits back in his chair and lets out a sigh before pulling his gun out from his jacket pocket. He rests the gun in his right hand as he opens his desk drawer with his left. Several bullets lie inside the dusty drawer. Ace loads his gun. Once his gun is loaded, he focuses his attention on a half-full bottle of whisky which is on his desk. He pours himself a glass and begins to sup.

Within a few short minutes, Ace's hangover from drinking the night before forces him to sleep. That's pretty much the only way he manages to sleep these days, through his bad habits forcing him to. He doesn't usually dream but this time, he does.

In Ace's dream, he finds himself standing on a busy platform at a train station. He stands confused as strangers rush past and bump into him.

"Watch it," he calls out. He doesn't understand why he is here and why no one can hear him. He looks frantically around for answers. Then, out of the corner of his eye, he sees something very warm and familiar to him. Brunette hair that he can never forget. The woman is dressed in a purple dress and as she turns around, her blue sparkling eyes strike him like a bullet through his heart. It's Ava.

"Ava! Ava!" He shouts out but nobody hears him. In the mass of people, his voice is lost. He begins to rush over to her as the train appears in the distance heading for the platform.

Weaving through the jungle of people, he panics as he sees the train pulling up. After shoving a few more people to the side, he finally reaches her.

"Ava, it's me," he softly says.

Ava turns her head and looks at him with an expression of confusion.

"Ava, it's me, Ace," he says again.

"Sorry, I don't think I know you," she replies.

"Yes, you do, Ava. It's me."

"I don't know you," she replies again as the train doors open and she begins to board.

Desperate and fearing that he may lose her again, Ace reaches out his hand and grabs her arm.

She quickly turns around and pushes Ace back. "I don't know you. Leave me alone," she says before boarding the train and leaving Ace behind.

Ace stands back as his heart breaks once more. He goes to get onto the train but the doors quickly close. He stands alone on the platform as he watches the train set off on another journey.

Ace wakes from his dream with tears rolling down his face.

Dream aside, Ace puts all his focus and determination on one mission. To silence Smithson.

4 pm. Ace, with AJ and McHay by his side, arrives outside of the Smithson household which is located on the outskirts of Manchester. The three sit in Ace's car which is parked adjacent to the three-story house. McHay and AJ are in their new attires of black blazers and a white shirt without a tie. Ace, however, is not in his blue three-piece suit. He is in his usual leather jacket, shirt, and tie attire.

"So, this guy, what exactly has he done?" McHay enquires.

"Did I not say?" Ace replies.

"No. You don't really say anything anymore," McHay takes a dig at Ace.

"He's a rat. That's all there is to it."

"Are we here to kill him?" AJ, sitting in the passenger seat, asks.

"No, we are here to scare him."

"Why do they call them 'rats' anyway? I've always wanted to know?" AJ asks.

"Because they squeal when pinched and do whatever they can to survive," McHay educates.

"I see. So, I take it this guy has been going to the police about Paulie?"

"Yes," Ace confirms.

"Whether we scare this guy or not, the pigs have a tight grasp on Paulie at the minute. They raided two of his pubs last night," McHay comments.

"Regardless of that, we have a job to do."

"Then let's go and do it," AJ remarks.

The Three Grifters make their way and ring the doorbell to Smithson's house. After a few seconds, the door opens and before them stands a twenty-four-year-old, blonde woman. This is Smithson's youngest daughter.

"Hello, how can I help you?" She asks staring bizarrely at the three men.

"We are here to see your father," Ace brusquely responds.

"Who are you sorry?"

Not wanting to waste any time with unnecessary conversation, Ace fiercely grabs the girl by her hair and drags her inside the house. AJ and McHay are dumbfounded at Ace's bellicose manner but they follow. The girl screams and attempts to throw punches at Ace but is unsuccessful. Ace drags the girl right into the living room where Dan Smithson is sitting watching some old-school wrestling on his television.

Smithson immediately jumps up out of his chair but McHay pushes him back down into his seat.

"Get your hands off my daughter!" Smithson shouts.

"Very well." Ace throws the girl down hard on the couch.

"Who are you and what do you want with us?" Smithson rages.

Ace removes his gun from his jacket and aims it at Smithson who is now petrified. AJ looks slightly concerned that Ace might disobey Paul's orders not to kill.

"We are here on behalf of Paul Moonie."

Upon hearing Paul's name, Smithson is terror-stricken. He slowly turns pale as he knows exactly what this visit is about.

"Look, I don't want any trouble here," Smithson pleads.

"Then you know what you have to do, stop giving the police information," AJ says as he steps in, fearing Ace will go too far with his handling of the situation.

"I'm sorry, I truly am. They didn't give me much choice."

"There's always a choice, trust me," Ace replies.

"Please, I made a mistake."

"More than one from what I have been told," Ace remarks.

"Sorry?"

"From my understanding, you gave the police information on Paul in exchange for the police to drop the several charges of sexual harassment you have against you," Ace reveals.

"What?" Smithson's daughter is in disbelief at what she has just heard.

Smithson sits in silence.

"You see that, fellas? The police aided the crook in order to get what they wanted. They are no different to us after all. There is no good or evil in this world, gentlemen. Just choices," Ace declares.

"It seems gangsters have more honour than the police," McHay adds.

"Please, Sir, do not kill me. I won't contact the police again, I swear."

"You are pathetic." Ace strikes Smithson across his face several times with the end of his gun. Ace is caught up in the moment, he can't stop himself from striking Smithson.

Instantaneously, Smithson feels an uncomfortable pain in the left side of his chest. He leans forward holding it tight.

"Dad, are you okay?" His concerned daughter asks.

Smithson feels light-headed and short-breathed. He falls off his chair and drops to the floor. His daughter stands in an attempt to help him but Ace grabs her and launches her back down on the couch.

"Acey, he's having a heart attack," AJ informs. His worries about Ace taking it too far have come to fruition.

"Shit. What do we do?" A perturbed McHay queries.

The grounded Smithson looks up at his daughter as he begins to fade.

"We can't do anything," a cold-hearted Ace replies as his eyes are glued to Smithson.

"Ace, he is dying. We need to call an ambulance," McHay stresses.

"Are you thick? We call an ambulance, and we might as well turn ourselves over to the pigs! Fucking think, McHay!" Ace snaps.

"The man is dying, Ace!" McHay shouts back. AJ races over as he can see that Smithson's movements and struggles are slowing.

"There is nothing we can do."

"For fucks' sake, Ace! This is too much." McHay spins Ace around and gets in his face.

"Yeah? And what are you going to do about it? Hit me like you did Amanda?"

"Fuck you."

"Guys!" AJ intercepts the bickering. "He's dead."

Smithson's daughter lets out a deafening cry as she runs over and falls to her knees beside her dad's freshly deceased body.

"Fuck," McHay says.

"You monster! MONSTER!" Smithson's daughter gets up and hits Ace several times in his chest.

AJ pulls her off him and pins her up against the wall. "Calm down!" He instructs her.

"We need to get rid of the body fast," McHay claims.

"No, we leave it here. He died of a heart attack, there was no foul play here. But she, she will have to come with us," Ace speaks.

"I will never go with you. You will all pay for this! Murderers!"

"Very well." Ace raises his gun and aims it at her head.

"Ace, we can't kill her!" AJ, still having the girl up against the wall, takes in a nervous gulp. "Her blood stains will show foul play." AJ thinks something up quickly as he doesn't want an innocent life to get caught up in Ace's relentless actions. AJ believes that the killing of Smithson's daughter is not necessary.

"You're right," Ace says before picking up a table lamp from the coffee table and hitting Smithson's daughter over the head with it, knocking her unconscious. "We will bring her back to the club with us then," he announces.

"Are we in the business of kidnapping now, Ace?" AJ, feeling uneasy about the whole situation, asks.

"We do what we must. Now, let's move."

The Three Grifters arrive back at 'The Rogue' at around 5.30 pm. They arrive through the back entrance to avoid being seen carrying Smithson's unconscious daughter in with them.

"Take her to my office and handcuff her to the radiator. The cuffs are in my second drawer," Ace orders McHay and AJ.

"We will tape her mouth too," AJ responds.

"Where are you going?" McHay wonders.

"To find Paulie and let him know of our current situation."

McHay and AJ enter Ace's office and handcuff the girl's right wrist to Ace's radiator which is located opposite his desk. They stand back and take in the sight of the bloodied girl.

"How did it come this?" McHay says aloud.

"We do what we must, Vino. It's a better option than her being shot dead."

"I mean what has happened to us? We used to be clean and smooth, now it's just mess after mess. This poor girl has no idea what she has just entered."

"What do you think will happen to her?" AJ asks.

"It's hard to tell these days. If she's smart, she will keep her mouth shut and move away. If she's not, then I wouldn't be surprised if they feed her to Peppa."

"Poor thing. I really thought for a second that Ace was going to kill her. He lost his way in there."

"Things shouldn't be like this."

AJ pats his hand on McHay's shoulder. "We do what we must, McHay," he says in a soft tone.

"We need to keep our eyes on Ace."

"What do you mean?"

"I mean we need to really look out for his best interests. Where we can we need to keep booze away from him, and just like you did in the house saving her, we need to step in and stop him from making things worse."

"I agree, Vino. We will."

Ten minutes pass and Ace enters his office.

"What did he say?" A keen-to-know McHay asks.

"Smithson's death can't be tracked to us so that's all fine, and in terms of her, like me, he doesn't trust her to let her go. So, we will have to come up with a solution," Ace informs them.

McHay takes a quick disquiet glance at AJ.

Ace sees this glance and is triggered by it. *Have they been questioning how I do things? Are they turning against me?* He clears his throat. "What was that look about?" He calls them out.

"Sorry?" McHay replies.

"That look you just gave AJ. Do you not agree with me? Do you think that you are better than me?"

"Jesus, no, Ace! He didn't mean anything like that," AJ defends McHay as he sees Ace's paranoia begin to surface its ugly head.

"He's a grown man, he can speak for himself, AJ," Ace says as he approaches McHay face-to-face. "Speak, Vince."

McHay stays silent.

Ace slaps him across the face and says, "Use your voice, Vince. Come on." He slaps him again.

"Don't overthink it," McHay says with resistance.

Ace slaps him once more and says, "I asked you, do you think that you are better than me?"

"No."

Ace delivers yet another slap before asking, "What?"

"No."

"You're too quiet, Vince." Ace strikes him with a final slap.

"No, I don't think that I'm better than you, Ace," McHay spits out in a louder voice. His right cheek is red raw now.

Ace acerbically and lightly taps McHay's cheek with his hand. "Thank you." He can feel the heat come from McHay's marked face.

"I wonder how long it will take for someone to find Smithson's body," AJ wonders.

"It doesn't matter, that's irrelevant to us. Thank you for today, gentlemen. McHay, you may leave. AJ, stay, I need to talk with you," Ace says. McHay leaves.

"What do you need to talk to me about, Acey?" A slightly on edge AJ questions.

"I want to make this clear to you, AJ. I love you like a younger brother but do not ever oppose me as you did at Smithson's house again. I will not stand for it to happen again, okay?"

"Okay," AJ simply says. AJ doesn't know what to think of this. For Ace to speak like this to him is out of character. He thinks Ace has lost his mind.

"I know your intentions were good but there is no room in this life for good intentions. No matter how hard it may be or how foggy the mission has become, sometimes we have to cross that line for the greater good. When that time comes in your life, you will understand."

"I understand, Ace."

"Good."

Once AJ leaves the office, Ace runs his hands through his hair as visions of Ava's cut-up body creep through his mind uncontrollably. He holds his hair tight to make the thoughts stop. It doesn't work. He closes his eyes shut but this only makes the images of her savaged body clearer. A tear falls from his eye as he screams out for it all to end.

XXI
'Dissension'

A few days have passed since Smithson's death. Smithson's daughter is still cuffed to Ace's radiator and Ace has been supplying her with two meals a day as well as several glasses of water, yet he hasn't spoken a word to her not once. His paranoia about her presence has grown exponentially. He can't trust her to let her go free as he fears she will go straight to the police and get them on charges of kidnapping and possibly manslaughter.

She sits having just eaten a cheese sandwich with her one free hand and looks up at Ace who is sitting in his navy-blue three-piece suit at his desk looking over financial documents for the club. "I have been here for three days now and you haven't once spoken to me. You've not even asked me what my name is," she says trying to get some sort of conversation out of him.

Ace ignores her and carries on reading through his documents.

"Oi, I'm speaking to you. The least you can do is give me a conversation. I'd rather talk to you than sit in silence," she continues. Ace still doesn't talk. "Rude. Well, my name is Liberty. I am twenty-four years old and a dentist receptionist. Your turn." Ace ignores her yet again. "I'll start screaming if you carry on ignoring me."

Ace puts his documents down, stands up, and makes his way over to Liberty. He kneels before her and picks up a slab of duct tape which he removed from her mouth so she could eat. He puts it back over her mouth. He then sits back at his desk.

An irritated Liberty begins to kick down on the floor and scream. Her screams come off as more of a loud mumble due to the tape covering her mouth, however, it annoys Ace nonetheless. Ace slams down on his desk and heads back over to her. Without any hesitation, he kicks her several times in her stomach before he removes her tape. "What is your problem? No one is going to hear you down here. You are in the basement, you stupid bitch."

"Finally, you talk to me. How are you?" Liberty sarcastically asks wincing from the pain in her stomach.

Ace slaps her across her face so hard that his hand leaves a little imprint.

"Child," he says before spitting in her face.

"Why do you have me here?" Liberty enquires.

"I'm not playing games." Ace stands and heads back to his desk.

"Do you think I'm going to go to the police about my dad? If you let me go, I promise you I won't. Just let me go, please. I can't stay here."

"Shut up, I'm working." Ace picks his documents back up.

"You do realise that when they find him, they are going to look for me. They will know that something isn't right. If you let me go, I can act oblivious to it all and say I was staying at a friend's house after we got into an argument. Please, Sir," she begs.

Ace puts his documents down and looks at her. "You have been here three whole days and that's the best you come up with? Did you really think I would buy into that crap?"

"Please, let me go."

"I don't see that happening."

"What are you going to do to me?" Fear takes over Liberty now as she ponders her fate.

"That is a question I have no answer to at this time," Ace replies. His words send shivers down Liberty's spine.

"Do you want to kill me, is that it?"

"I don't want to kill anyone but circumstances arise, and I have to do what I have to do."

"Please, I am only twenty-four and I have so much to live for. There are so many things I want to do," she says. "Is it sexual? Do you want me to do a sexual favour for you in return for my freedom?"

"No, I am not your father."

"You didn't know my father!" She shouts at the top of her voice.

"AND YOU DON'T KNOW ME!" Ace shouts even louder, which scares Liberty more. "Killing you doesn't matter the slightest to me. I have killed before you and I will kill after you. It's the life I live."

Liberty detects pain in Ace's voice.

188

"That's why you haven't been speaking to me, isn't it? You don't want to get to know me or get attached to me because then killing me will make it personal. You know it's wrong but you feel you must do it. You are trapped, aren't you?"

"Do not try that therapist shit on me, child. I will not think twice about putting a bullet through your head. You know nothing," Ace sternly says. He stands up and heads for the door.

"Where are you going?"

"To make a decision as to whether you live or die today." Ace slams the door behind him. What will he decide?

Ace heads upstairs to the club's main floor where he sees Paul Moonie speaking to some members of his staff helping to prepare for opening in an hour's time. Ace approaches Paul who has just finished ordering his staff around.

"Paulie, I think I have a solution to our problem," he says.

"Okay, come this way." Paul leads Ace to a nearby booth where they both sit down. "What do you have in mind?"

"I think we need to kill her. She's a smart girl and we can't afford for her to trick us into letting her go. She will compromise us," Ace shares his opinion.

"I get that, Acey, I do, but she's so young."

"Timmings was young. Look what he was capable of. We can't let history repeat itself. The girl knows who we are and what we do. She's seen our faces. She can have us on several charges and bring your empire crumbling down."

Paul sits back and takes a minute to think. "Look, Ace, I will give my opinion right now but ultimately you guys got into this absolute fuck fest of a mess so the final call will be yours. There are options to get around this, we can drug her, bribe her, or straight up send her someplace far away from here. I, personally, do not want her blood on my organisation's hands. But I trust you, so the final call is yours."

"Paulie, I understand but I just can't afford her out there. I would be looking over my shoulder for the rest of my life."

"It's not much different to how you live now, Acey." Paul laughs but sees the seriousness in Ace's eyes. "Look, do what you feel is best but just make sure whatever you do doesn't compromise my organisation." Paul believes that Ace's paranoia has gotten the better of him. Just like Hunter said it one day would.

"Then I will kill the girl."

"If you feel that it is the right decision, then do it. I trust you. But don't tell me how or where because I don't want to know. It has to be clean."

Ace already has the place and method in mind.

As this conversation between Ace and Paul Moonie is transpiring, AJ enters Ace's office to drop him off two more bottles of whisky.

"Do you condone this?" Liberty asks AJ as he places the bottles on Ace's desk.

"Do I condone what?" AJ replies.

"Me being held here. This isn't right."

"Whatever you are trying, it isn't going to work with me."

"I'm not trying anything. I remember it was you who stopped him from shooting me. You're not like him."

"You know nothing about me." AJ heads for the door.

"Please. You know that this isn't right."

AJ stops himself from leaving and turns to face Liberty. "You talk too much."

"You are a good man. I can tell that. Please, please let me go. I will run away and never come back to Manchester again I promise."

"I can't do that."

"Yes, you can. You stopped him from killing me once, do it again," she pleads. "Do you really want the blood of a twenty-four-year-old on your hands?" She attempts to inflict guilt upon him. "What did I ever do to deserve this?"

"You did nothing, it's just the way things are."

"It doesn't have to be like this."

"Yes, it does."

"Be the change. Help me, please. I beg of you."

AJ is conflicted. Liberty doesn't deserve to suffer at the hands of Ace's erratic and weak mind. He is out of control and AJ has an opportunity to save a life, a life that has no business to be in danger here.

"I'm sorry that this has happened to you."

"Then let me go."

AJ looks down. He can't let this young girl die, what kind of man does that? "If I do this, you must never return to Manchester. Ever."

"You have my word. Thank you so so much."

The second that AJ heads over to Ace's desk drawer to receive the key to the handcuffs, he hears the door begin to open. He quickly slams the drawer back shut and steps away from the desk. The door opens and in walks Ace.

"AJ, what can I do for you?" Ace asks upon seeing AJ standing in his office.

"Acey, there you are, I was just nipping down to see if you have seen McHay," AJ thinks up fast.

"He's gone to pick up some barrels. He should be back any minute."

"Very well."

"Well, have you made your decision?" Liberty asks Ace.

"I have." Ace slowly pulls his gun out of his inside blazer pocket. AJ stands behind Ace and looks at Liberty riddled with guilt and kicking himself for not acting sooner.

"So today is the day I die?"

"Today is the day you die," he replies. "AJ, you can go now."

Still standing behind Ace, AJ silently mouths 'I'm sorry' to Liberty with a tear in his eye as he heads for the door and leaves the office.

"Please, don't do this. Just think of the people you love, what will they think? Think of your girl what will she think? Your frie…" Liberty gets cut off.

As soon as she mentions 'your girl', Ace drops his gun and grips her tightly by the neck beginning to choke her. He looks directly into Liberty's eyes as he chokes the life out of her. He is acting like a man possessed. Possessed by the guilt of his lost love. Ace sees Liberty's young life slowly drain from her being. He feels nothing. His hands are so tight, fuelled with anger and rage. Liberty attempts to fight back as she lunges her sharp nails vigorously deep down the left side of Ace's face.

This only angers Ace more so he grinds down on his teeth as he goes deeper with his grip. It doesn't take long before Liberty dies in his unyielding grip. Ace is still choking her dead body when he releases that she has gone limp. He throws her neck back and stands up. He looks down at the young girl he has just murdered. Not one feeling of remorse hits him. An innocent comment just merely mentioning Ava, not even by name, got this young ambitious life murdered in such a horrific way. Poor Liberty didn't even know Ava.

Ace heads over to his desk, perks his rear end on the edge of it, and downs a mouthful of whisky from one of the bottles that AJ brought in. He doesn't tend to the blood pouring from his face where Liberty scratched. He is numb to it. Deep down, Ace despises what he has become but he genuinely feels that there is no way out for him. He sees Liberty's murder in the same light bankers see money, just a regular day at the office.

The doorknob on Ace's office door turns. The door opens and Vince McHay walks in. McHay is instantly met with the sight of Liberty's body and is nauseated.

"Close that door," Ace orders him. Ace doesn't sound stressed or frantic, he is calm and collected. McHay closes the door and looks at Ace in disgust.

"You killed her."

"I did."

"Why? She didn't need to die."

"I couldn't trust her to keep her alive."

"No, Ace. She didn't need to die. You are a paranoid mess."

Ace takes another swig from his whisky bottle. "Maybe. Or maybe I'm a man who wanted to bring goodness into this world but this world ate at him and broke him down so much so that the brutal killing of this twenty-four-year-old girl does absolutely nothing to him. Nothing." Ace takes a final swig which finishes the bottle off. "Or maybe I'm a visionary living in a world full of the blind like yourself. Blind to the harsh truth that you can trust very little in this world and in order to survive, you have to sacrifice your ambitions, nature, and morals. How dare you stand there and look at me in disgust. She's not the first and she won't be the last. Maybe I am a paranoid mess or maybe I am a realist who knows how to survive in this world."

"How can you not see that you have drifted so far away from yourself? I don't know who you are anymore. This is sickening, Ace, and if you really do feel nothing at the sight of this dead young girl who had so much left to give, then you truly did die with Ava."

Ace clenches his fist up. "Do not bring Ava into this. I'm the only one here who has the Goddam bottle to do what needs to be done."

"Ava is all of this!" McHay shakes his head; he genuinely fears that Ace has gone too far and lost all control of who he once was. He has reached the point of no return. "This is too far, Ace. I'm telling you now if anything remotely like this happens again, I am out."

"Out? Are you threatening to leave me?"

"Yes. You always used to say how Hunter turned us into people we were never meant to be. Well, let me tell you, we were never meant to be this."

Ace grinds down on his teeth again in indignation as a result of McHay implying that Hunter had better control over the group than he does. "I never told you what actually happened to Hunter that night did I, McHay?"

"I don't want to know, Ace. I just want you to realise that you have lost yourself and if you don't sort your head out you will destroy us all."

"I took him into the woods and shot him dead. I watched him as he lay dying and then I put another bullet in his head. I was glad to."

Tears begin to slowly form in McHay's eye. "You bastard. He thought the world of you."

"He took the world from me."

"You are the godfather to his son, how could you?"

"I didn't even shed a tear," Ace lies. "That kid is better off without him, just like we are."

"You know you don't mean that. You know what it's like to lose a parent at a young age, yet you still took a little boy's father from him." McHay wipes his tears. Ace has only told him about Hunter's death in order to hurt him. He now knows that Ace is beyond saving. "I won't do this anymore, Ace. I'm out. Done. Me and you, me and this organisation, done."

Ace stands up straight and puts his hands in his trousers pockets. "You're walking out on me?"

"We are done," McHay states. "You going to kill me as well now?"

"You disappoint me, McHay. But then again, I always knew you were weakest. Adapt or perish, right?"

"Fuck you." McHay spits on Ace's shoes before he turns to the door and leaves.

"You won't survive without me!" Ace shouts. Then, out of rage, Ace hurdles his bottle of whisky, which shatters on impact as it collides with his closing office door.

McHay walks with a strong purpose upstairs to the main floor of the club. He sees to the left of him, AJ sitting in a booth with a bottle of beer in one hand and a beer mat he is fiddling with in the other. McHay hesitates to approach him as he looks in deep thought but gives in in the end. He heads over and stands at the booth. "AJ."

"McHay, everything alright?" AJ looks up and asks.

"No. Look, AJ, me and you have never really liked each other," McHay begins.

"I actually don't mind you, Vino."

"Regardless. I'm out of here and I think it is in your best interest to do so as well."

"Out of here? You're leaving?"

"Yes. I'm done, AJ, for good. He is out of control and I know what's coming. His self-destruction won't just affect him, he will take us all down. He can't be helped, AJ. If you know what is good for you, then you will leave and head far away out of his reach."

"Vino, come on, man."

"Don't try to reason with me. My mind is made up. You know how bad he has become."

"I can't believe you are leaving."

"He's killed the girl."

AJ hangs his head low. "I know," he says.

"I know we didn't ever see eye to eye, but ever since that day when you took out Ackhurst, I always respected you, AJ." McHay offers out his hand to shake AJ's. AJ reciprocates and the two shake hands.

"Good luck, Vino."

"You too, man." McHay leaves the club for the last time.

As soon as McHay leaves, AJ heads down to see Ace in his office. Averting standing on the broken glass from the shattered whisky bottle, he steps into the office. He looks down and sees Liberty's deceased body. A great sense of guilt overcomes him. He feels almost ashamed to be associated with the vile monster who did this. "I've just seen McHay," AJ says to Ace who is sitting at his desk. "He told me he's done."

"He is weak. Not like me and you."

"Do you think he will come back?"

"No."

"He has to come back. We are meant to be the 'Three Grifters'. We need him."

"We will be just fine."

"Are you going to have him killed? Like the girl?"

"No, I have enough on McHay as he does on me. He's not stupid. Going to the police will only put him in the same place. What did he tell you?"

"He told me that you had gone too far and lost control."

"And do you agree with him?"

194

AJ hesitates to answer straight away. Ace looks up at him. "I don't," AJ replies even though he does agree with McHay.

Later in the night, Ace, now sporting a brutal 15cm tall scar down the left side of his face from Liberty's nails, decides to make a stop at the 'The Blue Moon' on his way home. He makes this stop alone.

Soaking wet from the rain, Ace enters the warm pub at 11 pm.

"Just you tonight, Ace?" The barmaid, Eden, calls over.

"Just me. A whisky please."

"I'll bring it over."

Ace sits down in the group's usual booth. As he sits down, he looks over at the empty seats in the booth and questions where everything went wrong. He longs for the times when he, JJ, and McHay would come down here and spend many of their nights talking rubbish and having a laugh. How it should be. He remembers the time when the gang all cheered and celebrated the news of Hunter and Lizzy's pregnancy. He looks up to the empty seat opposite him, the seat where Hunter once sat and patted him on the shoulder to go and get the round in. Good times. All gone.

"So, you're drinking again?" Eden places Ace's whisky down on the table. "Is everything okay?"

"When I was younger, Eden, on my walk home from school, every day I would walk past a pub called the 'Bull's Head'. Each day, without fail, I would see this man completely drunk stumbling out of that pub stinking of booze and looking a mess. I would look at him, each day, and wonder to myself how can anyone let themselves become like that. I wondered why someone would rely on alcohol so much so that they lose touch with reality and themself. Well, now I know why." Ace takes a swig of his whisky. "I hope that you never have to find that out yourself, because when you do, there's no going back." He takes a mouthful of his whisky. "People are too easy to look at people like that and judge, rather than ask why and offer help. Everyone has a story."

Eden pats Ace on his shoulder. "Get some rest, Ace. You need it." She then heads back to the bar.

Ace drinks his whisky sitting in the lonely booth where he once shared some of his best nights with his once closest friends. Now they are just distant memories of a time that is deeply lusted for. They are just nostalgia now.

XXII
'McHay's Escape'

Since his departure from the 'Three Grifters' a few weeks ago, Vince McHay has gone on the run. He feared that Ace's paranoia would once again get the better of him and he would come calling for McHay's blood. Leaving his home and all his belongings behind, McHay made his return to Leeds. The very city he started his journey in.

He is taking refuge with an old client he and Hunter acquired during their business in the city. McHay and this client, Joe Kelly, grew a strong bond before Hunter and McHay left for Manchester. The short, thin-built, glasses-wearing, and well-educated Joe Kelly has given McHay his basement to live in until he sets up his new life in the city. To ensure that Joe, his wife and two little girls are safe, McHay has told them not to tell anyone about taking him in and he has kept the details about his return to the city very close to his chest. As far as the Kelly family are concerned, McHay is back in Leeds because he became homeless after he lost his job in Manchester.

It's June 20th and the city is calming down into relaxation after a warm busy day. The time is 6 pm and Joe Kelly has just finished his shift as a car salesman and has returned home. The first thing he does is wash a fresh set of bedding for McHay. He piles the bedding into a basket and heads down into the basement where McHay sits at a small old dining table reading issue number 20 of 'The Mighty Ten' comic book series written by creator Ryan Kevin Sutcliffe and called 'The Mighty Ten Disbanded'. This issue is a famous issue where the mighty heroes disband and wage battle against each other.

"Kids these days have no idea just how awesome those comics were," Joe laughs.

"They don't write them how they used to that's for sure." McHay puts the comic down on the table and looks over at Joe who places the basket of bedding down on McHay's pull-out bed.

"My daughters wanted no part of them," he laughs. "I bought them the whole first 50 issue set and they didn't read a single one."

"They don't know what they are missing, Joe."

"You're dam right there," Joe laughs. "Hey, I forgot to ask before, whatever happened to your boss? I think he was called Hunter?" Joe asks.

"Yeah, he was called Hunter. He, err, he got caught up in some bad business."

"The same bad business you are running from?"

"What makes you think I'm running from anything?"

"Vince, I hadn't seen you or even heard from you in years. Then one day, you show up on my doorstep needing a place to stay. You must have been desperate to get out of Manchester."

McHay lets out a sigh. "I'm sorry for just showing up, Joe. But I can't tell you about my time in Manchester or why I'm here. It's for your own good," McHay responds.

"Vince, you are sleeping in the same home as my wife and my two little girls. If you are in danger, I think I need to know why."

"I'm not in danger here. I would never put you or your family at risk. I'm here to start fresh, to live a normal life."

"It seems like you are here to stay under the radar from someone. Who?"

"Stop digging, Joe. Me, you, and your family are safe. It won't be long before I get my own place and you will never have to see me again. Just trust me on this one, okay?"

"Okay. Any sign of trouble though and you will have to go. I can't put my family at risk."

"There won't be any trouble. You have my word."

XXIII
'Stepping Out of the Shadows'

A few days later, Joe's wife, Sarah, heads down into the basement to see McHay after Joe has headed out to work. She sits on the edge of the pull-out bed and softly taps McHay to wake him up. McHay wakes and is slightly curious as to why Sarah is here. However, he is not too surprised. For the past week, he has been overhearing several heated arguments between Joe and Sarah. Fearing that he was being a burden and the arguments were about him, McHay listened in on them. He soon learnt that the arguments were over Joe losing out on a promotion to his boss's lazy and useless nephew. Sarah was annoyed that Joe didn't put up an argument or defend himself to his boss rather than just allowing it to happen.

"Sorry to wake you, Vince."

"It's fine. What's going on?"

"I was hoping to get a quick second of your time and ask you for a favour."

"You both have done so much for me. I will do anything I can to help you out."

"Thank you. I don't know if Joe has mentioned it to you but he lost out on a big promotion to his boss's nephew. We needed that promotion to help pay off our bank debts and now they are threatening us with bailiffs. Not to mention his boss had promised Joe he would be getting the promotion. Is there any way you could pay a visit to his boss and try to persuade him to give it to Joe? I wouldn't normally ask but we really need the money that comes with that promotion."

"Sarah, I get it, I really do, but I don't see how I could change his boss's mind."

"Vince, please. Joe has told me about your previous business here and what you and your boss got up to. You are the last chance we have to get out of our debt. Please do not take away a roof over my children's heads."

"Sarah, I could try but at the end of the day who am I? Why would he listen to me?"

"Take charge, Vince, and stand up for your friend. We have given you a home and the only thing I ask in return is for you to try. But if that's too much, and if you want to keep running rather than stepping up, then that's fine." Sarah stands up to leave.

McHay thinks for a moment. Sarah has finally made him realise that it's time to stand and step out of Hunter's heavily influenced shadow and be a man of his own. Not a sheep but rather a man who rises to the occasion on his own two feet. Taking charge of the man he wants to be.

"Sarah, I'll pay a visit to his boss."

11.30 pm. Vince McHay stands outside the entrance of 'Roddy's Deluxe Cars', the small but popular car dealership. 'Roddy's Deluxe Cars' has been a mainstay in Leeds for the past two decades and is run by the stingy, short, and balding owner, Rodrick Evans. Evans has a reputation for being rude when dealing with customers and is known to through what people describe as a 'hissy fit' when things don't go his way. His temper is as short as his build.

McHay stands before the entrance doors of the dealership. He closes his eyes, takes in a deep breath, and counts down from three before confidently entering with a determined look on his face. He refuses to leave here without accomplishing his mission. He must succeed in this job because, in his mind, this is him finally stepping out of the follower shadow and asserting himself as his own man.

"How can I help you, Sir?" The brunette receptionist asks him.

"I have a meeting scheduled with Mr Evans. Where can I find his office?"

"Let me just check his appointment book. What is your name, Sir?"

"I don't have an appointment. In fact, this is quite an emergency. I'm his nephew's lawyer and I'm not at liberty to tell you my means of being here. I just need to speak to Mr Evans."

"Lawyer? Sorry, I didn't know. It's the first door to your left over there." She points McHay in the direction of Rodrick Evans' office.

"Thank you." McHay heads in the direction of the office.

Without knocking, McHay bursts straight into the office where he sees the short and balding Rodrick Evans filling his mouth with a chicken and mayonnaise sandwich as he reads a newspaper.

"Sorry, who are you? You can't just storm in here," an irritated Evans says.

"I just did."

"Oh, you're a funny guy, are you? Well, we will see how funny you are against my security."

"I wouldn't do that if I was you, Mr Evans. We have business to discuss."

"Business? What business? I don't even know who you are."

"Is that your daughter?" McHay points at a framed photograph of a young blonde girl dressed in a graduation gown placed on Evans' desk. "Sally, right? She graduated with a law degree last year, didn't she? Tough business to be in that. What a beautiful smile though, a smile too beautiful for law."

"How do you know my daughter?"

"If you don't agree to my demands here today, Mr Evans, you will never see your daughter's beautiful smile again. In fact, no one will."

"What did you just say? Who are you to come in here and threaten me?" Evans throws his sandwich down on his desk.

"I'm the man you want to please if you wish to see your daughter alive again."

"Bullshit!"

"Do you really want to take that risk? Outside of this building, my associate has your daughter in the back of a van, and if he doesn't see me leave here in the next ten minutes with a smile on my face, then he will put a bullet in her head."

"You are lying."

"Well, in," McHay checks his watch, "around nine minutes time we will see, won't we?"

"How do I know you're not lying?"

"You don't. But I'm telling you right now your daughter will die if you don't believe me. The choice is yours."

"Okay. Okay. Why are you here?"

"Because you lied to my friend."

"Sorry?"

"You promised Joe Kelly a promotion and instead you went back on your word and gave it to your dipshit nephew. The Kellys needed that promotion to keep the bailiffs away and you took that from them."

"It's just business, that's how it goes."

"Not when you make a promise. I think for your daughter's sake, you had better fix this."

"What do you propose I do?"

"Give Joe the promotion, not your dickhead nephew."

"It's not that simple."

"I'll tell you what is simple, the fact that in eight minutes my associate will put a bullet in your daughter's skull! Fix this!"

"Okay, I will give Joe the promotion."

McHay smiles. He has succeeded. "That's what I thought. Oh, and if I find out you don't give Joe the promotion, or if you tell Joe about my little visit here today, I won't wait ten minutes next time. I will personally take your daughter's life and burn this shithole to the ground. He needs this win. Pleasure doing business, Mr Evans." McHay slams the office door shut on his way out.

He stands in the car park and takes in a breath, feeling for the first time in a while, proud of himself. He loves the feeling of taking control of his own life and figures that it's about time things changed. There is no van in sight in the car park, it was all a lie to get Evans to agree to the promotion. McHay played him.

XXIV
'Keys to the Empire'

July 20th

A day that will live in Manchester's history in infamy. The day a god was silenced. A day that almost nobody saw coming…

From the early hours of the morning, the sun has brought great warmth across the busy city. The city's morale is at an all-time high on this scorching summer's day. But for one man, morale was about to take a cold turn.

Since McHay's departure from the group, Ace and AJ have so far managed without him. The club's popularity has continued to grow and McHay's position as doorman was easily replaced within a few days after he left. Ace immediately appointed AJ as the head of the doormen. Upon hearing about McHay's departure, Paul had gone to pay him a visit at his home to persuade him to return but he had already gone by then.

It's 11.01 pm and Ace is exiting his apartment block with his car keys in hand. Ace is unsurprisingly hungover from drinking heavily last night at 'The Rogue'. To his concern, he sees Paul Moonie pacing up and down in front of his car. This is unusual for Paul to pay a home visit to him and the last time he did, it resulted in Hunter's death.

Paul looks up and sees Ace. "Acey, quick, get in."

What's going on? This is strange. Is he going to whack me? Is this how I go? Ace is taken aback by Paul's surprise visit here this morning. He believes that whatever this is about, it cannot be good news. Ace unlocks his car door and they both enter.

"What's going on, Paulie?" Ace asks.

"They've got me, Acey. The bastards have found a way to get me."

"Who?" Ace says with concern in his voice. There are many people out there who would love to see Paul Moonie gone. Too many to count.

"The pigs. That shitbag commissioner. I have been tipped off that today he is arresting me and my brothers."

"Shit, Paulie. Is there not a way we can get out of this?"

"Not likely, my good man. He's got us on tax evasion." Paul sits back in the passenger seat and laughs. "After all the shit I have done, tax evasion is how they get me. There has to be something poetic in that."

"This isn't good, Paulie. What do we do?"

"There is only one thing we can do. My empire needs a new ruler. Ace, you are the only man I trust to take that helm."

Ace doesn't know what to say. He is extremely grateful that Paul entrusts him with so much responsibility but at the same time, he doesn't believe that he could live up to Moonie's reputation. "It would be an honour, Paulie, but are you sure I'm the man you want in charge?"

"Acey, I have never doubted you once. There is nobody else I can trust to run my organisation until I'm back."

"How long will you be in there for?"

Paul smiles. "I don't know for sure, but shit, Acey, I'm Paul fucking Moonie. Whatever time I get won't be the same as the general pricks in there, not after the favours I've done for the judges over the years."

"That commissioner needs a bullet in his head."

"He's just doing his job. I lost the chase. Anyway, Ace, don't take any shit from anyone whilst I'm away. And if they do give you shit, then make them regret every step of their life that has brought them to you. And always remember, rule with an iron fist and don't do anything that I wouldn't do." Paul offers out his hand. "I'll see you on the other side, my friend." The two shake hands and Paul exits the car.

Rather than drive to the club, Ace heads in the direction of the graveyard where Ava's body lies in rest. Rain begins to pour down.

Ace stands in the pouring rain staring at the grave that reads: 'Beloved daughter, friend, and girlfriend. In loving memory, our Ava'. As he stands staring at her carved-in name, the rain pelts him, but he is too numb to feel it. Regret, guilt, and sadness plague his existence now. He wants to say a few things but finds himself unable to speak. This is the first time he's visited her grave. As he continues to stare down, he wonders what life would be like if she hadn't been murdered that day. A life where he wouldn't have killed Hunter, turned to booze, and destroyed himself and his relationships.

A life where the idea of happiness wasn't a long-faded memory to him. He also feels guilt as every time he remembered Ava these past few months, he was instantly reminded that she was gone and was brutally taken from him, so after a while, he stopped reminiscing. Deep down, he knows that she would hate the man he has become and that kills him every day.

1 pm. Word has soon spread throughout Manchester that all three of the Moonie brothers have been arrested. This is soon confirmed by Police Commissioner Cody Kenyon on a live television interview outside of the police station.

"I can confirm that the rumours are true. At around 12.30 pm this afternoon, we arrested Paul, John, and Jack Moonie on the charges of tax evasion. I am pleased that I was able to deliver on my promise to the people of Manchester that we would take down these criminal brothers," Cody confidently announces to the thousands of viewers.

"What a load of dogshit," AJ, who is standing with Ace watching the television in Ace's apartment, says. "Well, you're the man now, Ace." AJ knows that this only means that things will get worse with Ace as now there is no one above him to reign him in. Things are about to take a turn for the worse. McHay got out at the right time. He takes in a nervous gulp.

XXV
'To Restart a War?'

It is now August and has been four weeks and two days since the Moonie brothers were arrested. In these four weeks, Ace has fired a combined total of twenty people throughout Paul's organisation. Many of which he saw as weak, untrustworthy, or they simply opposed his views and direction. AJ has slowly come to understand why McHay left. He himself hasn't left though and he remains Ace's right-hand man and head of security.

In fear and paranoia that 'The Rogue' may lose customers due to Moonie's arrest, Ace has begun to allow drug dealers to conduct business inside the venue to try and get more people in. This is ridiculous and unwarranted though as the club never lost customers from the arrests. Once again, Ace's paranoia has gotten the better of him.

'The Rogue' is crammed with people on this summer's Saturday night. Business is continuing to boom here. The dancefloor is full and people are finding it difficult to move around there due to the heavy volume of people. By allowing dealers in, Ace has in turn expanded and grown the club's popularity. On the flip side, there are also more people getting lairy and being thrown out due to fighting. The minute you bring drugs in is the minute trouble follows. Nevertheless, the club is at its peak popularity.

Ace enters the main floor having just come up from his office. Shaking hands with strangers whom he has never met, nor will he ever have the intention to get to know, he makes his way over to AJ who is on shift and standing at the bar watching over the main floor.

"Bloody busy one again, Acey," AJ says.

"Good. By the way, Bradley Owens is meant to be coming here tonight for a meeting with me. When he's here, I want you to pat him down and escort him to that booth over there. That's where I will be."

"You got it, Ace. You expecting trouble tonight?"

"I don't know. We haven't heard from Owens in over a year. I have to be ready for anything."

"I see. I'll pat him down and send him straight over." AJ doesn't know if this is Ace being paranoid again or if Owens does act as a threat.

An hour soon passes and Bradley Owens enters 'The Rogue' with two other members of his crew. AJ greets Owens and quickly pats him down. But before he escorts him to Ace, he informs Owens that his men will have to wait at the bar. They oblige and AJ takes Owens to Ace.

Owens arrives at Ace's booth. The two shake hands and sit down. Ace has AJ stay and stand at the booth to protect him from anyone who may approach them. AJ stands with his back to Ace and Owens guarding the booth.

"Look at you, Ace, who would have thought it? You're a king who rules an empire now," Owens opens the conversation.

"A lot has changed, Owens. I was surprised to learn that you requested this meeting with me tonight," Ace replies.

"Surprised? Why? We are good friends, Ace. This could just be a catch-up."

"But it's not, is it? There is always a catch with you, Owens."

Owens laughs. "Caught red-handed! I do have a reason for this meeting today, yes. But I don't really feel comfortable with your man there." Owens points at AJ.

"Me and AJ are one of the same. He is there for our protection. Now, talk to me."

"Okay, very well, as you know when Paul came up with a solution to bring peace between me and the Red Syndicate, he gave me control in Ordswall and them in Beswick."

"I do know, yes."

"Well, two weeks or so after Paul got arrested, there were some sightings of a dealer in Ordswall. Now, this dealer didn't match any description of any one of my boys. So, we did some digging, and this bloke, well, this bloke is a member of Red Syndicate. I believe that now Paul Moonie is out of the picture, Red Syndicate plans to take Ordswall."

Ace itches his beard as he thinks. He knows that this will be an issue and will break the treaty that Paul implemented. He also knows that if he can't control this issue and Red Syndicate does take Ordswall, he will look weak in Paul's eyes. He can't stand for this. "That is a problem. A big problem."

"I know. That's why I've come to you. I propose to you that I take the guy out and send a message to Red Syndicate to stay in their lane."

Ace sits there and thinks some more.

"Right now, they don't see you and Paul in the same light. You are fresh and weak to them. You need to make a statement that you are no pushover. Let me take him out and send that statement."

Ace continues to think and weigh up the situation.

"You need to show people that you take no shit. Take Moonie's reputation and make it your own," he goads. "Let me take him out."

"Take him out? What, for a meal? No, you butcher that fucker. Make him wish he was never born, then, in his last breath, kill him," Ace aggressively orders. It's clear that Owens' words have triggered Ace into wanting to show everyone that he is just as dangerous as Moonie and he's not a feeble figure in the city. A decision made from his insecurities.

"So, I have your permission?"

"Yes." Ace and Owens shake hands and Owens leaves. Is this Bradley Owens purposefully feeding on Ace's paranoia in order to help him against Red Syndicate? Or is this Bradley Owens running to Ace out of fear of Red Syndicate? Some may say it's both.

"Acey, can I speak to you?" AJ asks who has just heard the conversation.

"Sure, take a seat," Ace says. AJ sits down where Owens was just sitting.

"Ace, I don't think that this is a good move. Owens killing the Red Syndicate member could restart the war. Not only that, but we will be slap bang in the middle of it this time," AJ highlights his concerns.

"AJ, the Red Syndicate will know their place. They won't want a war, not after the last one caused so much damage. They will see that Owens and his men won't stand for it and they will know that I am not a soft touch. We will show them their place. Trust me, that's all it will be."

AJ isn't sold. "Ace, all I'm saying is that Paulie left his empire in your hands to protect. This may just burn it down."

Ace sits back and pulls his face at AJ. "After all we have done, do you really think I am going to let that happen?"

"There are other ways to sort this that's all I'm trying to propose to you, Acey. I mean how do we know Owens is telling the truth about them breaching the treaty?"

"AJ, some men in this world only learn when they're hit in the face."

"I'm just not sure they are the men to hit," he says. "Surely we could negotiate with them?"

"AJ, my mind is set and there is no changing it. Stop worrying."

AJ sighs. He knows that arguing is going to get him nowhere. "Fair enough," he simply replies.

Through his internal anguish and pain, Ace has lost all touch with who he once was. So much so that he won't even listen to reason anymore. Has he become the man he always hated in Hunter? His loss, guilt and regret have brought on his own self-demise. There is no return for him.

XXVI
'The Crumbling of an Empire'

'It's not the power that destroys us, it's the lust for it.'

It is now October and following Bradley Owens murdering the member of the 'Red Syndicate' who was selling drugs in Ordswall, the war did break out once again. Ace was wrong and AJ was right.

In these months, Ace has joined the war with Bradley Owens and is set on the demise of the 'Red Syndicate'. However, they are losing. Losing drastically. The 'Red Syndicate' have taken most of Ordswall as well as the lives of several of Owens' men. This war has been far more destructive and lethal than the one before with even the police being killed upon arrival to break up the fighting on the streets. Unlike the previous war, there is no Paul Moonie to save the world this time.

It's 11.05 am. The morning is dull and grey clouds lay stale over the sky. Sam has just opened up at 'The Moonie'. He's just finished sweeping the floor and is about to start wiping the bar down when the doors forcefully fling open. It is uncommon for people to come drinking here so early in the day. Sam's attention is peaked even more when he sees a slick, black-haired man enter wearing a red trench coat and holding up a black bin bag which has blood dripping out of the bottom. It's 'Red Syndicate' member, Ryan Kelly. The red trench coat triggers panic in Sam; he knows who Kelly represents. "I don't want any trouble, Sir," he says with his lips trembling in fear.

Ryan Kelly approaches the bar and rests the bin bag on it. Whatever it is inside the bag it has a peculiar shape that Sam can't quite guess the identity of. Kelly winks at Sam before he turns and leaves the pub.

Not knowing what to do, but knowing that whatever the bag contains is not good, Sam decides to take a little peek at the contents of the bag.

"AHHHHHHHHH!" He screams out at the top of his voice as Peppa's decapitated head stares up at him. He vomits all over the bar.

It's now 12.30 pm and Ace has called for a meeting in his office between himself, AJ, and Bradley Owens. This comes as a result of a car bombing Red Syndicate acted out last night which killed four of Owens' men, including his right-hand man, Bill Picker.

Owens is pacing up and down in the room as Ace stands behind his desk awaiting AJ's arrival.

"Four of my fucking men, Ace. Four. We have to hit them hard," Owens stresses.

"Picker's and the rest of your men's lives will be avenged, Owens. I assure you."

"This war has gone too far. I've lost 80% of my business, my home, and my life as I knew it. What's Moonie said about all of this?"

"As far as I know, he doesn't know about it. That's how it will stay. We will win this, Owens."

AJ enters the room looking just as agitated as the other two. Like Owens, AJ is uneasy about a victory for them in this war. A war that he never wanted part of in the first place.

"Gentlemen, how are we?" AJ asks.

"Shitter than shit, my friend," Owens answers.

"Let's begin," Ace opens the meeting. Not one of them is sitting down, this is a tense time for each of them.

"What do we do? They are hitting us so much harder than we expected," Owens shares his concerns.

"We have to keep pushing them," Ace responds.

"With what, Ace? I have lost most of my men and resources. We don't have much left!" Owens snaps back.

"We can't give in now, Owens, they will keep coming for us," AJ adds.

"You're not the only one suffering here, Owens. We have lost massive amounts of business and run the risk of losing it all. This needs to end for the greater good. We only do that by winning," Ace says.

"Well, what more can we do? We have pushed and pushed and barely made any movements. We tried to take areas of Beswick but failed all whilst they annihilated our territory in Ordswall," Owens claims.

"I'm sick and tired of this, Owens. You lose your arse at the first sign of trouble. You lost someone close to you in Bill Picker. Well, look at me, Owens. Look at all those I have lost. Make Picker's death mean something. If we give in and accept a defeat, then your right-hand man died for absolutely nothing," Ace attempts to light a fire in Owens.

That's the most sense he's made in months, AJ thinks.

"You're right. Sorry. So, what's our next move?" Owens asks.

"I have a plan. All these attacks are notable for one thing, the absence of their leader, Finn O'Sullivan. He's sending orders from the shadows because he's weak. Rumour is the fire that killed JJ left O'Sullivan limp in his legs, he now has to walk with a cane. So, what I am presenting to you both is that we send AJ down to Beswick to scout out and find information on O'Sullivan's whereabouts and when we know, we execute," Ace lays out his plan.

"Why AJ?"

"Yeah, why me, Ace?"

"Because I trust you with my life. The only one in this world I trust with my life. And me and Owens are too high profile to be seen in Beswick. They will kill us the minute we step foot there," he reasons. "Keep a low profile and find out any information by any means necessary."

"So, we find where O'Sullivan is and then we take him out?" AJ checks.

"Yes."

"Do you think it will be just as simple as that?"

"I don't know, AJ, but it's the only card we have left to play," Ace says.

"I can't lose any more men, AJ. This is our last gasp," Owens states.

"Head down tonight. Scout out and do what you must to find where he is," Ace orders.

"But what about the Halloween party? You will need me on the doors," AJ asks referring to 'The Rogue's' big Halloween party tomorrow night. A party that is intended to bring people and money back into the club after its decline in profits due to the ongoing drug war. Even dealers don't do business in there any more out of fear of becoming involved in the war.

"You have bigger fish to fry, kid," Owens says.

"Forget the party. I can't see it being busy anyway. Let's get this done."

"Okay," AJ says. "I will find the fucker."

A slight relief comes over Owens. "Look at us Ey, people will start calling us the 'New Three Grifters'," he comically claims in an attempt to lift the depressing mood.

AJ looks at him and shakes his head. "You would never survive as one of us."

"Oh yeah, and why's that?"

"Too much baby oil to start," AJ mocks Owens and his excessive use of baby oil that he applies to 'impress the ladies'.

After taking the banter from AJ, Owens shakes the hands of both men and leaves the office feeling a lot better than he did when he entered.

"Before I head back up, Acey, I need to talk to you about something."

Ace knows this must be important as AJ's tone has acutely changed to more serious. "Sure."

"There is word going around that O'Sullivan has been telling people that he plans to burn 'The Rogue' down."

Ace laughs at the very prospect of O'Sullivan attempting something so bold. "He wouldn't dare. He knows that if he comes for this place, he is directly shitting in the eye of Paul Moonie. He frankly doesn't have the balls for that."

"I don't know, Ace. I think that we should add extra security around the club in case."

"AJ, trust me, it's all talk. O'Sullivan wouldn't dare. Small fish don't fuck with big fish."

"If you say so, Acey."

"I do."

October 31st

Halloween Night. Bradley Owens stands in his expensive penthouse and pours himself a glass of red wine to ease his nerves. He takes his glass and looks out of his large window overlooking the city. What a sight it is to see at night. Budlings with lights on, each window serving as a doorway into someone's life, someone's story. All his current problems are irrelevant to each of them. *How lucky*, Owens thinks to himself. Over the past few weeks, Owens has come to regret his actions killing that 'Red Syndicate' member and re-starting the war. He feels responsible for the men's lives he has lost. He takes a sip of his wine in the hopes that the alcohol will ease his guilt.

Knock. Knock. Knock. He is broken from his trance of reflection by a sudden knocking at his door. Owens quickly turns, puts his glass on the side, and opens his cabinet drawer where he pulls out his handgun. He cautiously approaches the door. "Who's there?" He asks loudly. There's no answer, just another knock. "Listen, fuck head, if you don't identify yourself, I will shoot!" Owens is panicking. A few short moments of silence ensue before BANG! Whoever is on the other side of the door has fired a gun and shot Owens in his right knee. Owens hits the floor holding his knee. He looks up and sees the doorknob turning.

With his other hand, he holds up his handgun. Trembling a little. The door springs wide open and Owens gets a full view of the perpetrator who fired the gun. It's Finn O'Sullivan, the leader of the 'Red Syndicate'.

"Well, hello there, Mr Owens." O'Sullivan, who is standing with a cane in his left hand supporting him and a revolver in the other hand, laughs.

"You mother…" Owens is cut off as O'Sullivan fires two more shots in his head which kills him there and then.

"Fucker." O'Sullivan chuckles. Without hesitating, he leaves the penthouse closing the door behind him. His sights are now set on heading to 'The Rogue'…

11.30 pm. 'The Rogue' isn't busy at all. The main room has around twenty-five people in it, some dressed in costumes for Halloween. Business is far from booming which is what Ace anticipated.

Ace sits in his office with a bottle of whisky to the left of him as he looks over financial documents for the club, checking profits made this month. Suddenly, the thumping noise of the music playing on the dancefloor up above him stops. He waits a few minutes for it to start up again but it doesn't. This is unusual. The DJs that they hire are usually professional and well-known DJs. Mistakes are very rare. Ace curiously stands and makes his way upstairs to the club's main room.

To Ace's shock and horror, the club is now completely deserted. The DJ is gone, the customers are gone, and the bar staff are all gone. *What's going on?*

"Here he is. The man himself." Finn O'Sullivan comes from around the corner and several other Red Syndicate members follow behind him dragging across the floor the two bouncers that were on the door. The bouncers have bloodied and battered faces.

Ace immediately draws his gun from his blazer pocket.

"Easy now. There are more of us than you," O'Sullivan says.

Ace steps forward and realises he is standing in something wet. He then gets a whiff of petrol up his nose. The 'Red Syndicate' have poured petrol all over the club's floor.

"I'm no genius but if I were you, I would lower my gun. You must be careful where you shoot these days as you never know what fire you are about to start." O'Sullivan laughs as he pulls out his lighter.

Ace slowly lowers his gun in the hopes that O'Sullivan doesn't drop the lighter and start a fire.

"Is it just me or are you getting a serious case of déjà vu here?" O'Sullivan refers to the fire that killed JJ. "Well, I've not been here with this Ace, no, this Ace is different. They told me, my boys, that you had changed. They said that you're as bad as the Moonies now. And now I see you up close in the flesh, I must agree. What happened to the man I met in the betting shop that night?"

"He adapted," Ace scornfully replies.

"For the worse I see. Maybe it should have been you who died that night. Maybe that would have done you a favour."

The sad reality is that Ace agrees with O'Sullivan's words here. "Maybe so. But here we stand."

"It's amusing to me that even in the face of death, the great Tony 'Ace' Johnson still thinks he stands a chance. Your time is up, pal. It's all over."

"I'll kill you." Ace spits down.

"I wouldn't be too sure. Bradley Owens once said the same thing and I've just put two bullets in his head."

Ace is slightly stunned by this news but he doesn't let it show. He won't expose any weakness to O'Sullivan. "I am no Bradley Owens."

"Granted." O'Sullivan turns and looks at his fellow members. "Owens was a far bigger threat." They all laugh.

"Let my boys go. This isn't about them," Ace says in reference to the two bouncers that 'Red Syndicate' are holding hostage.

"Now where's the fun in that? It is Halloween after all," O'Sullivan says before pulling out his gun and pointing it at the grounded bouncer to his right. "Trick." He then points the gun to the floored bouncer to his left. "Treat."

"Stop playing games."

"Trick or treat? Which one do you want? The other will die."

"This is about me, not them. Let them go."

"Not going to happen. Make your choice Acey boy."

"You're out of line."

"And you're out of time." O'Sullivan shoots both bouncers in their skulls.

"NO!" Ace calls out. "Just wait till Paul Moonie hears about this."

"About what? About how you allowed for the war that he ended to be restarted? Or about how you let his club, which he spent thousands on, burn to the ground? It's safe to say that daddy won't be too happy with you. Not that it matters though. You won't live to tell the tale."

"That's not going to happen."

"I don't get you. You really are thick, aren't you? Even if, and it's a big if, you make it out of here, you are still a dead man. The minute Moonie gets out of prison, he will hunt you down and slaughter you. Just accept the fact that you have lost. Just like you lost your girl."

Ace grinds his teeth together and erratically fires his gun, quickly sending a bullet straight into O'Sullivan's shoulder. The other members draw their weapons but O'Sullivan orders them not to shoot. O'Sullivan winces a little and holds his shoulder tight, applying pressure to ease the bleeding.

"Teach him a lesson," O'Sullivan orders. Two 'Red Syndicate' members then run over and tackle Ace down, kicking his gun across to the other side of the room. They begin a ghastly assault on him. Pummelling him left, right, and centre. Ace doesn't fight back. They then prop him on his knees and strike him over and over in his face, busting him wide open.

A fresh coat of blood trickles down his face as O'Sullivan, holding his shoulder as blood pours from his small wound, slowly heads over to him. The bloodied Ace looks up at O'Sullivan standing tall with his cane.

"Look at you, you don't even fight back anymore. What happened to you?" O'Sullivan says.

Ace spits up at O'Sullivan but soon gets a receipt in the form of O'Sullivan swinging his cane hard across his face.

"Come on, boys, he's already lost." O'Sullivan leads his two men back to where they were originally standing. Ace remains on his knees with blood pouring down his battered face.

O'Sullivan looks Ace directly in his eyes, sarcastically blows him a kiss, and then drops the lighter on the petrol trail. The fire travels rapidly across the club. The 'Red Syndicate' then flee, leaving Ace behind to die.

This is like reliving an awful nightmare for Ace, but instead of running free, he just stays knelt. Kneeling still and looking into the rising flames which are soon approaching his position. As the flames race through the petrol trail, he wonders for a moment whether he should just lay down and let them engulf him, ending it all and finally having a way out of all the madness. He is conflicted to live or die but he then thinks of AJ and how he needs to live to be there for him and in turn honour his best friend, JJ. He stands to his feet in discomfort and turns around just before the flames reach him. Throwing himself through the door on the back wall, Ace makes his way out of the back exit of the club.

Once safe, he then stands at a distance and watches Paul Moonie's empire crumble to ash.

The fire brigade comes but it's too late and they are unable to save 'The Rogue'.

It's all over. Ace takes in a nervous gulp. The old Ace would have never have let this happen, and he knows it.

XXVII
'End of the Road'

Upon hearing the news about the fire at 'The Rogue', AJ heads round to Ace's apartment where he enters and finds Ace sitting on his couch downing a bottle of whisky.

"Hey, Acey, I heard about the club. Are you okay?" AJ says as he sits at the table opposite Ace on the couch.

"Do you have a location on O'Sullivan's safehouse?" Ace asks after finishing a swig of the whisky.

"No, but I think I'm coming close."

"Good. The second you know, you come to me, and we will kill him. Then we will wipe the rest of them out one by one." Killing O'Sullivan isn't enough for Ace, he wants them all to suffer.

"We're going after all of them now?"

"Every single fucking one."

Holy shit, he's insane! AJ thinks. "Has Paulie heard about the club?" AJ asks.

"No, but it's only a matter of time before he does."

"Shit, we are dead."

"No, we're not. I've thought this through."

"Great, what's the plan?" AJ hopes Ace has a solid plan to get them in the clear with Paul. But then again, he can't remember the last time Ace had a solid plan for anything.

"I will kill him."

Ace's words catch AJ off guard as he sits back and says, "What?"

"When his release day comes, whenever that may be. You arrange to pick him up and I will hide in the back of the car. Then I will pop up behind him and choke him."

AJ doesn't believe what he is hearing. He thinks that Ace truly has lost it. AJ doesn't for a second believe Ace will ever kill a man like Paul Moonie and to even suggest it is beyond lunacy. It's delusional to say the very least.

"You're quiet. Why?" Ace wonders.

"It's just a lot to take in, that's all, Acey."

"We are giants, AJ. Fucking giants." Ace takes another swig from his whisky. "I want you to carry on your search for O'Sullivan. That's our first step."

"I will, Acey, I will. Do you really think you could kill Paulie?"

"I know I can, AJ. It's either we kill or be killed. That's how it's always been."

Twenty Years Ago
September 2nd 1967

Fifteen-year-old Tony Johnson has just entered his first school lesson, 'History', of the fresh academic year. Shy, nervous, and scared, Johnson looked over the flood of his fellow pupils all finding their seats and caught a young JJ Reeves sitting on his own. Johnson, whose only friend in the school was JJ, raced over and sat next to his best friend. All of Johnson's school life he has been a victim of bullying and until last year, he had no one to call a friend. He was always anxious about meeting new people and found it difficult to mix. He was all alone. That is until he met JJ.

It was a warm summer afternoon and Johnson was kicking about a football in the schoolyard by himself. A group of three slightly older pupils saw this and decided to kick Johnson's ball over the school fence and onto the road for their own amusement. They then resorted to name-calling Johnson which soon evolved into physicality as they began to push and kick him down to the ground. By sheer luck, JJ passed by and witnessed all of this. In JJ's eccentric fashion and even though the three boys were older and substantially larger than him, he shouted at them as he charged over, looking like a soldier on the battlefield.

"Do you want some as well, you freak?" One of the boys asked JJ who continued to shout and cause a commotion so loud that a nearby teacher, who was on duty watching over the children during the break, heard and rushed over. The three boys fled like cowards on the teacher's arrival. JJ looked down at the floored and crying Johnson and offered out his hand to pick him up. From this moment, the two bonded like brothers.

Two minutes after Johnson took his seat next to JJ, the tall, slim-figured, and black-haired Mrs Lord entered the classroom. Mrs Lord was new to the school at this point and wanted to get to know her pupils more. To do so, she asked each student their name and their dream job.

Ten pupils later, she arrived at the quiet Tony Johnson.

"And you, dear, who are you?" She asked.

Johnson nervously perked himself up in his chair. "My name." Johnson stopped himself as he sounded groggy. He quickly cleared his throat before he continued. "My name is Tony Johnson and when I'm older, I want to be a comedian."

"A comedian? That's different. Tell me, Tony Johnson, what makes you want to be a comedian?"

"Well, comedians make people smile and laugh. They make people happy. I want to do that."

Mrs Lord smiled. *What an innocent and kind child*, she thought to herself. "I can tell, Tony Johnson, that you are a very kind and special soul. Never lose sight of that, young man."

Johnson smiled and sat back comfortably in his chair.

Back to the Present Day
November 2nd 1987

Ace sits in his apartment at his table, head in his hands and back arched over. Behind him, on his television, the news is reporting on Bradley Owens' murder. Ace doesn't turn around to watch, he just listens in as he sits there.

"At this current time, we have no idea who is responsible for Mr Owens' murder, but many speculate that the Red Syndicate are the ones who carried out this killing. With Owens' awful and tragic death, one must ask, does this finally bring to an end the horrific drug war? Only time will time. This has been Alec Kinderman reporting at 'News This Noon'."

"All this death," Ace says to himself knowing deep down that things should have never come to this.

All of a sudden, AJ quickly and excitedly hurries through the apartment door.

"Acey, Acey. I've found him. I've found O'Sullivan," he says with a wide smile on his face.

Ace perks his head up with a focused and determined look on his face. Like a hunter who has spotted a deer through his scope. "Where?"

"Apartment 114 Brickson Lane, Beswick."

"How do you know he's there?"

"At first it was word of mouth but then I staked the place out. I followed him up to room 114. He's there, Acey. We have him."

"Is he alone?"

"Surprisingly, yes. No men outside or in. It's like he doesn't even trust his own men to know where he is based."

Ace stands and pats AJ on his shoulder. "You did good, AJ. Let's finish this."

"How do you want to go about this?" AJ asks. "Quiet or loud?"

"We reign hell on the bastard." Ace goes into his blazer pocket to retrieve his gun but soon remembers he lost it in the fire at 'The Rogue'. "Shit."

"What is it?"

"My gun. It was in the fire." Ace thinks for a second before continuing. "I guess I'll get it done the old way." He heads over to his kitchen and opens a drawer where he pulls out a sharp steak knife.

"So, what's the plan, Acey?"

"We force our way in and beat the ever-living shit out of him. Then, I slowly cut him inch by inch, limb by limb, until he begs us to kill him. That's when you put a bullet in his head. Job done," Ace reveals his ruthless plan.

AJ is slightly disturbed by Ace's brutality but he doesn't let it show.

"Do you have a silencer?" Ace asks.

"Yes."

"Good. This is a residential area, so we must be as smooth as possible. Once he's dead and cut up, we will put his parts into bin bags and bury them in the woods I buried Hunter in."

"Let's end this then."

AJ is driving them both over to Brickson Lane, Beswick. The journey is silent and tense. For Ace, this is all about ending the war once and for all and re-establishing his dominating grip over Manchester. He knows that in order to do this, O'Sullivan needs to die and thus he intends to, along with AJ, be the one responsible. Kill or be killed.

They stand before the door of apartment 114 Brickson Lane. It is time. As they are standing before the door, AJ looks over at Ace whose eyes are glued straight ahead like a shark who has spotted an injured swimmer in the distance.

"Let's finish this, Acey," AJ says before loudly banging on the door several times. "Room service, motherfucker!" There is no movement from the inside so AJ bangs on the door once more.

Tired of waiting for an answer, AJ tries the door handle. It opens. AJ looks over at Ace surprised.

"Today, he dies," Ace simply says before stepping ahead of AJ into the apartment.

The apartment is clean and homely, which is not what Ace was expecting. He heads to the first door to his left and enters. It appears to be an office space with an oak desk, bookshelf and drawn curtains covering the window. This isn't anything like Ace imagined for O'Sullivan. The room is populated with old books, a few plants, a handful of lava lamps placed on various shelves, and a large steel safe.

And then, out of the corner of Ace's eye, he spots a small framed photo of JJ on the desk. "*What the fuck?*"

As was the plan all along, the sound of a gun loading can be heard from behind him. He knows what this means. His eyes widen in shock. The realisation heartbreakingly hits him.

"Well played, kid. Well played." Ace places his hands down on the desk. He hangs his head low.

With his silencer equipped, AJ is holding his gun up, aiming it at the back of Ace's head.

"The knife. Throw it over to your left," AJ orders.

Not putting up a fight, Ace removes and throws his steak knife to the left of him. "It had to be you, didn't it?"

"Welcome to my second flat. It's the end of the road, Ace. It was always going to end like this. I had you from the very beginning."

"You son of a bitch," Ace's soft and defenceless tone is the tone of a man who knows that he's defeated.

"All I had to do was act and talk like my brother, and your guilt did all the rest."

"I loved you like a brother."

"And that's why it worked. Pulling you apart came easy to me. I soon realised that all I had to do was just hand you a bottle of whisky."

"After everything we have done together, as the Grift…" Ace gets cut off.

"This was always the plan, Ace. I came to you to end you. Didn't you question how I got your address in the first place to send you that letter? Tell me, how did a man like me play you, the most paranoid man in the city? I'll tell you how. All the guilt you carried blinded you. You have brought about your own demise, Ace. You."

Ace lets out a sigh. "I had my suspicions, AJ. I just hoped that, for JJ's sake, they were just that. Suspicions."

"Don't bring him into this. You have no right to mention his name anymore!"

"I loved your brother."

"LIAR! You are the reason he's dead! If he had never got involved with you, then he would still be alive."

Ace attempts to process what is happening right now and then a horrendous thought comes through his mind. "How much did you plan? Did you..." He stops himself for a moment. "Did you have her killed?"

"Enough of the talk, Ace."

"TELL ME!" Ace shouts with all the strength in his lungs before he slams down on the desk. "Just tell me. Please. Did you have Ava killed?"

AJ sighs. He isn't proud of what he's about to say. He did what he did to avenge his brother and had to do whatever he could to break Ace. "I told Timmings where you lived and he did the rest. I was also the one who told Ava's parents where you lived."

Ace slams his fist down on the desk in a furious fury once more.

"Don't you fucking move or I'll shoot you right now!" AJ shouts. "I didn't know that he would kill Ava. The understanding we had was that he was going to beat you. He lied to me. She never deserved what happened to her and for that I am sorry."

"How fucking gracious of you." A tearful Ace turns to his right side and spits down. "Targeting me for your brother's death is one thing but she never deserved to be brought into this."

"I know. I never wanted that. But this isn't about her, it's about you. And I want you to suffer and pay for JJ's death."

"You crossed the line."

"Sometimes you have to cross that line for the greater good. You taught me that."

"I will never forgive you for her death."

"Well, looks like we are even then because I hate you for taking my brother from me."

"She was pregnant."

"What?" A tremendous wave of sorrow hits AJ.

"A few days before she died, I found a pregnancy test in the bathroom bin. She was pregnant."

AJ is taken back by this. "I didn't know. I'm sorry for that, truly. I never meant to hurt her. It was you I was after. She was a good woman and would have made a great mother." He feels a great shame take hold of him.

"Yes, she would have."

"All that hatred you have for me now is what I have felt for you ever since the night JJ died."

"Your brother's death affected us all."

"Save me the bullshit. He died because of you! You took him from me! If you really cared for him, then you would have told him to sort his act out and leave behind this way of life a long time ago."

"There wasn't a man I cared more for than your brother! Don't ever talk to me about care. Where were you all this time he was with me? Did you ever try to talk him out of working with me and Hunter? I think fucking not."

"YES! Yes, I did! Time and fucking time again I told him to leave you and Hunter behind, but he never listened," AJ says shaking with anger and with tears in his eyes. He takes a deep breath to calm himself from his fit of pique before continuing. "He was too blinded by his loyalty to you. And what did it cost him? His life. That's a recurring pattern for people who love you though, isn't it? My brother, your parents, Hunter, and Ava. That is all your doing. You killed them all."

Ace sighs. "You know what, if you would have said all that to me a year ago, then I would have beat the ever-living shit out of you and left you for dead in a pool of your own blood. But now, well now, I'm thinking that maybe you're right."

"You are a plague, Ace, to everyone you love."

"I never asked for any of this, AJ."

"You could have stepped away," AJ says.

"I couldn't."

"I think you should know that I also gave O'Sullivan Bradley Owens' address. That was me too."

"You rat bastard."

"The war had to end and it was only ever going to end one way."

"McHay was always on the fence about you. He was right this whole time."

"I don't take joy in the pain that I've caused, Ace, I truly don't. I did what I did for JJ. My brother."

"He would be ashamed of the man you are."

"So would Ava of you. Don't you stand there and try to act like you are above me? I did what I did out of purpose. You've done all you've done out of guilt, regret, and the inability to accept the fact that you are the problem. Look at all those lives you have taken, all those innocent lives who died as a result of your trauma. You deserve every bit of this."

AJ's words resonate with Ace. All that has been said about him he's already known. He knows the monster he has become. "I know." He slowly turns around and sees that AJ is shaking as he holds his gun. "You're shaking."

"I've thought this moment through in my head so many times and now I'm actually here, I fucking hate the fact that I'm struggling to pull the trigger."

"You're conflicted."

Although AJ's hatred has brought him to this point, he and Ace did bond like brothers and that bonding has made it harder for AJ to finish his plan and fire that bullet. He places his other hand on the gun in an attempt to stabilise himself. Now both of his hands are holding the gun but he's still shaking.

"I'm not conflicted. I will kill you. I just hate the fact that I know for the rest of my life, I will feel the guilt of your death. I shouldn't feel guilty for you."

Ace slowly grabs AJ's hands which are holding the gun and he rests the gun's nose on his chest. "You are right, AJ. About it all," Ace acknowledges everything AJ has said. "Let me be with her." Ace looks into AJ's eyes begging him to pull the trigger and fire the bullet into his chest. AJ hangs his head low and looks at the floor.

AJ feels chagrin for thinking twice about killing Ace. He collects himself, thinks about his brother and remembers just why he is doing this. He looks up into Ace's eyes and says, "She won't want you." AJ fires two bullets into Ace's chest. He then grabs Ace's dying body and rests him across the desk.

In agony, Ace looks up at AJ and reaches out his hand before pulling him closer. Still tearful, blood pouring from his chest and fading fast, Ace grabs AJ's head, pulls it closer to his and tells him, "I'm sorry. For everything."

AJ slowly stands back as Ace passes away. One single tear falls from AJ's eye. It is finally done. The mission is complete. He doesn't feel pride in finishing his plan nor does he feel guilt for killing Ace. He doesn't know what to feel. He looks at the photo of JJ which overlooks Ace's head and he feels nothing.

He walks back and slumps into the wall where he slowly descends and sits on the floor staring ahead at the desk.

Ace was the one who loaded the ammunition and AJ was the one who fired the bullet that killed the 'Three Grifters'. A group built to last, but never stood a chance. That was always the plan. Trust can be a dangerous game.

The 'Three Grifters' will go down in history as one of the most fearsome factions in the United Kingdom. The stories of their antics will be told for generations in Manchester. But now, that is all they will ever be. Stories. Stories that, in time, will become faded and forgotten. Plagued by guilt, regret and a betrayal, was this always going to be how they ended? Every day has a sun set, and every story has an ending. And for this story, it was AJ who drew the curtain down. The 'brother' who played the ultimate distraction. The poison from within.

How the mighty have fallen.

After recollecting his thoughts and downing a bottle of rum, AJ leaves his apartment and heads to a nearby telephone booth. Inserting his ten-pence coins, he looks around to see if anyone can see him dialling. No one is in sight.

"Hello, it's me, AJ. Yes, I'm fine. It is done. The weeds are gone."

XXVIII
'A Ghost in the Shadows'

December

It's a cold winter's afternoon and snow has begun to fall across the UK. After several weeks of looking and planning a way out, AJ has booked a flight to California, USA. This is where AJ hopes to start fresh and put all of the 'Three Grifters' business in the past with no worries. His flight is in two days' time. He has finished his plan and intends to cut all ties he has ever had with his previous business and life here in Manchester. His apartment is nearly empty now with all his items and clothes packed in a suitcase.

After a long day of packing, AJ strips down to his boxers and jumps into bed. It's 10.30 pm. He longs for an escape in the form of a dream but ever since he murdered Ace, he has been waking up several times throughout the night sweating. He hopes this will fade out in time and it's just all in his head. But tonight, he will be met with a physical reason to sweat…

5.30 am. AJ wakes up for the third time in a panicked frenzy having just dreamt about the day he killed Ace. In his dream, he finds himself standing in the same position shooting Ace over and over like it's playing on a loop in his mind, a loop that he can't stop. He sits up in bed, wipes the sweat off his forehead, and switches on his bedside lamp.

"AJ Reeves, it's been a while," a voice says. A voice that AJ had forgotten. He rubs his eyes and sees a figure sitting in his chair adjacent to his bed holding up a gun. It's too dark to make out any features on the figure.

"Hello?"

"We have a lot of catching up to do."

AJ recognises the voice now. "McHay?"

"The penny drops. I think we need to have a chat."

AJ gulps. "What do you want?"

"First of all, I want you to put the light on. I want to see you clearly."

AJ steps out of bed and switches the main bedroom light on. He heads back and sits on the edge of the bed. "Why are you here, McHay?"

"I think you know why, AJ. Two weeks ago, my friend was found dead with two gunshots in his chest. He was found in the rubble of 'The Rogue'. The pigs say the body looks to have been placed there a few days after the fire, and I agree."

"McHay, plea…"

"Shut up. I had it called from day one about you but nobody listened. You killed him and I want to know why."

"McHay, it's not entirely like it seems. You knew what he was like yourself."

"Why did you kill him?"

"Why do you care that he's dead? You knew how bad he got and you left him."

"I lost respect for him, and I even grew to dislike him. But at the end of the day, when it's all said and done, I will always love that man. After everything we have done together, all the jobs, all the laughs, all the loss. After all of them years it's hard to forget someone and truly cut them off. And no matter what he did, I know that he would have taken a bullet for any one of us. So, help me piece this together. Why did you do it?"

"You don't have a brother, do you, McHay?"

"Ace was a brother to me."

"Then you know the rage and vengeance you feel now looking at me, the man who killed him. Do you feel it slowly take over you? You want, no, you need to make me pay. Well, that's how I felt every single day after JJ's death."

"What does JJ have to do with this?"

"JJ is all of this. Ace killed him."

McHay gives AJ a glance, looking at him like he's stupid.

"Don't act numb. That night in the betting shop, Ace killed my brother."

"JJ died saving Ace. Your brother meant the world to Ace."

"That's not true."

"Listen, you schmuck, I saw it happen. JJ saved Ace's life by putting his own at risk. Do you really think I'd have stood by Ace all this time if he killed JJ?"

AJ feels sick to his stomach. His mind is clouded with confusion. Has he really just murdered a man in cold blood over a lie? AJ leans back and doesn't know how to react to this revelation.

McHay sees the regret quickly overcome AJ.

"Who told you that Ace killed JJ?"

"McHay, you have to believe me, I was told that Ace killed him that night in the fire."

"By who?"

"I was told Ace was paranoid of JJ taking his place in Hunter's organisation."

"Ace was a paranoid man but never because of that. You have been lied to. I want to know by whom."

"It doesn't matter."

"AJ, someone close to me has been murdered over a lie. So do not sit there, as I hold a gun to you, and fucking tell me it doesn't matter! Who had you kill Ace?"

"You don't want any part of this, McHay. Let me sort it."

"I won't ask you again, AJ. I'm pointing a gun at the head of the man who killed my friend. What makes you think I won't pull the trigger?"

AJ looks down before letting out a sigh. He realises that he is a pawn in a game at this point. A game way bigger than him or McHay or even Ace. "Simon Stark. He was the one who made me believe that Ace had killed my brother."

McHay loosens the grip of his gun and he sits back in confusion, looking like he has just seen a ghost. That name has him taken aback. "That's impossible, Simon Stark is dead. I should know, I was the one who killed him."

"No, you didn't."

"He was Hunter's old business partner. After things went sour, Hunter had me torch his home with him inside it."

"He survived, McHay. The worst that fire did was paralyse him from the waist down. He faked his death and stayed low."

McHay leans back in his chair with a look of shock.

"Years before the fire, he began to date my mother and helped raise me. In the end, he and my mum split when she wanted to move to Manchester. I hadn't heard from him in years, I even thought that he may have died. Then, a few days after JJ died, he reached out to me and told me about his business with Hunter and that Ace was responsible for killing JJ. He'd been keeping tabs on you all for years and he came up with a plan that would give us both the justice that we needed. He would have me tear Hunter's organisation down from the inside and in turn, kill Ace once it was done."

McHay is shocked. All these years he had to deal with the guilt of killing a man only to find out that he survived. "He used you as a pawn to get his revenge on us after all of these years."

"He wanted Hunter gone and I wanted Ace gone. It just made sense. I thought I could trust him. He's like a father to me."

McHay leans forward in his chair. "He played us all. Did anyone else know that he survived the fire?"

"I don't know. I do believe he sent Hunter a letter once though, a few years after."

"Hunter knew?"

"That's why he left Leeds."

"He never told me," McHay says in a sombre tone. "All this time I thought I killed him."

The room falls silent for a few short moments before AJ says, "I can't believe Stark lied to me. He told me that he had been shown CCTV footage of Ace throwing JJ into the flames. I trusted him."

"He lied. I was in the building that night."

"I killed Ace for nothing." AJ sits there feeling betrayed and full of regret.

"You were blinded by grief and vengeance. You were vulnerable and he played on it. Where is he now? And don't shit me, AJ."

"He lives on a farm in a town in Yorkshire, Walsden I think."

"This is how it's going to go, me and you will go to Walsden, and we will kill Stark. Together as one."

"How are we going to take him out?"

"Not with this," McHay says holding up his gun. "When I left Manchester to head back to Leeds, I was in a rush and I didn't bring any ammo with me. I only have one bullet in it. I had hoped to start fresh and leave this life behind, only taking the gun in the off chance that I would need it to defend myself. But that was unlikely, so I never bothered fully loading it. Then ever since I read the headline on Ace's death, I knew who I was saving that bullet for."

AJ doesn't argue, he understands McHay's grief. "So, what happens when this is done?"

"Then, I do what I have to do."

"Fair enough." AJ knows what this means. The realisation that he brought upon the demise and destruction of a man over nothing more than a lie nearly cripples him.

"I guess Stark wasn't the man you thought he was, huh? Does Paul Moonie know any of this?"

"No. Stark and I didn't anticipate Paul Moonie becoming associated with the organisation. Moonie's involvement made Stark nervous but it ultimately worked out well for him as Moonie had Hunter killed."

"Motherfucker. Tell me though, were you ordered to kill me?"

"I was ordered to kill you, yes. But I never planned to. To me, your death was unnecessary. Hunter and Ace were the ones who needed to pay."

"You could just be saying that because I'm here holding a gun up to you."

"I could. But when you left, I informed Stark of your departure, and he ordered me to track you down after killing Ace and finish you off. A week after Ace's death, I contacted Stark and told him I had you killed."

"Well, he's about to be see a ghost. Come on, AJ, one last dance."

XXIX
'The Parting of Ways'

Walsden is a small yet beautiful town around half an hour from Manchester via train and around an hour's drive. Surrounded by several breathtaking hills and a heart-warming community, Walsden is a small yet very homely place.

After an hour's drive, AJ and McHay arrive outside of an old farmhouse on the snowy tops on the outskirts of Walsden overlooking the rest of the village.

"It's bloody freezing," McHay says as they exit the car.

"It's bloody Britain."

"Don't get smart. How are we going to do this anyway?"

"I'll do it. I need to do it." AJ pulls out his gun and loads it.

Suddenly, a thin, brown-haired woman exits the front door of the spacious farmhouse wearing a blue gown. She sees AJ and McHay and is curious. "Good afternoon, gentlemen. Simon didn't tell me he was expecting company today," she says.

"We're just old friends paying a long overdue visit, that's all," McHay quickly responds.

"Ah, I see. Well, I'm his private carer, Ruby," she introduces herself.

"Nice to meet you, Ruby," McHay replies.

"And you two are…"

"Late," AJ rudely replies before heading towards the front door. He is focused on putting an end to the life of lies he has been forced to live for the past year. He's on a mission and wants this done as soon as possible.

"Sorry, Ruby, he's an arsehole." McHay soon hurries behind AJ as Ruby enters her car and leaves.

The two enter the house without knocking.

"Nice to see that he's done well for himself," McHay says with sarcasm as he points out the expensive interior of the farmhouse.

The inside of the house has several paintings hung on the expensive wallpapered walls, a huge candlelit chandelier and stone statues in the hallway which lead directly into the living room. Here is where they find the crippled Simon Stark sitting in his wheelchair with a tray of food on his lap watching television.

Simon Stark is halfway through his bowl of cereal when McHay calls over, "Morning TV is just shit, am I right?"

Simon turns his head around and drops his food tray at the sight of McHay standing there with AJ next to him.

They can see that Simon has several scars across his face, scars which he acquired in the fire that McHay set those years ago. His hair is almost fully grey and he is wearing an open dark grey blazer with a faded white shirt under it. An attire that he was known for back in the day.

McHay switches the television off and draws the curtains.

"What is this, fellas? AJ, my boy, why are you here?"

"You sound like you're panicking, Simon," AJ responds. "You should be."

"You must have known that one day the past was going to catch up to you, Stark," McHay chips in.

"I don't understand what is happening here."

"Oh, you do. We are here to kill you," McHay replies. "To do the job right this time."

Simon turns to AJ with eyes like puppy eyes. Knowing that he can't physically out-fight the two, he desperately tries to grasp any sympathy he can out of AJ. "AJ, my boy, that cannot be true."

"You lied to me, Simon. You made me take the life of a man who didn't need to die," AJ, with a face of regret-fuelled determination, says.

"I would never lie to you, AJ."

"Ace didn't kill my brother."

"Is that what he's told you? That fat piece of shit over there? You can't believe him, AJ. He and Hunter tried to have me killed remember?"

"Fuck you, Stark. Ace did many things but killing his best friend wasn't one. JJ was a brother to him," McHay adds.

"You're out of time, Simon. Your lies have cost me so much. More than you will ever know. I have done things that will never leave me. I have hurt people I cared about and I have killed those who called me family. All in the name of a lie." AJ's anger turns into emotion. His voice slightly cracks as he speaks. "How could you? I will hate myself for the rest of my life because of you. My own brother would hate me for what I've done. You used me as a pawn for your own game of vengeance." A tear drops from his eye as he raises his gun.

"I didn't make you do anything that you didn't already want to do."

"You manipulated me."

"Hunter and his organisation had to die."

"No. No, they didn't. You did." AJ's grip on his gun tightens. "You deserve every part of this," he says. McHay steps in and lowers the gun.

"Let's make him suffer," McHay says as he pulls a lighter out of his pocket. AJ nods in approval.

"After all I've done for you. You ungrateful shit! If it wasn't for me, you would have turned out just like your deadbeat brother," Simon maliciously says.

"Go fuck yourself, Simon." AJ kicks Simon hard in the middle of his chest sending him and the wheelchair falling backwards to the ground.

McHay heads over to the grounded cripple. "It's getting warm in here," he says before flicking up his lighter and lighting the bottom of Simon's pants up in flames. They plan to burn him alive.

Distressed, Simon crawls out of the wheelchair and drags his body across the floor as the fire slowly rises to his chest. He screams and cries in the burning pain as the flames reach his upper half. The scorching blaze destroys his clothes and begins to toast his skin. AJ and McHay stand there watching him crawl and burn before their eyes.

"Come on, we've seen enough," McHay says to AJ.

"No, I have to see this." AJ can't take his eyes off Simon burning alive. His screams are going right through him. It's hard to see, especially after everything Simon did for him when he was a child. But AJ knows that those time are gone. Simon Stark is a monster. Simon Stark is the conductor of the symphony of pain. Simon Stark is the string puller of this whole story.

It doesn't take long before Simon Stark burns to a crisp. AJ and McHay agree that they should set ablaze the rest of the farmhouse which is exactly what they do. They then, as the farmhouse burns behind them, drive out further onto the hillside.

AJ stands admiring the magnificent view which overlooks the village of Walsden. He takes a deep breath in like a weight has just been lifted off his shoulders as the farmhouse burns in the very far distance.

"Some view, isn't it?" AJ says. He doesn't get a response, so he turns around only to be met with the sight of McHay holding his gun up at him.

"I told you, one bullet," McHay says.

"You did," AJ replies as he turns back around to look at the view. "Go for the head, please. Make it quick." He closes his eyes in preparation. He quickly reflects on his life and his regrets. He remembers a time with his brother when they were very young playing with toy cars in their garden. Followed by the time JJ had taken him out on his first night out when he turned eighteen, and how they almost got into a fight with a rugby lad after JJ kissed the lad's girlfriend. Then his time as a member of the 'Three Grifters' sitting in 'The Blue Moon' drinking with Ace and McHay. Then lastly, the time Ace took him back to his apartment after he killed 'The Silencer' and gave him a beer. If only things could have played out differently. Happy endings don't exist.

He accepts that this is how it ends now. The end of the road.

McHay loosens the grip of his gun and lowers it. "In all the time that I've known you, in there, I finally saw the real you. I know you did what you did because you were manipulated and thought you were avenging your brother. In that position, I would have done the same thing. I know you genuinely do regret what you have done," McHay says.

AJ slowly opens his eyes and faces McHay. "Thank you, Vino. I am so sorry for what I've done."

"It was Stark, not you. You proved that to me in there. And Ace was the dragon that only his own mind could slay. Even if it wasn't you pulling the trigger, someone else would have before long."

"I will never be able to repay you for this."

"You can and you will. You will run. Run far away from here, as far as you can, and never return. You have a second chance now, don't waste it."

The two admire the view standing at the edge of the hill looking over Walsden.

"Who knows, just maybe, maybe in some other universe out there things worked out differently and the three of us were still doing our thing." McHay pauses and smiles at that idea. "We would have ruled the world."

"You're dam right, we would have. But that's not the reality we live in."

"Unfortunately, not." McHay takes a moment before he continues. "And maybe if I had stayed around, I could have stopped you and put an end to Stark sooner. Ace would still be here and you would still be standing by his side. I failed you both, and I'm sorry."

"You have no reason to apologise, McHay. The Ace you loved died a long time ago. It would have always ended badly."

"Maybe. So, what will you do now, AJ Reeves?"

"I'm going to California. I've got a neat little apartment in Los Angeles, and I'll start from scratch. Live a simple life, find a wife, and settle down."

"Where anyone can become someone, ey."

"And you?"

"Well, I can't go back to Manchester and be there when Paulie gets out, and I think he will be able to track me in Leeds so that leaves me looking to start fresh as well. But I won't be going to America like you. I have some connections in Newcastle, so I might head there."

"Still in the game?"

"I don't think I can ever leave the game, AJ. I tried it once and look where that brought me." McHay laughs. "For what it's worth, what he said in there about you turning out like your brother, that wouldn't be such a bad thing at all." McHay's words make AJ smile.

AJ removes his gun from his pocket and throws it down into a small bush in front of him. He shakes McHay's hand one last time before he starts to walk away and head back to his car.

"Take care, man," McHay calls behind him.

"You too, Vino."

XXX
'What Comes Now?'

The Epilogue

So, there it is, that's how the mighty fell. That's how the 'Three Grifters' journeyed from a successful group into an unmitigated disaster. That's how Tony 'Ace' Johnson, a man forever plagued by his guilt and regrets, brought about the demise of the once-feared faction.

The 'Three Grifters' were feared, ruthless, and dangerous. But above all else, they were bonded by the blood they shed. The 'overthinker', the 'experienced follower', and the 'betrayer'. The ticking timebomb ticked on for some time. They had good times, sad times, and everything in between, but their fate was ultimately always sealed, just two of them didn't know it until it was too late. The story of guilt, regret, and betrayal.

For every 'happy ending', there must be a bit of sadness along the way.

After all the pain and suffering he caused, the only person who attended Ace's funeral was Dorothy, Flacco's mother. Paul Moonie was informed of Ace's death the day after his body was discovered. He was given the opportunity, with police supervision, to pay his respects at Ace's funeral but he refused to go after learning of the news of Ace re-starting the drug war and the fiery fall of 'The Rogue'. 'Red Syndicate' claimed responsibility for Ace's death, even though it had nothing to do with them. It was just another trophy in their cabinet to use for bragging rights and to gloat their power.

In 1992, Paul Moonie and his two brothers were released from prison. Paul soon came to the harsh realisation that Manchester had changed and entered the 90s without him. A lot had changed in the time he was behind bars and he and his brothers found themselves starting back up from scratch. They had to take the rubble that was once their empire and rebuild it. Speaking of which, the land where 'The Rogue' once stood has now been reformed into a block of flats. It took the brothers some time to re-establish themselves, but eventually, they prevailed. Even though Paul wasn't there to witness the change in Manchester, he did help inspire it. Club owners modelled themselves on Paul's game-changing strategies and took great inspiration from 'The Rogue'. Manchester wouldn't be what it is today without Paul Moonie.

As for McHay, he did indeed move to Newcastle where he managed to set up his own debt-collecting business and he made several high-profile connections throughout the city. It's here where he took two young men under his wing, James Furnell and Jude O'Neil. With Furnell and O'Neil at his side, McHay soon rose through the ranks of Newcastle and became a respectable man within the city. He became a leader and an intimidating presence there.

As for AJ Reeves, he now resides in Los Angeles, California, where he works as a taxi driver and lives with his wife, Scarlet, and his three children, Jace Jasper Reeves, Alexa Ava Reeves and Vincent Reeves. His family knows nothing of his past in the UK, and that's how he intends to keep it.

THE END
Thank you for reading.